Also by the Author

The Erin O'Reilly Mysteries

Black Velvet

Irish Car Bomb

White Russian

Double Scotch

Manhattan

Black Magic

Death By Chocolate

Massacre

Flashback

First Love

High Stakes

Aquarium

The Devil You Know

Hair of the Dog

Punch Drunk

Bossa Nova

Blackout

Angel Face

Italian Stallion

White Lightning

Kamikaze

Jackhammer

Frostbite

Brain Damage (coming soon)

Tequila Sunrise: A James Corcoran Story

Fathers
A Modern Christmas Story

The Clarion Chronicles
Ember of Dreams

Frostbite

The Erin O'Reilly Mysteries
Book Twenty-Three

Steven Henry

Clickworks Press • Baltimore, MD

First publication: Clickworks Press, 2024
Release: CWP-EOR23-INT-P.IS-1.0

Sign up for updates, deals, and exclusive sneak peeks at clickworkspress.com/join.

Ebook ISBN: 979-8-88900-017-4
Paperback ISBN: 979-8-88900-018-1
Hardcover ISBN: 979-8-88900-019-8

For Officer Paul Elmstrand,
Officer Matthew Ruge,
and Firefighter-Paramedic Adam Finseth,
killed in the line of duty in Burnsville, MN,
February 18, 2024.

Frostbite

Combine 1½ oz. tequila, ¾ oz. Crème de Cacao, ¾ oz. Blue Curaçao, and 1 oz. heavy cream in a shaker glass. Shake with ice for 10-15 seconds. Strain into a rocks glass over fresh ice. Garnish with a cherry and serve.

Chapter 1

"The National Weather Service has issued a winter storm warning for the greater New York City area, with predicted snowfall in excess of twenty inches. Temperatures are expected to plummet well below zero, with a wind chill in the negative double digits. All residents are advised to remain indoors and refrain from unnecessary travel."

The weatherman's face was grim.

"We're not joking, folks," he continued. "This is going to be a nasty one. Stock up on food, make sure your heating is working, and hunker down."

A chorus of groans and boos met the man's words. Someone threw a crumpled-up napkin. It ricocheted off the big-screen TV that hung on the Barley Corner's wall. Several anonymous voices expressed unflattering opinions of the weatherman's appearance, personal habits, and sexual preferences.

"At least the kids can look forward to a snow day," Erin O'Reilly said, swirling the half-empty glass of Guinness in her hand. She was sitting at the bar next to Morton Carlyle; boyfriend, reformed gangster, and friendly local pub owner.

"But not you poor blighters," Carlyle observed. "Neither

snow nor sleet nor gloom of night..."

"You're thinking of the Postal Service," she said. "But you're right, the NYPD never closes. I'm just glad I'm not working Traffic. Those guys are going to have a nightmare."

"I'd imagine that's what's got these lads all in a tizzy," Carlyle said. "Two-thirds of them are truckers. They've cargo to move and their living to earn, whatever the weather boffins say. Have you ever tried handling an eighteen-wheeler on an icy highway?"

"No," Erin said and shivered. All this talk of snow and ice was making her feel cold.

"Nor I," he said. "But according to Wayne McClernand, it's an experience best avoided. Are you sure you're going out tonight? Wouldn't you rather put your feet up with another bowl of Marian's Irish stew?"

"You know I would," she said, looking regretfully at the empty bowl on the bar in front of her. "But it's not up to me. This is an important meeting. You know why."

Carlyle nodded. "I'd be happier if you could do it over the phone, but I understand."

Erin shrugged. "It's the Job," she said, standing up.

Rolf uncurled himself from the base of her stool. The German Shepherd stretched and yawned, opening his jaws amazingly wide. Then he positioned himself at Erin's hip and stared up at her, waiting to see what she'd do.

"Call me when you start for home," Carlyle said.

"I'm meeting my people, not yours," she said quietly. "I'm in no danger."

"Not from your folk, perhaps," he said. "But there's the weather to consider. There'll be widows made on the roads tonight, I've no doubt."

"In that case, you've got nothing to worry about," she said, grinning at him.

"And why's that?" he replied.

She leaned in and kissed him on the cheek. "Because we're not married," she said. Then she winked and left the pub.

*   *   *

"We've got to stop meeting like this."

It was cliché, but the only thing Erin could think of to say. She was still tense from driving through the snow, and meeting with her undercover handler wasn't exactly relaxing. Neither was the venue. Phil liked to meet in parks and other outdoor locations, preferably under cover of darkness, but the weather had wrecked that plan. So now they were standing on a subway platform, pretending they didn't know one another, while Rolf hung out next to Erin and waited for something interesting to happen. The station was otherwise deserted, except for a homeless guy who sat against the far wall with his upturned hat in front of him, hoping for the charity of strangers. He appeared to be asleep.

"How was the drive?" Phil Stachowski asked. He didn't look like an NYPD Lieutenant. He looked like a down-on-his-luck community-college professor, one who taught English Literature to bored freshmen. He was balding and slightly overweight. His mild, pleasant face was screened by wire-rimmed eyeglasses. He was wearing a shabby topcoat, and Erin knew if she looked under it she'd find an equally shabby tweed jacket with leather elbow patches and a pair of corduroys. If he even bothered wearing a gun, she'd never seen it.

"A little rough," she said. "Not as bad as I thought. Most of the other drivers listened to the news and they're staying home. I'm surprised the subway isn't busier."

"The city's shutting down," Phil said. "The snow's coming pretty hard."

"It's as bad as I've seen it," she said. "My niece and nephew are over the moon. The governor's already closed the schools."

Phil smiled. "Christmas comes a little early this year," he said. "My girls are happy, too. When I left, they were already planning a whole family of snowmen they're going to make in the park."

"How old are they?" she asked.

"Nora's ten and Grace is twelve," he said. "I'm trying to enjoy the pre-adolescence as long as I can. I just know the next time I blink, they'll be into boys and wanting to borrow the car."

"So what'd you want to talk about?" she asked.

"We're putting pieces in motion," he said. "Finally. We're setting up surveillance on the O'Malley leadership, round the clock. I've got a team of guys from my house."

Since Phil had just been talking about his family, his reference to his house confused Erin for just a second. Then she realized that of course he was talking about his police precinct. The cold must be slowing her wits.

"Are they solid?" she asked.

"I've worked with them for years," Phil said. "And they're discreet. They've all worked undercover assignments for me, so they know the drill."

"What do they know?" she asked. Paranoia was tickling the back of her neck.

"Nothing about you," he assured her. "All I've told them is that we're setting up a watch on the O'Malleys. I didn't tell them about the upcoming arrests, and I haven't breathed your name, or anything else that would compromise you. As far as they know, this is just a watchdog detail, gathering information."

"What's the real purpose?" she asked.

"To track their movements," Phil said. "When we come down on Evan O'Malley and his underlings, we need to make sure we get all of them at once, or as many as we can. You know what'll happen as soon as we start making busts."

"Everyone else will scatter," Erin said. "They'll run or they'll hide and it'll take forever to root them out."

"Right," he said. "We'll have a fair amount of manpower on this, so spreading some information around is unavoidable. Don't worry, it's compartmentalized. Like I said, you haven't been mentioned, or even suggested."

"You're known for running undercover operations," Erin said. She knew she was probably borrowing trouble, but she couldn't stop herself. "Won't they suspect you've got an informant in the O'Malleys?"

"Possibly," Phil said. "But your position is rock solid. Remember, as far as the Mob knows, you've killed for them."

"But what about Carlyle?" The worry showed in her eyes.

"Erin, it's natural to feel some nerves at this point," he said. "I'd be lying if I said there wasn't any risk, but I don't think either of you is in any more danger than you were a week or a month ago. This is just the next step."

"I don't like it," she grumbled. "You may trust these guys, but I don't even know them."

"They're good police," he insisted.

"They'd better be," she said. "You could be betting my life on them."

"It'll be okay," Phil said. "I'm going to talk to some of them in person tonight. If anything feels off, I'll take care of it. Remember, you can call me if anything comes up; anything at all. I've got your back, Erin. No matter what."

*　*　*

The drive back to the Barley Corner was worse. The snow was really coming down now, whipping across Erin's windshield in lines of brilliant white. She couldn't see more than a few yards. She went at a crawling pace, wondering if she might not be better off leaving the car somewhere and walking. Even though most of the other drivers were also being sensible and driving slowly, she still lost count of how many times she squeaked through close calls and near misses.

A big SUV tried to take a turn too tightly in front of her and spun out clean across the intersection, narrowly avoiding wrapping itself around a lamppost. Two taxis had somehow managed a head-on collision on a one-way street, though they appeared to have been going slow enough that no one had been hurt. An NYPD Patrol car was already on scene, two cops trying to separate the taxi drivers. Their muffled argument filtered through Erin's window as she passed them.

When she finally saw the Barley Corner's lights through the swirling blizzard, she breathed a sigh of relief. A drive that normally took twenty minutes had taken almost an hour. She steered into the parking garage across the street from the pub and eased the Charger into its designated space. Then she sat back in her seat and rubbed her hands. Her knuckles ached from gripping the steering wheel so tightly.

"That's it," she told Rolf. "I'm not going anywhere else tonight. I don't care if Canada declares war on us. I don't care if it's the second coming of Christ Himself out there. The goddamn Rapture can wait till tomorrow."

Rolf nosed her cheek and panted happily. He didn't know what the big deal was. He loved snow.

Erin climbed out of the car, adjusted her jacket, and hurried across the street toward the warm welcome promised by the pub's glowing windows. She was already thinking about a hot shower, or even better, a long soak in Carlyle's tub. Maybe she'd forget about her usual evening glass of whiskey and have a cup of hot cocoa instead. Carlyle would be happy to give her a nice, relaxing back rub. Then they could curl up on the couch together and...

She opened the Corner's front door and her happy train of thought went right off the rails. Waiting just inside was a wiry, dark-haired Irishman with a black glove on his right hand and horrible, puckered scars masking the right side of his face. His eyes, so dark brown they looked black, zeroed in on her like a pair of pistol barrels.

"Snake," she blurted, reflexively using the man's Mob nickname. "What're you doing here?"

"O'Reilly," Gordon Pritchard rasped. His vocal cords had been permanently scarred by the same gasoline bomb that had ruined half his body. "The boss is in back. We need to talk. We got a problem."

Erin followed Pritchard to the back room, trying to hold down a sudden surge of uneasiness. She wished she was wearing her special bra, with its recording microphone stitched into the underwire. But she hadn't expected an encounter with Evan. The O'Malley chieftain ought to be at home, riding out the storm like a sensible human being. Something really important must have happened.

She glanced down at Rolf. The dog padded along beside her; solid, warm, and reliable. He was a comfort.

The back room at the Barley Corner was a place for private card games and meetings. It was small, dimly lit, dominated by a heavy wooden card table topped with green baize. At the table, facing the door, sat Evan O'Malley. He was alone.

"Evening, sir," Erin said, speaking as lightly as she could.

"Good evening, Miss O'Reilly," Evan said. "Please sit down." He spoke politely, but he remained seated, hands clasped on the tabletop. His eyes were midwinter blue, holding no hint of warmth or humanity.

"Rolf, *sitz*," she said, giving the K-9 his German "sit"

command. She slid into the chair opposite Evan, though it put her back to the door and to Pritchard, neither of which made her comfortable.

"It's an unpleasant night for traveling," Evan said. "Where have you been tonight?"

"Police business," she said, giving what she hoped was a casual shrug. "Just meeting a contact. Who else are we waiting on?"

"Nobody," Evan said.

She blinked. "What about Cars?" she asked.

"Mr. Carlyle is otherwise engaged," Evan said. "It's you I've come to see."

Erin schooled herself to stay calm. It didn't mean a thing. There might be any number of subjects Evan would want to talk to her about. But he had to at least suspect whatever he said to her would be repeated to Carlyle. The two of them were a unit as far as the O'Malleys were concerned.

"What can I do for you?" she asked.

Evan's stare drilled into her like twin icicles, sucking the heat out of her heart. "You can tell me about Philip Stachowski," he said.

Chapter 2

Every month or so, Evan O'Malley held a poker game. All his senior bosses were expected to attend. The buy-in was one or two thousand dollars. Erin played with Carlyle's money and reported her winnings or losses to Phil, so she had no real skin in the game. It was an opportunity to sit around a table with a group of violent sociopaths, drinking good booze and trying not to say or do anything that would get her killed.

These games held several purposes for Evan. He kept his fingertips on the pulse of his organization, getting a sense of the morale of his underlings. He could see who was getting along with whom and which gangsters weren't on speaking terms with one another. He might spot any initial rumblings of discontent, so he could head them off before mutterings turned into rebellion.

But first and foremost, it let him observe his minions up close and learn their tells. By watching them play cards, Evan could find out how they reacted when they were lying. He could watch their reactions to surprises, both good and bad, and catalog them. Then, when something really important was on the line, he'd be able to read the truth in their faces.

Erin had played cards with Evan more than once, but never for stakes like these. She didn't have a prayer of hiding her surprise at Phil's name. Shock merged with a visceral jolt of pure terror, which turned instantly to despair. If Evan knew about Phil, it was safe to assume he knew everything; the undercover operation, the faked murder of a witness, Carlyle's treachery. Carlyle might already be dead. It was over. She'd gambled and lost everything.

The only play left when you were holding lousy cards was to bluff, and bluff big. Her chips were already on the table, but just maybe Evan didn't know every card she was holding. Carlyle had taught her that the best way to lie was to tell the truth, but to tell it in a way that would lead the enemy off the scent.

"You mean Lieutenant Stachowski?" she replied, somehow keeping the tremor out of her voice. "NYPD? Works out of the Ten?"

"That's the very man," Evan said. "You know him?"

"I've never worked out of the same house," she said, keeping to the technical truth. "But I know the name."

"Do you know what he does?" Evan asked.

She shrugged. "I've heard he runs undercovers," she said. "It's a tough gig, but they say he's good at it."

"Have you met him?"

Yeah, an hour ago, she thought. "I have," she said. It was a dangerous thing to say, but a blanket denial would be more dangerous. If one of Evan's people had seen her with Phil, he'd know she was lying, and that would be fatal. She was walking a tightrope, one with no safety net. The hairs on the back of her neck were standing on end. Gordon Pritchard was behind her. He'd have a gun and she knew he'd use it. If she made one wrong move or said one wrong thing, the last thing she saw would be her own blood spraying across Carlyle's nice clean tabletop.

"What's your read on him?" Evan asked.

A faint glow of hope flickered to life in her heart. Was it possible Evan didn't suspect her? But if so, why was he asking about Phil? "He's a little strange," she said. "He doesn't look like a cop, or act like one."

"How so?"

"He's soft," she said. "He struck me as kind of a wimp. Too much of a nice guy to be a hardcore street cop."

Evan nodded. "But he's smart," the O'Malley boss said. "And he's dangerous. Not in himself, but in what he can do. Is it true he's never lost an undercover officer?"

"That's what they say," she said.

"He's got somebody inside," Evan said.

"Inside where?" she asked. It was a stupid question, she knew that as soon as it spilled over her lips. She saw the flash of contempt in Evan's eyes and knew she deserved it. The answer was painfully obvious.

"Inside my organization," he said.

"That seems unlikely," she said.

"Why do you say that?" he asked, raising an eyebrow.

"I'd have heard if there was another cop," she said, which might or might not be true. "How do you know? What did you hear?"

"I have sources," Evan said. "But they're frustratingly vague at times. Mr. Stachowski has poked his nose into my business. I need to know what he knows and who he has."

"You want me to find an NYPD mole?" she asked, and she didn't need to fake the disbelief in her voice.

"That's precisely what you're going to do," Evan said coldly.

"There's no way," she said.

"You seem to be operating under a misapprehension of your position," he said. "You're going to do this for me, not because I'm telling you to, but because you're doing it for yourself as well. Think about it; you're a part of this organization. You've done things that will cost you a great deal more than that gold badge of which you're so very proud. If we fail to unearth the traitor, I may go down, but I won't be going alone. Do I make myself clear?"

Erin swallowed. "Perfectly, sir."

He allowed himself a frigid smile. "Excellent," he said. "I'll expect prompt results."

"I think you misunderstood, sir," she said. "I wasn't refusing. I was trying to tell you, I don't think this is possible. Lieutenant Stachowski is in an entirely separate chain of command. I don't report to him, and I sure as hell don't outrank him. If he runs undercovers, he's going to be a pretty cagey guy. He isn't going to just spill the name of one of his officers, particularly if he already suspects me of being involved with you. That's not exactly the best-kept secret in New York."

"You have access to the NYPD's inner workings," Evan said. "Find a way. I have full confidence in you. If you succeed, you'll have my gratitude. If not, my displeasure may be the very least of your worries."

Erin licked her lips. "I'll get right on it."

"Excellent," he said again. "I'll let you get to work."

He stood up and walked around the table, extending his hand. Erin got to her feet and shook with him. His fingers were cool to the touch. It was like taking the hand of a room-temperature corpse. He went to the door. Pritchard opened it for him and they left.

As the door clicked shut behind them, Erin leaned forward, her shoulders shaking with suppressed laughter. She wasn't prone to hysteria, but this was genuinely funny. She'd heard of succeeding too well at a job. Now she'd done such a good job convincing Evan of her *bona fides* that he'd tasked her with tracking down the mole in the O'Malleys.

"Talk about putting the fox in charge of the henhouse," she gasped to Rolf, who cocked his head curiously. He didn't get the joke. But then, he'd never had much sense of humor.

The laughter died in her throat as fast as it had come. There was only one way Evan could have heard about the penetration of his racket. If he knew this much, it was only a matter of time before he learned the rest.

"Shit," she said. "I have to tell Phil. He's got a leak."

Erin reached into her jacket pocket and came out with a cheap cell phone. It was a prepaid burner with only one number saved on it; Phil's. She dialed it and listened to the ring tone, thinking what she needed to say. At least she knew he'd be awake. Not that it mattered; he always took her calls, no matter what time it was.

The phone rang a third time, then a fourth.

"Come on," she muttered. "Pick up."

A fifth ring buzzed in her ear. She answered it with a chain of quiet profanity.

The call connected. Erin thanked God and opened her mouth.

"Please leave your name and a brief message," a recorded voice said. It was a neutral female voice, nothing to connect it to Phil. He was way too canny to attach his name or any identifying information to his voicemail.

"It's me," she said, trying to match the unemotional inflection of the recording. "Call me as soon as you can."

Then she hung up and stared at the phone. Phil had never failed to answer; never. He'd promised he'd always be there.

"Now what?" she asked the world.

Rolf laid his chin against her leg, letting her know she wasn't alone.

But it suddenly felt very much like she was.

*   *   *

The bar had mostly cleared out, the Corner's clientele making their way to whatever home or motel they'd chosen to ride out the storm. The few customers who remained were either O'Malley associates or guys who had nowhere else to go.

Erin didn't care about the patrons. She scanned the room and saw the one face she'd hoped to see. The hard-faced young man with the cool, steady eyes was standing against the far wall, carefully positioned with lines of sight to both the front and rear entrances. His clothing was perfectly composed except for his sport coat, which hung open to allow easy access to the pistol she knew he was carrying.

"Ian," she said, walking quickly across the room to meet him.

"Situation?" he asked, not wasting words. He didn't miss much, and he knew her well enough to recognize her agitation.

"Where's Carlyle?" she asked.

"Mr. Finnegan called him to a meeting," Ian said. "Mr. Carlyle told me to stay here, keep an eye on things."

"Any idea where?"

"No. Trouble?"

Her eyes darted around the room and back to Ian.

He nodded, though she hadn't said anything. "Orders?" he asked quietly. In dangerous moments his Marine training, never far from the surface, took over.

Erin shook her head. "I don't know what's going on," she said. "But we need to be ready."

"Always ready," he said. "Can call in a couple more guys if we need them."

"Don't stir anything up," she said. "Just tell Carlyle to call me the second he gets back."

"Affirmative. He may want your coordinates."

"I don't know where I'll be," she said. "But I'll have my phone."

He didn't like it, she could tell by the slight narrowing of his eyes. He knew, or suspected, everything was a long way from okay. But Ian was a good Marine and didn't protest. He just nodded and went back to watching the room while Erin zipped up her jacket and led Rolf back into the blizzard.

She'd told Ian the truth; she really didn't know where to go. She had to get in touch with Phil, but she didn't know how. The only thing she did know was that she couldn't do it sitting around on her ass at the Barley Corner. Every street instinct was screaming that hours, maybe even minutes, were critically important.

She had to sort through her priorities and make the right decision. Leaving the voicemail had been a mistake. If Phil's communications had been compromised, somebody else might be listening to his messages. She hadn't left her name or any other information, and her phone was untraceable, but her voice was identifiable. Paranoid? Maybe, but she couldn't afford to be sloppy.

Precinct 10, Phil's house, would have his contact information. She knew the phone number she'd used was another burner cell; Phil was too good at tradecraft to use his personal phone for undercover work. She didn't have his personal cell, nor his home phone. Or she could call Dispatch and ask them to patch her through. But either of those approaches would leave a trail through the NYPD. Dispatch would record the call, and she had to assume the mole on Phil's team could access Departmental phone records. It wouldn't be the first time a criminal had hacked into the NYPD's database. She recalled an earlier incident which had led to an attack on a fellow officer's home. She and Officer Firelli had barely survived a fight which had left a crooked detective dying on Firelli's kitchen floor.

"Damn it," she said under her breath. She hurried across the street, avoiding a sedan that skidded halfway through the intersection on the red light. Snow was already two inches deep and still falling fast. She ducked into the parking garage and started up the stairs to the second floor, where her Charger waited for her. Rolf took a moment to shake the snow from his thick fur and followed.

If she couldn't safely go through police channels, she had one other option. It wasn't a great one, but beggars didn't have a whole lot of choices. She slid into the driver's seat of her car, brought up her onboard computer, and punched in Phil's name. The thought of the attack on Firelli's house had given her an idea. The Stachowski family home was listed in the NYPD's records.

"Great," Erin muttered when she saw the address. "Just great. All this and now we've got to get to Jersey. In a snowstorm. At least there won't be any snow in the Holland Tunnel. Why couldn't he live in Manhattan?"

Rolf poked her ear with a very cold, very wet nose.

"Right," she said. "The Island's expensive, I know, and cops don't make much money. Maybe I should just call them."

She shook her head, dismissing the thought at once. "No. The drive is risky, and it's going to take forever, but Evan's got Phil under surveillance. If the bad guys are onto him, they might have his phone tapped. Damn it, they might be watching his house, too. Jesus."

Rolf didn't have any advice to offer, so he licked her ear instead.

"You're right," Erin said. "The weather's so lousy, nobody's going to be camped out at his house. Besides, we're not talking about a huge number of bad guys. It's not like they've got teams of surveillance guys with nothing to do but hang around in a storm. Let's go."

She put the car in gear and hoped she'd make it. Phil lived across the Hudson River in Hoboken. It'd take half an hour even under ideal conditions. Tonight that meant at least an hour, probably more like ninety minutes. She shouldn't be driving to Jersey on a night like this. She shouldn't be driving anywhere. But what choice did she have? Conditions would only get worse as the night wore on.

Did they really have Phil's phone? Was she just being paranoid, and risking getting stuck or, worse, crashing her car?

She dialed Phil's home phone number. If he picked up, that meant he was safe and she'd hang up. If his wife answered, she could pretend to be someone else and find out where Phil was.

A recorded voice said, "We're sorry. Your call cannot be completed as dialed."

"Damn it," Erin said. Was it the storm? Had she misdialed? Or was the Stachowskis' number wrong? It didn't matter. All it meant was, she was going to Jersey whether she wanted to or not.

Erin gritted her teeth and started driving.

Chapter 3

Getting to the Holland Tunnel wasn't so bad; Erin had never seen less traffic on the Manhattan streets. After that, the tunnel itself was almost pleasant. The road was dry and she was able to turn off her wipers. But coming out on the New Jersey side of the river was awful. The snowfall seemed to have doubled in intensity while she'd been underground. She leaned forward, clutching the wheel and peering into the swirling white. Wasn't white the color of death in China?

Visibility was so bad that she had to rely on her phone's GPS to tell her which turns to take. She couldn't see the street signs until she was practically on top of them. She steered by instinct and experience.

"This is nuts," she said. "We're going to crash into something and die."

Rolf thrust his head between the seats and watched the snow, eyes bright, mouth slightly open. He'd never seen anything quite like it. He could feel Erin's tension. This was an exciting drive.

Erin finally guided the Charger onto Ogden Avenue in Hoboken. The plows hadn't come down this street yet and the snow was several inches deep. She blessed her four-wheel drive as she carefully drew up to the curb. She couldn't leave the car on the street for long; the Hoboken cops were likely to give her a ticket.

She laughed quietly at the absurdity of the thought. She wasn't getting a ticket, not tonight. The tow trucks would be busy all night hauling motorists out of ditches. Hoboken PD would have their hands full. Nobody would have time to mess around with a Manhattan cop who'd wandered into the wrong neighborhood. She left Rolf in the car and hurried up the stairs to the Stachowskis' front porch.

The house was brick, about a hundred years old, lined up in the middle of a row of nearly-identical homes. The porch roof was supported by brick columns, overlooked by a bay window. Tasteful little white Christmas lights were strung around the window, twinkling into the snowy night. The front door was solid hardwood, pierced by a small window at eye level.

She rang the doorbell. After a moment, she heard the faint scrabble of claws on woodwork. Then a yellow, furry face sprang into view as a large golden retriever stood up on its hind legs to see who the visitor might be. It gave her a big, goofy grin before its breath fogged the glass.

The lock clicked and the door opened a few inches. The retriever's muzzle worked its way out in the vicinity of Erin's knee. A woman peered out at her.

"Yes?" the woman said.

"Ms. Stachowski?" Erin guessed.

"That's right," the woman answered. "I don't think I know you."

"I'm with the NYPD, ma'am," Erin said, showing the gold shield at her belt. "I'm sorry to bother you, but I'm trying to get in touch with Phil."

"He's not home," Ms. Stachowski said.

"Do you have any idea where he is?"

Phil's wife considered her for a long moment. She had keen, intelligent eyes. "And what's your name and shield number, ma'am?" she asked.

Erin approved of caution. On any other night, she would have silently applauded it. Now, however, all she felt was a rising impatience and concern. Did she dare tell this woman her name? Even that would be a breach of undercover protocol. But then, being here at all was a dangerous risk.

The best thing, she decided, was to come at the situation from another angle. "I'm Detective O'Reilly," she said. "Major Crimes. Shield four-six-four-oh. I'm working a case I was hoping to get his help on. I need to talk to him tonight, if possible."

"Don't you have his phone number?"

"I actually don't," Erin said, offering a shamefaced smile. "I did try your landline, but it didn't go through. And Dispatch is really busy on account of the storm, so I thought, as long as I was in the area..."

"Of course," Ms. Stachowski said. "The landline is down. I think the storm must have done something to the lines. The city keeps saying they're going to bury the cables, but there's never enough money in the budget. Why don't you come in for a minute? I'll get you his cell number. Don't mind Bradley, he's a big marshmallow."

She stepped back from the door and opened it wider. Bradley greeted Erin by jumping up on his hind legs, planting his paws on her shoulders, and giving her face a friendly slurp. He somehow managed to stay balanced on his back feet despite his vigorously wagging tail, which made the entire back half of his body shimmy from side to side.

Erin maneuvered herself around the retriever into the house. It was warm and cozy, reminding her of her brother's brownstone. Phil obviously wasn't living off a surgeon's salary; the furnishings were less expensive and the building itself more worn, but the place had the air of a happy home. A pair of pre-teen girls were sitting on the living-room couch, watching TV. The screen showed a black-and-white Jimmy Stewart, so Erin figured they were watching that Christmas classic, *It's a Wonderful Life*.

"You can call me Camilla," Ms. Stachowski said. "That's Nora and Grace. You've already met Bradley."

Bradley was following Erin very closely, snuffling at her pants leg. He'd identified Rolf's scent and was seeing what else he could learn through his nostrils.

"Hi, kids," Erin said. One of them glanced up and waved. The other took no notice.

"Let's go into the kitchen," Camilla said.

"I really should be getting going soon," Erin said.

"You came out of your way to get here," Camilla replied. "I know you said you were in the neighborhood, but you had to cross the river. I've got peppermint cookies fresh out of the oven and coffee on. Don't worry, it's decaf."

Erin would actually have preferred a caffeinated beverage. She had the feeling she might be up for a while. But something hot would be welcome anyway.

"That'd be nice," she said, following the other woman through the dining room into the kitchen. Before she quite knew what was going on, she found herself holding a plate on which sat a pair of warm cookies. They were shaped like candy canes and made of two ropes of dough, one red and one cream-colored, twisted together. They were sugar cookies flavored with peppermint extract and tasted exactly right for the holiday season.

"So, you know Phil," Camilla said.

"What's that?" Erin said, startled. She hadn't said anything of the sort.

"You used his first name," Camilla said quietly. "You didn't change to calling him Lieutenant Stachowski until later. And Phil doesn't work with Major Crimes. What's going on, Detective?"

Erin was slightly unnerved by Camilla's sharp, perceptive stare and the way she'd picked up on little details. Misleading her was going to be very tricky, and might be more dangerous than telling the truth.

"You know what your husband does with the NYPD, ma'am?" Erin asked.

Camilla nodded. "He handles informants and undercover officers," she said, swinging the door shut and cutting off the kitchen from the rest of the house. Bradley had managed to worm his way into the room just in time. The dog now sat with his nose as close as it could get to the cookies.

"That's right," Erin said. "I've got reason to believe somebody he's working with is a double agent."

"Is he in danger?" Camilla asked. She said it very calmly, but the muscles in her cheeks had tightened up.

"I hope not," Erin said truthfully. "But that's why I need to reach him. I got some information from another source that he needs to hear right away."

Camilla nodded again. "All right," she said. She pulled her cell phone out of her pocket and brought up the contact list. She pressed the call button and tilted it so Erin could see the screen.

"You don't need to—" Erin began.

"You said right away," Camilla said.

The phone rang a second time. Then a third.

"Maybe he's busy," Camilla said. "If he's meeting with someone, he might not be able to talk."

It rang again, then one more time.

"Stachowski," Phil's familiar voice said. "Sorry I missed you. Let me know what you need and I'll do what I can."

The phone beeped.

"Hi, Phil," Camilla said. "This is Cam. Someone was here looking for you. They've got your number now, so I hope they find you. Give me a call when you get this, okay? Love you."

She hung up and gave an apologetic shrug. "That's marriage to a cop," she said. "I'm sure you know what it can be like."

"Of course," Erin said, a little distracted. She was entering Phil's number into her phone. She saved it under "Brother Tommy." Her youngest brother had a tendency to change phone plans when he got too far behind on his payments and his previous plan got canceled. She already had four numbers saved for him, so it would serve as camouflage if anyone got their hands on her phone and hacked the security code.

"Detective?" Camilla said.

"Thanks for the cookies," Erin said. "I'll let you get back to your evening."

"What's the matter?" Camilla demanded. Her voice now held a cold, steely undertone.

"Probably nothing," Erin said.

"Then why are you worried?"

"I'm not," she lied.

Camilla crossed her arms. "This is my family, Detective," she said. "I have a right to know."

Erin sighed. "Ma'am, I'm not at liberty to say," she said, hating the sound of the words. "I don't have any reason to think your family is in any danger."

"I think you're lying," Camilla said.

Erin felt her own jaw tighten. She'd bluffed dangerous psychopaths for months, including earlier this very evening. Why was she having trouble with this ordinary housewife? "I'm telling you everything I can," she said. "All I know is that one of

Phil's—Lieutenant Stachowski's—officers may be playing both sides, and he needs to be careful. The bad guys think he's got some information that's dangerous to them and they want to know what it is."

"You think they might hurt him to get it?"

"It's unlikely."

"But possible."

"Yeah, it's a possibility. That's why I'm here."

"And if they'd hurt him, they might also come after his family, isn't that true? For leverage?"

Erin shook her head. "I don't want to scare you," she said. "Just keep your eyes open and—"

"We've got a gun in the house," Camilla said. "It's a double-barreled hunting shotgun. Phil taught me how to use it."

"Jesus," Erin said. "Be careful. Having a gun in the house doesn't make you safer, ma'am, especially if you've got kids. The chances of an accident are a lot higher than the chances it'll protect you."

"I'm not a child, Detective, and I'm not stupid," Camilla said. "It's locked up. But I can get to it quickly if I have to. I'm going to protect my family."

"Okay," Erin said, giving up. "But if you notice anything out of the ordinary, anything suspicious, don't just start blasting. Call 911. And remember it's usually better to run than to fight. Now I've got to go see if I can track Phil down. Do you have any idea where he might have gone?"

"He called me around five and said he had a couple of meetings after his shift," Camilla said. "He said he'd be back by eight."

Erin looked at the clock on the kitchen wall. It read 8:13.

"Road conditions are pretty bad," she said, knowing it sounded lame but saying it anyway. "He's probably just been delayed."

"Then why didn't he answer the phone?" Camilla asked. She still sounded calm, but her eyes showed the strain.

* * *

Rolf was waiting in the Charger, which was already coated with a thick dusting of snow. He gave her a thorough sniffing, acquainting himself with Bradley's scent, while she thought what to do. It had actually been a good thing for Camilla's phone to be the one that had called Phil; that way it couldn't be traced to Erin. She noted that Camilla had absorbed some of her husband's tradecraft. She hadn't mentioned Erin's name, nor even her gender, in the message she'd left.

She decided to try calling from her burner phone. That number might already be compromised, but if so, it wouldn't do any more harm. She put it to her ear and let it ring. When it rolled to voicemail, she hung up without leaving a message.

"He didn't take my call," she told Rolf. "And he always takes my calls. He called his wife to tell her when he'd be home. Now he's late, but he didn't call again to warn her. Evan knows Phil's watching him. The only way he'd know Phil's name is if one of Phil's guys is feeding him intel. So what does that tell us?"

Rolf cocked his head and perked his enormous ears.

"Maybe his phone died," she said. "But both phones at the same time? Unlikely. More likely he can't answer. Maybe he crashed his car."

Rolf listened to her theories. She was talking, and that meant she was planning. Planning often led to the good stuff, like chasing and biting, so he was willing to be patient and optimistic.

"Yeah," Erin sighed. "And maybe I'll hit the jackpot playing slots in Atlantic City. Something's seriously wrong. I need to find him."

And just how was she going to do that? She still didn't dare get Dispatch involved. She didn't want to leave a trail for some crooked cop to follow. And all the time the snow kept falling, covering her car deeper.

She had a phone number, but it was useless by itself. The NYPD had a team of phone operators who liaised with the Department. Those guys could locate a cell phone within a few meters. But they wouldn't do it for a random burner phone, not without a court order. That meant getting a judge's signature, which meant an even broader paper trail.

Erin only knew one judge she trusted enough to bring this to. Fortunately, it was a judge who owed her a favor. She picked up her phone and dialed.

"Good evening," Judge Ferris said in his mellow baritone. He rarely sounded upset or even excited. More than a half-century on the judicial bench had made him accustomed to trouble.

"Evening, your honor," she said. "This is Erin O'Reilly."

"Ah, the lovely Miss O'Reilly. What an unexpected and particular pleasure. How do I find you on this cold and wintry evening? If you are as wise as I think, you ought to be ensconced before a roaring fire with your faithful dog curled at your feet, a steaming beverage in one hand and a familiar and beloved book in the other, as I am myself."

"Not exactly," she said. "I'm in my car right now, in Hoboken."

"New Jersey? Good gracious, and I took you for a sensible young woman. Whyever would you go to such a dreadful place on such a night?"

"I need your help, your honor."

"I shall be only too gratified to come to your assistance, though I do hope it will not necessitate tramping through snow and ice. My arthritis is terribly aggravated by cold and damp."

"I need you to sign a warrant for a phone number."

"To tap the line?" The banter dropped out of Ferris's voice, replaced by the professional jurist who'd sat on the bench since before Erin was born.

"No, sir. I need to trace the number to a specific location. And it needs to happen fast."

"Who is the malefactor?"

It took Erin a trying to remember what a malefactor was. She came up with the definition of "bad guy," or maybe "evildoer."

"It's not like that," she said. "The phone belongs to an officer with the NYPD. I have to get a fix on him. I think he might be in danger."

"Surely if an officer's safety is at stake, the Department can trace his number," Ferris said. He sounded confused.

"It's a burner phone," she explained. "I don't think I can run a trace on his registered number."

"Why not?"

Erin drew in a deep breath and took the plunge. "It's Lieutenant Philip Stachowski. He runs undercover assignments. Going through official channels will compromise at least one ongoing operation and might get an undercover killed. I've got credible evidence that his team has been infiltrated."

"I don't suppose this evidence is something you're willing and able to produce?"

"Not immediately. It'll have to wait until the current investigation is closed."

"Are you citing the extenuating circumstance of operational security?" From Ferris's tone, it was too easy to imagine his sardonically raised eyebrow.

"That's right."

"What reason do you have to fear for Lieutenant Stachowski's safety?"

"This won't be in the paperwork," Erin said. "I got a tip from an underworld source that Lieutenant Stachowski has an officer undercover in the organization. That organization is aware of the penetration and they're trying to identify the officer. They know Stachowski's name. If they can't think of another way to get to the mole, they might come after him. He's overdue getting home and his wife can't reach him. Neither can I."

"Very well," Ferris said. "Send me the warrant. Assuming everything is as you've described, I'll sign it. But this is somewhat irregular."

"You're telling me. Thanks."

"My pleasure."

Ferris preferred to get his warrants the old-fashioned way, by hand, but he lived all the way down on Staten Island. There was no way Erin was going to drive that distance, through a blizzard, just to provide the personal touch the Judge valued so highly. She was able to fill out the request on her car's computer and send it electronically. Of course, for an old-timer like Ferris, technology only went so far. Erin knew he had an honest-to-God fax machine in his house that would spit out the paper copy, which Ferris would then read and sign with a fountain pen. No cheap ballpoints for Ferris.

She fired off the request and waited, trying not to squirm with impatience. It wasn't really a very long time, only six and a half minutes, but it felt longer. Then her departmental email informed her she had a new message, an electronic fax. She opened it up and saw Ferris's signature with its distinctive flourishing capital F.

After that it was time to call in the trace. Erin phoned the liaison team and gave them the number. They asked for the warrant and she forwarded it. The trace itself took almost no time at all. There was none of that Hollywood nonsense about needing half a minute to bounce the signal around. They simply triangulated the signal from nearby cell towers, using sensitive equipment to gauge the strength of the signal from each tower.

"We've got a location," the liaison officer reported. "The Carousel in the southern part of Central Park, give or take ten meters. Phone is turned on but not currently active."

"Copy that," Erin said. She aimed the Charger back toward the Holland Tunnel and put New Jersey in her rearview. Her wheels churned up fountains of snow. The temperature was falling as fast as the snowflakes; her car's thermometer read fifteen degrees and dropping.

"Why Central Park?" she asked Rolf.

The dog's tail started wagging. He knew the word "park." Those were wide open spaces where he went to run and play. He could fetch balls and sometimes go after guys in bite suits. Going to a park was definitely promising.

But if Erin had been a K-9 her own tail would have been tucked low, her ears flat against her skull. If Phil's phone was turned on, and if he was out of doors, why hadn't he answered it? He could have been in a car accident, but if so, why was his phone so far from the road? And if he'd been unable to answer in the moment, why hadn't he called her back?

Every passing minute made it worse. And here she was, on the wrong side of the Hudson. It'd take another hour to make it to Central Park. Anything could happen in an hour.

But she didn't see any choice. So she gritted her teeth and kept driving.

Chapter 4

10-13.

The numbers kept running through Erin's head. 10-13 was the NYPD code for "officer needs assistance." A 10-13 would bring every available cop in the area, a converging swarm of blue uniforms and guns. One of the things that gave a cop the necessary courage to run toward the sound of the gunfire was the knowledge that if it all went to shit, thirty-five thousand other cops were ready and willing to back you up.

Erin O'Reilly couldn't call for backup now. That would log a call to Dispatch, a call she wasn't prepared to explain. Some number of cops, she didn't know how many, couldn't be trusted. Evan O'Malley already knew too much. One more snippet of information might be the last straw.

The safest thing would be to turn toward the Barley Corner, forget about Phil's situation, and go home. If this whole thing turned out to be a big nothing sandwich, it would be the right decision.

But what if it wasn't?

"No," Erin said. "No way."

Rolf, not able to hear her inner monologue, was baffled. He figured she wasn't talking to him, since he hadn't been doing anything, so he lay down in his compartment and waited for clearer instructions.

The drive was endless. It was an awful combination of tense and tedious, like watching the dials at a nuclear reactor or standing guard at a supermax prison. Nothing much happened, but it always felt like something *could* happen, and she'd better be ready when it did. The constant vigilance but lack of any outlet for her nervous energy was exhausting. Her shoulders ached. She had to squint to see through the snow, and it made her eyes burn and her head hurt.

Somehow she made it to Central Park, a little before ten o'clock. Traffic was almost nonexistent, which meant the snow was just piling higher on the streets. She slewed the Charger into a parking space, guessing at the position of the lines, and felt a jarring shock when her tires slammed against a curb she couldn't see.

Erin cursed wearily. Then she wriggled out of her jacket, strapped on her body armor, and put the coat back on over it. When she picked up Rolf's K-9 Kevlar vest, the dog sprang instantly upright, tail lashing. The vest meant it was time to go to work.

Once they were geared up, she made one more call to the phone liaison team. "Any change in position on that phone?" she asked.

"That's a negative," the answer came. "The phone you're asking about is still showing at the Carousel, still turned on."

East 65th Street ran across the park, just a short distance north of the Carousel. The street lay in a sunken lane, stone-wall embankments on either side. Nobody had bothered clearing the snow, and it didn't look like anyone had driven on it, at least not for the past couple of hours. The Charger was up to the task, but the car's ground clearance was low enough that a hump of snow piled up at the front of the grille as she drove.

The headlights did basically no good, falling snow blocking the beams only a few yards in front of the Charger. Erin had to rely on her phone's GPS again to tell her when she was close. She was glad of the embankments, because as long as she stayed between them, she wouldn't run off the road and get stuck.

At last, the little electronic map in her hand told her she was next to the Carousel. She threw the car into Park. Then she opened the door, popped Rolf's compartment, and climbed out into the storm.

Icy needles peppered her face. She threw up an arm to shield her eyes. A short distance away, barely visible, the bulky shape of the Carousel squatted atop the embankment. Erin struggled upward, forcing her way through snow-covered underbrush.

Rolf plunged happily into a snowdrift. He raised a snowy head and shook himself vigorously, flinging snowflakes in all directions. His tail and ears were perked high. He was having a great time.

After a few minutes of hapless floundering, Erin managed to reach the metal railing that lined the sidewalk outside the Carousel. She hauled herself over it, cold and wet. Rolf jumped and scrambled after her. The sidewalk was also covered with a thick carpet of snow, but at least the footing was smooth and solid beneath it.

The Carousel was enclosed by an octagonal brick shelter, pierced by arches on all sides. The ride was closed, of course. The building was dark, the ticket booth deserted.

Erin climbed over the gate into the interior. Rolf scrabbled over it behind her. It was somewhat sheltered from the storm inside, though the wind whipped flakes in through the arches and made weird, eerie whistling noises. The garishly-painted horses on the carousel itself were dark shapes in the near-blackness.

"Phil?" she called, not really expecting an answer and receiving none.

She took out her pocket flashlight and twisted it into life, shining the bright LED beam around the darkened structure. She saw no sign of Phil, nor of anyone else.

"Damn it," she muttered. She reached for her burner phone. She poked Phil's contact number, calling the burner he used to talk to her.

It rang and rang, finally rolling to voicemail.

Erin cursed again, quietly but thoroughly. Then, without much hope, she dialed Phil's personal number, the one she'd gotten from Camilla. It started ringing.

She froze. The faint but unmistakable sound of a ring tone drifted through the icy air. It was nearby, but hard to place.

Erin quickly moved from side to side, trying to get a directional fix on the music. The tones were familiar, reminding her of a movie she'd seen as a kid, but she couldn't identify the song. That didn't matter; what was important was finding the phone. The sounds were coming from the direction of the carousel, she was sure of it.

She hurried to the carnival ride and dropped to her knees next to it. Then she ducked down and shone the flashlight under the apron of the turntable. Sure enough, she saw the little plastic rectangle of a cell phone.

It was a tight squeeze, but she was able to worm her hand under the carousel. She had to lie down flat on her stomach and reach as far as she could, her fingertips barely brushing the phone. Telling herself to be patient, not to snatch at it and shove it away, she began to carefully draw it toward her.

She'd heard stories of accidents involving mechanical devices like this one. Sure, it was turned off, but there might be some spring-loaded energy stored up in it. What if the carousel lurched into motion? It'd tear her arm clean off at the shoulder. A wave of claustrophobia swept over her. She clenched her jaw and held still until the feeling passed. Then she eased the phone another half-inch nearer.

That was enough. She had a grip on it. She dragged it free, sat up, and stared at it. The phone was a very ordinary model, surrounded by a plastic protective case. She took off a glove and swiped a finger across the screen. A security prompt popped up, demanding her access code.

"Figures," she said. Of course Phil wouldn't leave his phone unsecured. But what was it doing here? And what was she supposed to do with it?

"He's got bigger hands than I do," she said to Rolf. "There's no way his arm would've fit under there. And look at these scuff marks on the case. I think this got dropped and kicked under. That means either Phil did it himself, or there was some sort of struggle, or somebody else put it there to get it out of sight. No matter what, that means he was here and he was in trouble. But where'd he go? There's no damn footprints. It's snowing too fast."

Rolf waited patiently. He was used to Erin using him as a sounding board. He wasn't sure exactly what service he was providing, but as long as he was being helpful, that was good enough for him.

Erin looked at the dog. He was her best chance, maybe her only one.

Phil's phone rode around in his pocket all day long. His smell would be all over it. Erin extended her arm, holding the phone in front of the K-9's nose.

"Rolf, *such!*" she said.

Rolf's nostrils flared. He knew Phil's scent, had been around the man plenty of times. He tossed his head, trying to catch the elusive odor as the wind whipped around him.

No human could possibly follow a scent-trail in conditions like these. But human noses were pitiful things, good only for the strongest, most obvious smells. Rolf's olfactory receptors were thousands of times better. He could track a suspect across running water by the particles of sweat that hung in the air. He could find a body that had recently been buried under several feet of concrete. A little wind and snow made it harder, but far from impossible.

Rolf's entire body stiffened. He froze, one paw poised and pointing. Then he was off, leaping the gate and hurling himself into the December night, angling southeast.

Erin followed, but she slipped as she clambered over the gate. The loop of Rolf's leash fell from her hand. She started to call him back, but tumbled headlong into a snowbank and inhaled a mouthful of snow. She came up spluttering, lungs burning from ice in her throat. Rolf had vanished into the blizzard.

"Rolf!" she shouted hoarsely. *"Komm! Hier!"*

The wind snatched the words from her mouth and carried them away. Cursing again, Erin played her flashlight across the ground, looking for the fresh pawprints that would tell her where he'd gone. She found his trail, running straight down the sidewalk. Erin ran after him.

The going was hard. The wind was blowing from northeast, catching her in the face. Snow had gotten into the tops of her shoes and she could feel icy wetness seeping through her socks. Her jacket was totally inadequate for the conditions, as were her gloves. Every part of her was cold. Her fingertips and toes were already going numb.

Erin ignored all that. Her dog was somewhere ahead, racing headlong into God only knew what. She forced herself to go faster, slipping and stumbling. The path was lit, but the lamps gave only dim halos of radiance that faded after just a few feet.

A building loomed in front of her, a shape she could only guess at. As she passed under the arch of a covered walkway, gaining a little shelter, she heard Rolf barking. It was his shrill, penetrating bark, the one he used in searches when he'd located his quarry.

Erin put on a burst of speed, half-melted snow squelching in her shoes. Her flashlight beam danced with every step. She saw movement in the shadowed entrance of the gift shop, a gigantic silhouette of a dog, flung against the wall by her light, a spirit animal with a wildly wagging tail and tall, pointed ears.

Rolf was prancing excitedly in front of a huddled shape. It was a man, or the right dimensions for one, clad in a dark coat. It was lying face-down. Fresh snow was already covering it. The body wasn't moving.

"*Sitz!*" Erin gasped to Rolf, who immediately sat back on his haunches, tongue lolling, ready to be told what a very good boy he'd been. She tossed him his rubber Kong ball without even thinking about it, completing the ritual. Rolf snagged it in midair and gave it a joyful, rubbery squeak with his jaws.

Erin paid no attention to the K-9. She went to one knee beside the body, shining the flashlight toward its head. The reflected light was deep crimson. Blood had frozen in the thinning hair at the back of the man's head and on the collar of his coat, forming oddly beautiful ruby crystals.

She put her hand on the man's shoulder and turned him so she could see his face. His eyes were closed as if he was sleeping, but his temple was sheeted with blood. The side of his head was a red ruin, but in spite of the horrible wound, she knew him.

Phil Stachowski's skin was the color of the snow in which he lay. His flesh was cool under her chilled fingertips. He lay perfectly still.

Shock and cold made Erin clumsy. She fumbled her phone, dropping it twice. She finally got it to her face and dialed Dispatch. She knew, in some coldly rational corner of her mind, that she shouldn't, that it might blow her cover, but what did that matter now?

"Dispatch," the brisk, competent voice said in Erin's ear.

"This is O'Reilly," Erin said, recognizing her own shock in the way she was slurring her words. "Shield four-six-four-oh. I'm in Central Park, the Visitor Center off 65th Street. This is a 10-13. I've got an officer down. Repeat, officer down."

Chapter 5

When Erin had been a trainee at the Academy, she'd gotten a jolt from a Taser; five seconds of high volts, low amps delivered directly into her back by a pair of narrow metal darts. It was nothing personal. Every officer who'd be carrying a Taser needed to know exactly what it felt like to ride the lightning, so they'd know what they were dishing out to the perps and how the poor bastards could be expected to react. That was when she'd learned just how long five seconds could be. Time expanded. She distinctly remembered counting fifteen seconds in her head before the incredible, burning pain subsided.

Waiting for the ambulance didn't cause physical pain, but time stretched out the same way. The average response time for the FDNY's paramedics in Manhattan was a little over nine minutes. Conditions were much worse than usual, but traffic was better, which made it almost a wash. The flashing lights of the ambulance appeared through the driving snow almost exactly twelve minutes after Erin had made the call. It felt more like an hour.

She didn't know if Phil was alive or not. If she'd had to bet one way or the other, she would've put her money on "dead."

Her fingertips had lost sensitivity from the cold, so she couldn't say for sure whether he had a pulse. She didn't dare leave him for the time it would take to fetch the first-aid kit from the Charger, so she broke into the nearby Visitor Center and borrowed theirs. Then she realized there was almost nothing she could do for him anyway. The intense cold had already stopped the bleeding, so a bandage hardly mattered, and more invasive measures would have to wait for a surgeon.

Erin had to settle for breathing for him and doing chest compressions. His lips were cold on hers. She shoved her hands down against his chest over and over, finding the too-familiar rhythm of CPR. Sometimes it was enough to keep a man alive until the EMTs got there; more often it wasn't.

Two NYPD blue-and-whites arrived ahead of the ambulance, but there wasn't much for the Patrol officers to do either. Erin wasn't about to let anyone else handle the CPR, so they just established a loose perimeter and stood around getting cold.

Erin didn't let herself think. She just counted compressions over and over, gasping with her own exertions, sweating in spite of the cold, keeping going as the blue and red emergency lights glowed overhead and another pair of men struggled through the snow toward her.

A hand fell on Erin's shoulder. "We've got this," a paramedic said. "What's his status?"

"GSW to the head, nonresponsive," she replied mechanically. Nine times out of ten, those words were a death sentence.

"Copy that," the EMT said. He and his partner went to work, checking Phil's vitals and examining his injury.

"Got a pulse," the other medic announced. "It's weak. BP is real low but stable."

"Let's get him prepped for transport," the first EMT said.

"Northwell?" his partner suggested.

The first medic shook his head. "Bellevue," he said. "It's a little farther, but they've got a better trauma team. This guy needs the best we've got. How long has he been out here?"

"No idea," Erin said. "I'm guessing at least an hour or two."

"He's tougher than he looks," the second EMT said. "Or maybe he's just lucky."

"Don't call it luck," the first medic said. "Not yet."

Erin watched them load Phil onto the stretcher and carry him down to the ambulance. Then the vehicle slewed around in the snow, fishtailing and nearly clipping the embankment, and pulled away into the night. Still breathing hard from her CPR efforts, she looked dully at the surrounding scene. There might be all sorts of evidence, but the blowing snow had covered it. Her hands were completely numb in spite of her gloves. How cold was it? Single digits? Lower?

"Secure the scene," she told the Patrol officers, who nodded unhappily. "I'll get CSU to come out. Sergeant, you've got command."

"Yes, ma'am," the senior officer said.

"You talk only to Major Crimes on this one," she said. "Lieutenant Webb from the Eight will be here to take over from you. Until you see him, don't let anybody through. Not your CO, not the PC, not Jesus Christ Himself. You copy?"

"I copy," he said.

It was the best she could do. Erin put thoughts of the crime scene out of her head. She slid down the embankment to East 65th and started making her way back to her car. Rolf plunged through the drifts beside her, happily carrying his toy in his mouth. If he was cold, he wasn't showing it. She envied his fur coat.

Erin got behind the wheel and started the engine. The car warmed up fairly quickly, and soon blessed warm air started flowing through the vents . She peeled off her gloves and held her hands in front of the holes.

For a few seconds she felt nothing at all. Then the blood started tentatively making its way through the capillaries of her fingertips and the pain hit her.

She hissed sharply through her teeth. It was like being stung by dozens of hornets at once, all over her fingers. She gritted her teeth and held her hands there, toughing it out, telling herself that like a Taser jolt, it wouldn't last forever.

At some point, she realized the wetness on her cheeks wasn't just melting snow. She wondered whether she was crying from the pain in her hands or from what she'd just seen. Maybe it didn't matter.

Rolf nosed anxiously at her. He leaned forward through the hatch between the seats and carefully, gently licked the back of her right hand. His toy lay forgotten in his compartment.

"Good boy," she managed to say. The words caught in her throat and she choked on a sudden sob. "Oh my God," she whispered.

She couldn't afford to be weak, couldn't break down now. There were places to be, people to talk to. There'd be time to lose her shit later. Sean O'Reilly's daughter needed to step up now, she told herself.

"First things first," she murmured. She put the car in gear and started rolling. She was going to Bellevue Hospital. Phil wouldn't be conscious; hell, he probably wasn't alive. But he just might wake up before surgery, and if he did, she needed to know what he had to say. And she had to be there in case he pulled through.

While she drove, she had some telephoning to do. The first call would be relatively easy, the second and third would be complicated, and the fourth would be one of the hardest calls she'd ever had to make.

*   *   *

Lieutenant Webb had been asleep. It was obvious from the grogginess in his voice. But he woke up fast once Erin started talking.

"An NYPD Lieutenant?" he said sharply. "Shot?"

"That's affirmative, sir," she said. "East 65th, by the Visitor Center. We've got two units on scene, but I won't be there. I'm on my way to Bellevue to check up on him."

"Are you hurt?"

"No. I wasn't there when it happened."

"Then how… never mind. I'm on my way. I'll call Neshenko and Piekarski. Will you be at Bellevue?"

"For the next few hours, I think."

"Copy that. I'll be in touch."

"One down," Erin murmured as she hung up. Now things were going to get complicated.

*   *   *

"Holliday," the Captain said. To his credit, he sounded wide awake and alert.

"This is Detective O'Reilly, sir," she said. "I'm really sorry to disturb you at home, but—"

"What's the situation?" he interrupted.

"Lieutenant Stachowski's been shot," she said.

"How badly?"

"Pretty bad."

"Is he alive?"

"I don't know."

There were three seconds of silence. Then Holliday said, "Have you been compromised?"

That was the question she didn't want, because there was only one truthful answer. Erin swallowed.

"I don't know, sir," she said.

"Carlyle?"

"I don't know that either. I don't know what Phil said, or who went after him. It might be unrelated."

"And it might not. You get Carlyle into protective custody right now, and you get yourself somewhere safe immediately."

"He'll be safe enough," she said. "His place is a fortress and he's got good people."

"Good enough for this? If they know about him, they'll come for him with everything they've got."

Erin thought of Ian Thompson. *I'd like to see them try*, she thought. But Carlyle wasn't at home right now. "I'll call him," she said. "I'll warn him and ask if he's willing to come in. But if he does, that blows the operation."

"I'm aware of that, O'Reilly," Holliday said grimly. "And I'm also aware the operation may already be blown. Make the call. Where are you?"

"Streetside, on my way to Bellevue to check on Phil. I'll be safe there."

"I'll get additional officers detailed to the hospital. I'll spin it as protection for our wounded man. But stick close to the uniforms, O'Reilly. It's dangerous out there tonight."

No shit, she thought. "Copy that, sir," she said.

And that was the second call.

*   *   *

She wasn't sure Carlyle would answer his cell. The last she'd heard, he was with Kyle Finnegan, which hardly inspired confidence in his safety. Finnegan was utterly, violently insane. Erin had personally watched him pitch a man out a twelfth-story window and bite a chunk out of another man's face. If Finnegan had heard Carlyle was playing for the other side, Erin would never see her boyfriend again.

"Evening."

Carlyle's Irish lilt had never sounded so sweet. Erin blinked away fresh tears. "Evening," she said hoarsely. "Is this a bad time?"

"It's *sweet* of you to ask," he said. "I can't talk long, for I've other business tonight. But all's well with you? You're never far from my *heart*."

"I'm okay," she said, though her own heart had skipped a beat. "I just wanted you to know, I'm going to be out late, maybe all night."

"What's happened?" he asked.

"A cop got shot," she said, choosing her words carefully. "A Lieutenant from the Ten. He might pull through and he might not. But it's a Major Crimes case, obviously, and I've got to handle it very carefully."

"Understood. Take care of yourself, Erin. I'll keep the kettle on for you."

"How sweet," she said. "You're in my heart, too."

"Grand," he said. "Look after your business, darling. Ta."

And he hung up.

"Shit," Erin growled. Carlyle had used a code they'd worked out months earlier, but he'd modified it. If either of them called the other "sweetheart," it meant they were under duress. It was a call for help. Carlyle hadn't said that, but he'd been careful to include both parts of the word. She'd echoed them back to make sure he knew she'd heard them. But what had he meant?

She decided he'd probably meant he wasn't alone and couldn't speak freely, but he wasn't in any immediate danger. She'd meant to tell him about Phil, but his cagey words had warned her off. She'd settled for an oblique notification. He might have missed it, but she trusted Carlyle's intelligence and instincts. Both of them were playing hunches. If either was wrong, they risked everything. But Carlyle had done this dangerous dance since she'd been in high school. He was an old hand in a profession which was almost exclusively young men.

"Shit," she said again. But she'd rolled the dice and there was nothing to do now but see how they landed. Carlyle would have to look after himself. She was almost at the hospital and still had one more call to make.

*   *   *

"Hello?" the woman said. She'd pounced on the phone, answering before it finished the first ring, but now sounded hesitant. An unfamiliar number in the middle of an uncertain evening could mean anything.

"Ms. Stachowski?" Erin said. "This is Detective O'Reilly. We spoke earlier."

"Oh, yes, of course," Camilla said. "Have you heard from Phil?"

Erin closed her eyes for a moment, then had to open them again to watch the road. "That's what I'm calling about, ma'am," she said. "There's been an incident."

"What sort of incident?" Camilla asked. She was trying to speak calmly, but the undercurrent of raw terror in her voice tore little pieces out of Erin's heart.

"He's been shot," she said. "They've taken him to Bellevue Hospital. It's... it's pretty bad. But he'll get the best medical care available. If you have someone who can take care of the kids, you should probably get over there as soon as you can. I'm sorry."

The cheapness of her last two words was obvious to Erin, but what else could she say?

"Yes, I'll do that," Camilla said, suddenly brisk and businesslike. "Will you be at the hospital?"

"I should be."

"Then I'm sure I'll see you there. Thank you for letting me know, Detective."

Erin marveled at her. Camilla Stachowski was obviously one tough lady. It was amazing what you could do when your family was on the line.

The bright lights of the Bellevue ER beckoned to her through the snow. She swung into the parking lot. This lot, at least, was clear; emergency rooms were high priority for snow clearance. She unloaded Rolf and gave him a quick turn around the lot, letting him cock a leg at one of the lampposts. The ordinary everyday task of walking the dog steadied her a little. Then she led him inside.

The bustle of the ER was jarring after the snowy drive through the silent Manhattan streets. There might be a blizzard outside, but that didn't stop New Yorkers from getting sick and hurt. They might even be getting injured more than usual. Heavy snow led to car accidents, falls, and even heart attacks from over-exertion while shoveling. There'd be plenty of broken bones in New York tonight.

A cluster of dark-blue jackets had congregated at one end of the waiting room. Word always got around the NYPD fast when an officer was wounded. These cops had just come off duty, or had stopped in on the way to other assignments. A vigil had begun. It would last until Phil came out of surgery, or until he was pronounced dead.

Erin approached the group, making sure her gold shield was visible. The circle of cops opened to admit her.

"What's the word?" she asked.

"They just wheeled him into surgery," one of the cops said.

"He didn't look too good," another said.

"Bullshit," a third chimed in. "He'll be fine. You don't know Stachowski."

"What do you mean?" Erin asked.

The third cop was a grizzled veteran, a Sergeant with gray at his temples and scars on his knuckles. "I knew him back in the day," he said. "He don't look like much, sure, but that man don't know the meaning of fear and he don't know the meaning of quit."

Erin tried to make that description jibe with her own perceptions of Phil. He was good police, sure, but she couldn't picture him as a hardcore street officer.

"Nice guy," the Sergeant went on. "But don't let that fool you. He's got it where it counts."

He tapped his own chest expressively, right over his heart.

"Yeah, Sarge," the first cop said. "He's got heart. But he got shot in the *head*." He tapped his own finger on his temple.

"Don't matter how tough you are, you take one in the brain pan, that's it," the second cop said, shaking his head.

"Who's operating on him?" Erin asked.

"Doc O'Reilly," the Sergeant said. "I heard he's the real deal. A genuine grave-robber. Ain't nobody I'd rather have cutting on me or mine."

Erin drifted away from the other officers in the direction of the coffee dispenser. She got a paper cup and promptly burned her fingers trying to hold the hot drink. She hardly cared. The knowledge that her brother was the guy holding the knife was some comfort; Sean O'Reilly Junior was as good as they came.

She found a chair and tried to get comfortable. Soon enough she and her squad would start trying to figure out exactly what had happened in Central Park. But right now there was nothing to do but wait and pray.

So that was what she did.

Chapter 6

"Anyone sitting here?"

The voice startled Erin out of her reverie. She looked up into a round-cheeked, boyish face. The young man had a gold shield at his belt and a hesitant smile on his lips. He nodded to the open chair at Erin's right. Rolf was curled up at her feet, snoozing.

"It's all yours, Detective," she said.

"Carter," he said, offering his hand. "Lenny Carter, from the Ten. Narcotics."

"Erin O'Reilly, from the Eightball," she replied, shaking hands. "Major Crimes." His face might be youthful, but his hands were tough and his grip strong. His knuckles had fresh-looking bruises on them. This was no desk jockey; Carter was a street cop. She saw the gun at his belt and the bulge at his ankle that hinted at a backup piece.

"Nice of you to drop by," he said, taking the seat next to her. "You on the clock right now?"

"No," she said. "You?"

"Off duty," he said. "I'd rather be knocking back a couple at the bar, but what can you do? It's a hell of a thing. How do you know Phil?"

Tell all the truth you can, Carlyle whispered in the back of Erin's mind.

"I don't really," she said. "I kind of got roped into this. I'm the one who found him."

Carter pursed his lips and whistled softly. "Whew. That's rough. I heard he was in the middle of Central Park. How'd you stumble over him?"

"I was looking for him. I wanted to pick his brain about an old case."

Carter made a face. "I don't think his brain's in much shape to be picked right now," he said.

"Yeesh," Erin said. "That's not what I meant."

"I know, I know. Poor taste. Cop humor. But how'd you know where to find him?"

"When he didn't answer, I pinged his phone. His wife was worried about him."

"Oh yeah, he's married, isn't he," Carter said. "That's rough. Where's the wife now?"

"On her way here."

"That's good." Carter glanced at the swinging doors that led to Surgery. "I don't suppose they're letting anybody see him."

"Are you kidding?" Erin said. "He's practically dead. I thought he was gone when I found him."

"In this weather, with just a cell trace? You part Indian tracker, or what?"

"Rolf sniffed him out when I got close," Erin said. "And a damn good thing, too."

"Oh!" Carter exclaimed, taking in her and her dog with new eyes. "You're Junkyard O'Reilly!"

Erin smiled thinly. "That's what they call me on the street."

"I heard about you," he said.

"Only good things, I hope."

He smiled. "Tall tales," he said. "Is it really true you've had two car bombs blow up right next to you and walked away without a scratch both times?"

"Not quite," she said. "I got a little toasted. I haven't heard your name before. How do you know Stachowski?"

"I work with him all the time," Carter said. "Us Narcs do a lot of undercover plainclothes shit. He helps us keep our heads screwed on right. My squad's here with me."

"Yeah? Which ones are they?"

Carter pointed to the coffee machine, where three more men were standing. "The big guy is Erwin Katzenberg, we all call him Katz. The other two are Mingo Sanchez and Lieutenant Bowes. Del Ames is our fifth guy, but he couldn't make it."

"You guys must think a lot of the Lieutenant," Erin said. "To all come down here."

"Phil's one of a kind," Carter said. "It's funny; you wouldn't think a guy who runs undercovers would be such a straight shooter, but he is. Totally incorruptible. If he found a twenty lying in the gutter, he'd try to find the guy who dropped it so he could give it back. And he'd die before he'd sell out one of his guys. He was like a mentor to me. We're talking Obi-Wan Kenobi shit here."

"And you're Luke Skywalker?" Erin replied.

"Something like that," Carter said. "Say, what was it you needed to talk to Phil about? Could be I've heard something that'd help you."

Erin shook her head. "It's a cold case," she said. "Nothing current. No offense, kiddo, but you look like you were probably in grade school when it went down."

Carter grinned. "You know what they called me at the Academy? Baby Face Carter. They said I should've been a bank robber, like Baby Face Nelson, but I joined the cops instead. I swear, I'm older than I look."

"I hope so," Erin said, returning the grin. "Otherwise I'd think they were handing out gold shields as graduation presents."

It felt good to smile, to step away from the situation for a moment. She could still feel the desperate worry, the fear gnawing at the back of her mind, and she could see the lines of tension in Lenny's cherubic face. He was feeling it too. There was nothing worse than waiting to see if someone you cared about was going to make it. She'd been here too many times before.

The other Narcs came over and joined them. They reminded Erin of her friends Hank Logan, Zofia Piekarski, and their Street Narcotics Enforcement Unit; a tough, streetwise bunch of cowboys. Carter introduced her. They'd all heard of her by reputation and were impressed that she'd come to stand vigil with them.

"It's not a big deal, guys," she said, a little embarrassed. "My squad's going to catch this case, so I'm hoping he'll wake up and remember something."

"A guy gets shot in the head, he's lucky if he remembers his own name," Mingo said grimly. "I wouldn't bet on him knowing anything that's happened in the last twenty-four hours."

"And it wouldn't be admissible as evidence," Carter added. "He's likely to be pretty scrambled. Assuming he wakes up at all. He might think he remembers the attack, but for all we know he'll splice in somebody else's face in place of the shooter. Like, maybe he'll think his mom shot him or something."

"Moms shoot people," Katz said. "Remember that crack-whore in that basement that one time?"

"I don't think Stachowski's mom is going on my list of suspects," Erin said. "Thanks anyway."

*   *   *

Lieutenant Webb arrived about twenty minutes later, brushing snow from his fedora and the shoulders of his trench coat. He stomped his feet and rubbed his hands. Then he nodded to Erin, but went for the coffee machine before approaching her. Carter and his squad had drifted away and were hanging out at the other end of the room.

"I never should've left LA," Webb grumbled. "You know when it snows in Los Angeles?"

"I have no idea, sir," she said.

"Never."

"Never?"

"Well, we did have a little in '07," he admitted. "And I think it happened in '89. How are you doing?"

"I'm fine, sir."

He rolled his eyes. "Of course you are. Any word on our victim's condition?"

"Nothing. He went into surgery about an hour ago. Where's Vic?"

"He's either at the scene of the shooting, or trying to get there. I've never seen road conditions this bad. How on Earth did you find Stachowski?"

"I didn't," she said, putting her hand down and ruffling Rolf's fur. The Shepherd thumped his tail but didn't open his eyes.

"What do we know?" Webb asked.

"He's been shot in the head," she said. "Skull fracture and serious bleeding. He'll have brain damage." *If he survives*, she thought but didn't say.

"Handgun or rifle?"

"Impossible to say," she said. "But it was close range."

"Had to be," he agreed. "With the snow, the shooter couldn't have been more than a few yards away unless he made a really lucky shot. Did Stachowski get any rounds off?"

"I don't know," she said, speaking quietly. "He didn't have a gun on him. We need to secure the Carousel as well as the Visitor Center. I found his phone there. I think that's where things started. The phone was under the turntable. I think he was holding it and he dropped it. There might've been some sort of struggle. Then maybe he ran to the Visitor Center."

"Why would he go there?" Webb asked.

She shrugged. "They'd have a phone in the building," she said. "Or maybe he was trying to get somewhere there might be other people. I don't know."

"Had he already been shot?"

"Probably not. I didn't see a blood trail, but that would've been covered by fresh snow anyway. I can't imagine a guy running far with that kind of injury. He probably dropped the moment he got hit."

"So he ran into somebody at the Carousel," Webb said thoughtfully. "They had a difference of opinion. There was a fight, he got away, but someone, we're assuming the same guy, chased him down and shot him in the head. You figure they left him for dead?"

"Must have. He looked pretty bad when I found him."

"But what was he doing there in the first place?"

Erin pitched her voice even lower. "Meeting one of his guys," she said. "An undercover."

Webb nodded. "Maybe the guy's cover got blown," he said. "And the gang he was infiltrating followed him?"

"I hope so," she said. "Because otherwise..."

"Right," Webb said. "Have you ever read Nietzsche?"

"Isn't he the guy who said God was dead?"

"That's right," Webb said. "He also said, 'He who fights with monsters might take care lest he thereby become a monster. And if you gaze for long into an abyss, the abyss gazes also into you.'"

"Are you a bookworm now, sir?" Erin asked, raising her eyebrows.

"Hardly," Webb said. "That's from my freshman Psychology class in college. A depressingly long time ago. It's just about the only thing I remember from it. If I'd known I was going to be a detective someday, I'd have paid more attention in Psych class. Every cop ought to study it."

"But not so closely we become monsters," she said.

"It's a fine line," he agreed.

Webb's phone rang. He fished it out of his trench coat, glanced at the screen, and put it to his ear.

"What've you got, Neshenko?" he asked.

Erin was close enough to hear Vic's answer. He sounded grim, even by Russian standards.

"It's a damn mess," he said. "Can we give God a rip for contaminating our scene?"

"He's a little above our pay grade," Webb said dryly.

"There's probably all kinds of evidence," Vic said. "But we're not gonna find it till spring. Hell, I could be standing on it for all I know. We got tire tracks on 65th, but they don't do us any good. First they got covered up by fresh snow, then the bus ran right over them. No way of knowing what made them or matching them to a vehicle."

"No surprise there," Webb said.

"CSU is sweeping the area," Vic went on. "They're using metal detectors. They got three shell casings so far."

"Three?" Webb said. "I thought our victim was only shot once."

"Maybe our shooter's got real bad aim," Vic said.

"Plenty of shots go wide in a gunfight," Webb said. "What are the shells?"

"Nine-millimeter Parabellum," Vic said gloomily. "Just like everyone uses."

Erin and Webb nodded. It was the most common pistol cartridge.

"We can match the strike marks to the weapon," Webb said. "If we find it. I don't suppose you found a gun yet?"

"Oh, silly me," Vic said. "I totally forgot about the most important piece of evidence. The murder weapon. What the hell was I thinking?"

"So, no weapon," Webb said. He'd been Vic's commander long enough to develop resistance to the Russian's sarcasm.

"No weapon," Vic confirmed. "But we might still find it. The shooter could've tossed it away. CSU's looking near where they found the casings, but those things fly all over the place when they get ejected. Best guess is the shooter was standing pretty close to where Erin found our victim, under the awning, but that's just a guess."

"Sounds like that's where the shooting happened, at least," Webb said. "But get people to the Carousel. It may be part of the scene. O'Reilly found Stachowski's phone there."

"Copy that," Vic said. "Other than the casings, we got one hell of a lot of blood. Looks like it pooled and froze."

Erin shuddered. Phil's blood had cemented his head and upper body to the ice. She'd had to break him loose to turn him over and start CPR.

"Guessing it all belongs to our victim," Vic said. "Oh, speaking of his belongings, we did find his car. It's parked just up the road a ways. Locked. Patrol guys say it doesn't look like it's been tampered with. And that's about it."

"Keep looking," Webb said. "I know conditions aren't great."

"Not great?" Vic echoed. "They're shit, sir. With all due respect. Wait a sec. What's that, Zofia?"

There was a brief flurry of voices, unintelligible over the phone. Then Vic came back on the line.

"We got another one," he said.

"Shell casing?" Webb asked.

"Body. Looked like a shrub under the snow, but it's a dead guy."

"You sure he's dead?" Webb asked. "Because the last one wasn't."

"Oh yeah, he's dead all right," Vic said. "Bullet took the top of his head clean off. Everything above the eyebrows."

"Any idea who he was?" Webb asked.

"Zofia's checking with CSU."

"I'm sending O'Reilly to you," Webb said.

"You are?" Erin said.

"Of course I am," Webb said irritably. "You've got a dog trained in search-and-rescue, and we've got a scene where people are tripping over bodies. Get out there and help them. I'll stay here in case Stachowski wakes up and says anything."

"Sir," Erin said very quietly. "There's a possibility the guy who shot him is wearing a shield. He needs protection."

"I'll see that he gets it," Webb said. "Anyway, there's also a possibility the guy who shot him is the corpse airing out what's left of his brain in Central Park right now. Get moving. Get me answers."

"Yes, sir," Erin said. She twitched Rolf's leash, zipped up her jacket, and headed back out into the night.

Chapter 7

Erin had lied to Camilla Stachowski. It was an unintentional little lie, and probably wouldn't do much harm, but she'd still lied to a woman whose husband might be dying. She'd said she'd be at the hospital, and now she wasn't.

Webb would be there and he'd do what he could, but he wasn't exactly a comforting presence. And Erin had liked Camilla. She'd sensed a strength in the woman that had impressed her. She would have wanted to help, even if she hadn't felt partly responsible for what had happened.

"It wasn't my fault," she told Rolf, looking at his face in the rearview mirror. She sighed. Her words didn't sound even halfway convincing.

"It wasn't," she insisted. Evan O'Malley had ordered her to find out what Phil knew. For him to turn around and have Phil whacked was crazy. She'd certainly suspect him, and he'd know that. It didn't make sense. To murder an NYPD Lieutenant was to call down the wrath of God on his organization.

But she was sure the shooting was connected to her. The timing was just too damned convenient. Phil talked to his guys.

Word leaked to Evan. Evan talked to Erin. Phil was shot. What had he said to her? He was meeting "some of his guys."

"Either the dead guy's one of Phil's, or he's a shooter," she told Rolf. "Maybe both. But if he's a cop, we'll find that out soon enough. I wish you could tell a bad guy by the smell."

Rolf wagged his tail. He'd do his best.

*   *   *

The drive back to Central Park was every bit as arduous as her earlier excursions. Plows were trundling along the Manhattan avenues, piling up snow on the sidewalks and street corners, but the blacktop was slick with a slurry of snow, slush, and salt. Later, Erin supposed, front-end loaders and trucks would load it up and carry it off somewhere; to New Jersey, probably. She wondered what sort of interstate agreements covered the export of snow. Did you have to pay taxes on it?

She carefully navigated 65th Street, easing between police cars. She saw the coroner's van, which surprised her a little. She hadn't known Sarah Levine would be out and about so soon.

The Crime Scene Unit had set up battery-powered floodlights around the Visitor Center. Evidence techs were carefully sifting through the snow around the building. Two men were patiently sweeping metal detectors back and forth, like soldiers working their way through a minefield. In the middle of it all, Erin spotted the broad-shouldered bulk of Vic Neshenko and steered toward him.

Vic was talking to a woman and two men; a tall thin one and a short fat one. Erin was glad to recognize Zofia Piekarski, but less so to see Hank and Ernie. They were two of the least pleasant men working one of the least pleasant jobs the city had to offer. They drove the "meat wagon" that transported bodies to the morgue. A lot of guys turned to alcohol to dull the experience of bringing in the dead. Hank and Ernie used offensive humor as their coping mechanism.

"We're gonna have trouble getting him in the van," Hank said. "Look at the pose. Arms spread out like Christ on the cross. He's too wide."

"We could saw 'em off," Ernie suggested. "I got a hacksaw in back of the wagon."

"Why in God's name do you have a hacksaw in a coroner's van?" Vic asked. "Never mind, I don't want to know. Hey Erin, glad you could join us."

"Find any more bodies?" she asked.

"Just the one." Vic pointed. "The doc's taking a look now."

Sarah Levine was a short distance away, kneeling in the snow beside the corpse. Erin saw that Hank and Ernie, despite making their point with their usual lack of tact, were right. The body was spread-eagled on its back, frozen solid. The eyes were wide open and stamped with a shocked expression, which made sense. Losing the top of your head was a surprising experience.

"I walked right past him," Erin said. "I can't believe I missed seeing that."

"He was buried under the snow," Vic said. "Until CSU got their lights up, I wouldn't have known anything was weird either. Then I saw the fingertips sticking out of the drift. How's it coming, Doc?"

"I'll have to get him back to the morgue for a full postmortem," Levine said without looking up. "The tissues need to thaw before I can run bloodwork and perform the autopsy."

"Um, you did notice he was missing half his head, didn't you?" Vic said. "That's usually a pretty conclusive cause of death."

"You're making several assumptions," Levine said. "First, you're assuming he was alive when his skull was shattered.

Second, you're assuming no other fatal injuries. Third, you're assuming the postmortem won't turn up any useful evidence."

"Do you see anything interesting?" Erin asked.

"Every body is interesting," Levine said. "I learn from every cadaver."

"What've you learned from this one?"

"Detective Neshenko is probably correct," Levine said. "Cause of death is likely a single gunshot wound to the head. The entrance wound is just above the bridge of the nose. The bullet tumbled while transiting the skull, the slug flattening as it exited the rear, destroying the cranium. Death would have been instantaneous."

"Perfect headshot," Vic said. He sounded impressed.

"However, this victim has been shot twice," Levine said. "The other bullet struck the left side of the thoracic cavity, but did not penetrate significantly. That is academic, given the other wound. Judging by the dimensions of the entrance wounds, both bullets were medium-caliber handgun rounds, either nine-millimeter or thirty-eight caliber. The bullet from the body shot is likely suspended in his tissues, as there is no exit wound. It failed to pass through the rib cage."

"Why not?" Erin asked. "If he was close enough that the headshot overpenetrated, how come the other bullet didn't punch right through him?"

In answer, Levine laid a gloved finger on the dead man's chest. "Kevlar," she said.

"He's wearing body armor?" Vic said. "You don't see many perps carrying that shit around."

"This guy's a cop," Erin said quietly.

"You know him?" Vic asked.

She shook her head. Enough of the man's face remained that she probably would have recognized it if it had been familiar, but he was a stranger.

"How do you know, then?" Piekarski asked.

Erin didn't explain. She couldn't, not in front of so many people. "What's he got on him?" she asked instead.

"I haven't catalogued his effects yet," Levine said. "I'm planning to do that back at the morgue. But if it's important, we can do it now. The body's been photographed."

The days of chalk outlines were long gone; not that chalk would show up against snow anyway. Modern evidence techs preferred cameras. After carefully brushing the snow away, the CSU guys had snapped pictures of the dead guy from every conceivable angle.

Piekarski took a knee beside Levine, changed out her warm gloves for a pair of disposable rubber ones, and patted the body down, checking for bulges in the pockets. It was just like frisking a live perp, except that the dead guy didn't resist. "Got a holster here," she reported. "On the belt. Empty."

"But he's not holding a gun," Vic said. "And CSU didn't find one around him. Interesting."

"Two spare clips," Piekarski went on, holding up a pair of pistol magazines.

"Nine-mil?" Vic guessed.

"Yeah," Piekarski said, handing them to him.

"Glock mags," Vic said. He knew guns inside and out. Erin recognized them too. She carried a Glock 18 herself.

"He must've had the gun on him," she said. "A guy doesn't carry spare ammo without his piece."

"Maybe somebody got the drop on him and took it away," Vic said.

"Something in his hip pocket," Piekarski said. She grimaced. "I wonder what my mom would say if she saw me feeling up a dead guy."

"She'd say no wonder he's a stiff," Hank said.

"Say that again," Vic said softly, taking a step toward him.

"See, he's stiff because he's dead," Hank said. "But he'd be stiff anyway because—"

Then he saw the look in Vic's eye and, in a dazzling display of self-preservation, abruptly shut up.

"It's a wallet," Piekarski said, ignoring the men. She fished it out between two fingers and passed it to Erin, who flipped it open.

"Shit," Erin said. She was looking at the driver's license of Delbert Ames, whose face—the lower part, anyway—matched the body at her feet. But she was also looking at an NYPD calling card.

"What?" Vic asked.

"Did you find a shield?" Erin asked Piekarski.

"Not on his belt," Piekarski replied. She half-unzipped the man's jacket. There, hanging around Ames's neck like a good-luck charm, was a gold NYPD shield on a chain.

"Son of a bitch," Vic said. "We've got a cop-killer out there."

"We already knew that," Erin said.

"Stachowski's not dead, is he?" Vic replied. "Last I heard he was still breathing."

"Somebody shot him in the head," she said. "That's practically the same thing."

"And where's his own gun?" Vic wondered. "I was thinking they might've shot each other. Mistaken identity, tragic mistake, that sort of thing."

"Simultaneous headshots?" Erin said doubtfully. "I saw Phil afterward. He wasn't pulling any triggers after he got hit, and neither was this guy."

"Hey, it happens," Vic said. "There was this Civil War battle where they found two musket balls afterward, fused together. They'd smacked into each other in midair as the two guys were shooting at each other. Split-second stuff. It's a crazy world."

"It's also a cold world," Piekarski said, standing up and rubbing her hands together. "I'm freezing."

"I'm sure I didn't hear you complaining about being out in the field," Vic said, grinning. "Because last I heard, you were supposed to be on desk duty. On account of your delicate condition."

"Say anything about desk duty again and you'll be the one in a delicate condition," Piekarski said.

"Hey! Detectives!" a CSU guy shouted. He was standing near where Erin had found Phil. He had a metal detector in one hand and was waving the other.

Erin, Vic, and Piekarski waded through the snow to see what the fuss was about. They found the evidence tech pointing down at a little metal object nestled in a snowdrift.

"Glock 18," Vic said.

"About six feet from where Phil fell," Erin said.

"Too far for him to have just dropped it," Vic said.

"But if he was standing here..." Erin said thoughtfully. "Suppose he's on the sidewalk. Ames would be pretty close, just a few feet from him. They're walking together, maybe talking. Then a shooter comes out around the corner of the building right there."

Vic nodded. "They don't see him right away, on account of the snow," he said. "The shooter puts two in Ames, pop-pop; one in the chest, one in the face. Ames goes down. Stachowski turns toward him, sees he's dead, goes for his own gun and spins toward the shooter. But it's too late. Shooter is already throwing down on Stachowski. Puts one in his head. But Stachowski's arm has momentum, so his gun flies out of his hand and lands here."

"Could be," Erin said. "But then where's Ames's gun? If he didn't have the chance to draw, it'd still be in his holster."

"Maybe it didn't go down quite like that," Vic said. "It's just a theory. What did Stachowski carry? Glock like this one?"

"I don't know," Erin said. She stooped and took out her flashlight to get a better look at the pistol. "Got a serial number here," she said. She rattled off the digits.

Piekarski noted them down. "I'll run this in one of the Patrol units," she said, starting for the nearest parked squad car.

"You're right about one thing," Erin said. "There had to be a third guy here. Otherwise the geometry doesn't work. Neither does the timing."

"I never paid much attention to geometry," Vic said. "I only barely passed the class. See, Stacey Steiner sat next to me. She was this blonde cheerleader, had the best set of..."

"And that's all I want to hear about your high school days," Erin said.

"Eyes!" Vic said. "I was gonna say eyes!"

Erin turned to the CSU guy. "You get the pictures you need?"

The photographer had come over while they were talking and had snapped several shots of the handgun. The CSU man had placed a yellow plastic evidence marker next to the gun. Both of them nodded.

"I need to know how many bullets are in there," Erin said. "And if it's been fired."

"Copy that," the CSU guy said. "It'll be in the report."

"Levine!" Erin called. "Check Ames for GSR!"

"That's standard procedure in GSW cases," Levine said, slightly irritated. She hated being told how to do her job.

"You want to check Ames for gunshot residue?" Vic said. "Wondering if he got any shots off?"

"Mostly I just want to know who shot whom," Erin said, shaking her head. "Because right now this doesn't make any damn sense."

*   *   *

"I thought you didn't drink coffee," Erin said.

"There's a time and place for everything," Vic said. "It's too damn cold for Mountain Dew. It'd end up frozen, and Mom always told me not to eat yellow snow."

"It's better than what we used to drink at the Five," Piekarski said. She wrapped her hands around her cup. "Tell the truth, I'd drink battery acid right now if it was hot."

The detectives had retreated to a coffee shop across from the park to let their extremities recover. Erin couldn't ever remember being so cold. CSU was still combing the scene, though Ames's body had been carted away. Hank and Ernie hadn't needed to saw him to pieces after all; they'd managed to fit him into the back of the van by tilting the frozen arms diagonally. It had been a little weird—Vic had described it as being like trying to fit a couch into a U-Haul the wrong way round—but it had all worked out. Now Levine was presumably starting to thaw out the corpse at the morgue and the Major Crimes squad was thawing themselves in a less controlled environment.

"What can we tell Zofia about all this?" Vic asked.

Piekarski frowned. "About all what?" she asked, looking from Vic to Erin.

Erin took a look around the shop. It was deserted except for themselves and a barista who obviously wanted very much to be somewhere else. The barista was at the far end of the room, cleaning the counter and paying no attention to the customers.

"Okay," Erin said quietly. "I guess it doesn't make too much difference now. Word's getting out anyway, and you've got a right to know. But this stops here, at this table. You copy?"

"I copy," Piekarski said. Her eyes were serious.

"Phil Stachowski runs undercover ops for the NYPD," Erin explained. "He handles officers who infiltrate organized crime."

Piekarski nodded.

"The Irish Mob thinks Phil's got an agent on the inside," Erin went on. "They're trying to find out who it is so they can plug the leak. I think that's why Phil got shot."

"You think the Irish nailed him and Ames?" Piekarski asked. "Well, you've got contacts with the Irish, so I guess you'd know. But do you have any idea who we've got in their gang?"

Erin just looked at her.

"What?" Piekarski said.

"You really think you've got what it takes to make Detective, Officer Piekarski?" Vic asked with mock severity.

Erin saw the realization hit the other woman. She almost literally saw the light bulb go on over Piekarski's head.

"Oh my God," Piekarski said quietly, shaking her head. "I feel like such a moron!"

"Don't be so hard on yourself," Erin said. "If it were easy to figure out, we'd be in all kinds of trouble."

"In case you didn't notice, you *are* in all kinds of trouble," Vic pointed out. "Constantly."

"I just thought an undercover wouldn't be, you know..." Piekarski said.

"Openly wearing a shield?" Erin suggested. "Yeah, it's kind of unusual. That's why it's worked so well."

"But they know you're a cop," Piekarski said. "They've always known. So what's the big secret?"

"I've been playing a part," Erin said. "Pretending to be dirty. I've taken money. They think I've done some stuff for them."

"What sort of stuff?"

"We don't need to go into that," Erin said.

"It's need-to-know shit," Vic added. "I don't know half of it and I'm not supposed to know the half I do know. If it makes you feel any better, she didn't tell me, either. I figured it out myself."

"How?" Piekarski asked.

"For a while I thought she was a hitman for the Mob," he said.

"Hitwoman," Erin corrected.

"We've been over this," Vic snapped. "A hitman can be a woman."

"Jesus," Piekarski murmured. "So you've been working for the Irish, except not really, this whole time. That explains a lot. But wouldn't you be the first one they'd suspect?"

"That's the beauty of it," Vic said. "She's hidden in plain view. Like that sirloin letter."

Both women looked blankly at him.

"You know," he said. "That story by that creepy guy."

"That doesn't help, Vic," Erin said.

"The guy the football team's named for."

"I am so confused right now," Piekarski said.

"The Baltimore Ravens!" Vic said triumphantly.

"Okay," Piekarski said. "That's Edgar Allan Poe you're talking about. And I think you mean *The Purloined Letter*."

"Right. Purloined," Vic said. "What a stupid word. I read that in high school English."

"I hope Stacey Steiner wasn't in that class, too," Erin said. "I've heard she could be pretty distracting."

"Stacey who?" Piekarski said.

"Never mind," Vic said. "My point is, nobody could find that letter because it was right out there in the open. Like Erin. She can't be an undercover cop, they figure, because she's an obvious cop."

"I see," Piekarski said. "And this Detective Ames was the other undercover?"

"No," Erin said. "There is no other undercover. There's just me."

"Then why did they kill Ames?" Piekarski asked. She'd been a little lost before. The literary digression had left her utterly baffled.

"I don't know," Erin said. "It might not even have been the Irish."

"Why don't you ask them?" Piekarski suggested.

"That's nuts," Vic said.

"Vic, shut up and listen," Erin said. "You just made two mistakes. One, you called your girlfriend crazy. Never do that. And two, she actually has a good idea."

"She does?" Vic said.

"Yeah," Erin said. "Because Evan does think I'm playing for his team. If he didn't, he wouldn't have told me about Phil. So I'll ask Evan what's going on. He might actually know who did the shooting."

"What about me?" Piekarski asked.

"What do you mean?" Erin asked.

"Why'd you tell me all this?"

"You asked."

"Yeah, but I've asked what's going on before, and you've never told me. Why now?"

"Because it's almost over," Erin said. "We're bringing in some other officers while we get ready to shut the O'Malleys down. The rest of the squad's in on it, so now you are, too. But it's still top secret. You can't talk about it, even with other people who know about it."

"What if they come after Zofia?" Vic asked. "Now that she knows?"

"They don't know she knows," Erin said. "The only way they'd know that is if one of the people at this table told them, and we don't plan on it. This secret doesn't need to keep forever; just for a couple weeks."

"I can keep a secret," Piekarski said. "Like that one about Sergeant Logan."

"What secret about Logan?" Vic asked.

"I can't tell you," she said with a sweet smile. "Because it's a secret."

"What's the plan?" Vic asked Erin.

"We work this like any other case," she said. "First, let's circle back to the hospital and see how Phil's doing. Then I'll talk to the O'Malleys. I'd also like to know what Ames was up to, and why he was meeting Phil tonight. Somebody screwed up. Either it was Ames or Phil, but someone knew they were here and targeted them. No way was this random."

"Find the motive, find the perp," Vic said. "That's the first rule of being a detective, Zofia."

"I'm so glad you're here to tell me these things," Piekarski said, rolling her eyes.

Chapter 8

The cluster of cops at Bellevue Hospital had grown larger. About two dozen officers were now hanging around the waiting room. They were quiet, tense, and watchful. Every cop knew they might be the next one on the operating table themselves, if they were just a little slower or unluckier on their next shift. Lieutenant Webb was there, sipping bad coffee and clearly wanting a cigarette. In the corner, Camilla Stachowski was sitting in a chair next to a bearded man in black who sported a white clerical collar. The priest was holding her hand and talking softly to her.

Erin hesitated. She knew she ought to go talk to Camilla, but she shied away from the pain she knew she'd feel radiating off the other woman. Hating herself for her momentary weakness, she set her jaw and started moving again.

"Detective O'Reilly," a woman said brightly from her right.

Erin turned and saw a brightly attractive, perky face framed by carefully-styled blonde hair, accented by a little too much makeup. She cursed silently. She hadn't noticed the news van outside the ER.

"Holly Gardner," she said. The name came out like one of Rolf's warning growls.

"I'm honored you remember me," Holly said. "I was hoping you had a moment to tell Channel Six News something about this evening's tragic events."

"Of course you'd be here," Vic said. "Chase the ambulances far enough, they all end up here."

"And Detective Neshenko," Holly went on, undeterred. She gave him her most winning smile.

"Who's the bimbo?" Piekarski asked, taking in Holly's cosmetics and wardrobe. The newswoman was dressed in a skintight blouse, top two buttons undone in blatant disregard of the weather.

"Holly Gardner, Channel Six News," Holly said. "And you are, Detective?"

"I'm more trouble than you're worth," Piekarski said. "And I'm not a detective. Get your facts straight, prime-time bitch, and get out of our faces. We're working."

Vic pursed his lips in a silent whistle of admiration.

"What my colleague meant to say is, 'The NYPD does not comment regarding ongoing investigations,'" Erin translated wryly. "Excuse us, ma'am."

They left the newswoman pouting prettily. Vic and Piekarski peeled off to report to Webb, while Erin steered toward Camilla. She waited for a natural break in the conversation. After a moment, Camilla noticed her. Mrs. Stachowski's eyes were red-rimmed but dry. Her face was drawn so tightly, Erin could clearly see the outlines of her jaw muscles.

"Detective O'Reilly," Camilla said. "I was hoping our next meeting would be under better circumstances."

"I'm so sorry, ma'am," Erin said awkwardly.

"I was speaking to your commanding officer," Camilla said, nodding toward Lieutenant Webb. "He tells me you're the one who found Phil. If it wasn't for you, he'd still be lying out there, and he certainly wouldn't have survived. So thank you."

Camilla put out her hand and clasped Erin's between her own, giving it a squeeze.

"It was just good luck I found him when I did," Erin said. "And Rolf's nose."

"You gave him the best chance he could have," Camilla said. Her voice broke slightly, but she recovered. "You brought him here, among friends. And now I hear another officer has been found?"

"That's right, ma'am," Erin said. "Detective Ames. Did you know him?"

"No," Camilla said. "Because of the nature of his work, Phil didn't bring many of his people by the house. But I'm sorry there's been another loss to the Department."

"Have you heard anything yet?" Erin asked gently.

Camilla shook her head. "We're waiting," she said. "That's the hardest thing, I suppose. Once I know what I need to deal with, I'll find a way to handle it. But right now all I have are possibilities. I can't reconcile myself to five different outcomes at once. I feel like I'm flying to pieces."

"Where are the kids?"

"They're home. My sister's come over and she's staying with them. Poor things, they're scared out of their wits. I didn't tell them much, but that just gives them more to be scared of. They wanted to come with me, of course, but this is no place for children."

Erin swallowed the lump in her throat and nodded.

"Do you have any idea who did this?" Camilla asked.

"We're still gathering evidence," Erin said. "Can you think of anything that might help us? Anything at all?"

"I've told you everything I know about tonight," Camilla said. "Phil is such a kind, gentle soul. I can't imagine anyone wanting to hurt him."

Erin became aware of a shift in the room, like a ripple of water across the surface of a lake. Cops were standing up and turning, their eyes following a man who'd come from the operating room. He was walking toward the corner where Erin, Camilla, and the priest were waiting.

Doctor Sean O'Reilly Junior wasn't a particularly impressive-looking man. His face was pleasant, though he had his father's strong jaw. He was partway through yet another night shift in the Emergency Room and an aura of weariness surrounded him. It mostly resided behind his eyes, which were the same blue as his sister's. He wore rumpled surgical scrubs, spattered with blood that had doubtless come from Phil.

"Ms. Stachowski?" he said. "I'm Dr. O'Reilly."

Camilla sprang to her feet. Then she swayed and her eyes went out of focus. Erin reflexively reached out and caught her elbow, steadying her. The other police formed a loose ring around them, keeping a respectful distance.

"I'm Camilla Stachowski," Camilla said. Erin marveled at the woman's voice, which only quavered slightly.

"Would you like to go somewhere more private and talk?" Sean asked.

"You'd better just tell me now," Camilla said.

"All right," Sean said. "Let's sit down."

He sat on her right. The priest took her left hand. Erin stood back, wanting to ask her brother all sorts of questions but knowing this wasn't the time or place for it.

"Now talk to me," Camilla said. "How is my husband?"

"We've stabilized him," Sean said. "We removed several fragments of bone from the wound. There was some intracranial bleeding, but we were able to stop the flow. The neurosurgeon has arrived and he's taken over. I'm afraid it'll be several hours before he's finished. Dr. Yates is one of the best in the field. Your husband is in excellent hands."

"What's his prognosis?" Camilla asked.

Sean's mouth tightened. "It's way too early to tell, ma'am," he said. "He's suffered a massive traumatic brain injury, including severe damage to his brain tissue. The bullet went through a significant portion of brain mass, and until he wakes up, we won't be able to begin assessing the extent of the damage."

Camilla shuddered, but she grasped at the hope in Sean's words. "But he will wake up?" she said.

"I don't know," Sean said. "He's unconscious, and that's probably the best thing for him right now. It's possible for people to survive injuries of this sort, and even for them to make almost complete recoveries."

"Have you ever had it happen to one of your patients?" Camilla asked.

"No," he admitted. "But I've seen several cases in the literature. If you remember the Arizona Congresswoman who was shot a few years ago? She made an amazing recovery."

"Oh, yes, I saw that on the news," Camilla said. "But tell me, Doctor. Will the man who opens his eyes still be my husband, or am I going to see a stranger?"

"I wish I could give you an answer," he said. "Particularly the one you want to hear. But the brain is a funny thing, and we still don't understand nearly as much of it as we'd like to. All we can do is wait and see, and let Dr. Yates work. The good news is, with such a large hole in the skull, swelling will be less of an issue. The swelling after an injury can cause as much damage as the initial trauma. We would have needed to drill a hole if there hadn't already been one. Anything's possible at this point. But you do need to prepare yourself. If he does regain consciousness, he'll have a very long and difficult process of recuperation in front of him. It'll be hard for both of you, for your whole family."

Camilla's jaw set hard again. "I'll take care of him," she promised. "No matter what."

Sean nodded. "I wish I could give you better news," he said. "Now I have to go back and assist Dr. Yates. I'll let you know as soon as we have more news."

He got up and started back toward the operating room.

"Dr. O'Reilly?" Camilla said, standing.

He paused. "Yes?"

"Thank you," she said.

Sean gave her the best, most encouraging smile he could muster. Erin, who'd known her brother her whole life, saw through it and her heart sank. Sean didn't think Phil would make it. Or if he did, he might almost be better off dead.

Erin felt a pain in her palms. She looked down and saw, to her surprise, that her fingernails had dug channels into her own flesh. Her fists had clenched fearsomely tight. She'd been in a semi-daze of shock, horror, and fear ever since she'd gone looking for Phil. Now, finally, another emotion was taking over.

The last time she'd been this angry, her family had been in danger and she'd killed the man who'd put them there.

*   *   *

Erin called Carlyle from the parking lot. She couldn't sit for this conversation, or even stand still. She paced back and forth, wearing a path in the snow. Rolf pranced beside her, keeping his nose close to her leg, watching anxiously.

She didn't know what Carlyle's situation was. As far as she knew, Finnegan was keeping an eye on him for Evan. But then, maybe Carlyle was keeping an eye on Finnegan, too. The Mob was like that; a sort of perpetual Mexican standoff of paranoia and suspicion. But she didn't care if Evan found out about her call. She *wanted* him to know about it.

"I wasn't certain I'd be hearing from you again so soon, darling," Carlyle said. He didn't sound tense or upset; but then, he usually didn't.

"I need to talk to Evan," she said bluntly. "The sooner the better."

"Is this to be a private conversation?"

"Yeah."

"You're in luck. As it happens, I'm at his flat at this very moment, as are a few other acquaintances. If you'd care to drop by, he'll doubtless be pleased to see you."

"That's halfway across Manhattan," she said. "It'll take me a while to get there."

"No fear, darling," Carlyle said dryly. "I've a notion we're none of us going anywhere for a while."

"Then I'll see you when I see you," she said and hung up.

She went back inside to check in with Webb. She found him discussing the case with Vic and Piekarski.

"I've got a lead to follow up," she told Webb.

"Would this lead happen to have silver hair and a Belfast brogue?" Webb asked.

"As a matter of fact, yes," she said. "I think he's our best angle. Is that a problem, sir?"

"Yes and no," Webb said. "Let me put it this way, O'Reilly. There's two kinds of problems in this world. There's the kind I can do something about, like an error on my income taxes or a flat tire; and then there's the kind I can't, like world hunger, global warming, and your personal life. I try to devote my energies to the first kind. But we've already had too many cops shot tonight, so try to keep your head down. Where are you going to be?"

"Evan O'Malley's penthouse."

Vic snorted. "When you go hunting, you jump straight into the lion's den," he said. "Hell, you stick your head between its damn teeth. Okay, do you want to give me a lift, or should I trail you in my own car?"

"Vic, you can't come."

"You won't even know I'm there."

"Yeah, nobody'll notice the six-foot three Russian glaring at everyone over my shoulder," she said. "Seriously, Vic. You know what it's going to be like there."

He sighed. "Fine. But what am I supposed to do while you're talking to gangsters?"

"I'm the one you should be asking," Webb said. "Since I'm your commanding officer, in case you've forgotten."

"Okay," Vic said, turning to face him. "What am I supposed to be doing, sir?"

"We need a ballistics report on the gun that was retrieved from the crime scene," Webb said. "Compare it with the shell casings that were recovered. Get traffic cam footage from both sides of Central Park."

"It'll be a whole lot of snow blowing around," Vic predicted glumly.

"Probably," Webb agreed. "But it's worth a look. If we can identify another vehicle entering or leaving the Park, it'll be a big step in the right direction."

"Another vehicle!" Erin exclaimed.

All heads turned toward her. "Explain," Webb said.

"We only found one car," Erin said.

"Yeah," Vic said. "Stachowski's. So? The perp took his car with him."

"But what about Ames?" she replied. "How'd he get there?"

"He rode with Stachowski," Vic said.

"No," Piekarski said. "Erin's right. They were meeting at the Carousel. If they were carpooling, why bother meeting there at all? They could talk anywhere. Come to that, why was the meeting there?"

"Now I'm confused," Vic said. "Are you saying the perp took Ames's car? Then how'd the bad guy get there?"

"Maybe Ames was the bad guy," Erin said quietly.

"Then his car would still be there," Vic said. "Ames never left. He got his head blown off, remember?"

"He might have car keys in his pocket," Erin said. "Levine will find them if they're on him."

"What're you saying?" Vic said. "There had to be a third shooter, because both the other two were found at the scene, but they only had one car between them. Somebody else took a car away. But if he took Ames's car, what happened to his own? Shit, this is like one of those goddamn logic problems with canoes and cannibals on opposite sides of the river. I could never figure those things out."

"Those are easy," Piekarski said. "You just need to remember that people can ride back the way they came. The canoes don't have to be empty on the return trips."

Vic gave her a dirty look. "I bet you can solve those metal ring puzzles, too, can't you. And Rubik's cubes."

"Never got the hang of the cube," Piekarski said. "But you should see what I can do with a pair of handcuffs."

"Not on the clock, please," Webb said.

"That wasn't what I meant!" Piekarski said indignantly.

"O'Reilly makes a good point," Webb said. "There aren't enough vehicles. We know at least one other car was there from the tire tracks. Maybe multiple people were present. Suppose two perps showed up. They could've split up, one taking their own car away, the other taking Ames's car."

"Why would they do that?" Erin wondered.

"I have no idea," Webb said. "I'm just trying to fit the pieces into some sort of coherent picture. If you have a better theory, I'd be delighted to hear it."

"Maybe I'll have one later on," she said. "I'd better get moving."

"O'Reilly?"

"I know, I know. Be careful. I'm always careful."

"You say that," Webb said. "But I don't think you prioritize it."

"Sir, if being careful was my top priority, I wouldn't be wearing a shield," she said.

Chapter 9

Evan O'Malley had more than one home. Erin knew of three: his Manhattan penthouse, a stone mansion in Massachusetts, and a vacation place in the Hamptons. He also had a getaway in the Bahamas and several other properties owned through shell companies and fake names. When Corky had convinced Evan's bookkeeper Maggie Callahan to confide in him, all the chieftain's secrets had been laid open.

Erin herself had been to Evan's apartment, his house in the Hamptons, and his Caribbean tropical paradise. Of the three, she'd take the Bahamas in an instant, especially with the freak blizzard howling around her ears. As the night got later, the wind only blew colder and harder. She turned up her collar as she trudged to the front door of the apartment building.

Rolf followed in her footsteps, ears laid flat. Even he wasn't enjoying the snow anymore. He wanted to be home, curled up next to her on the couch.

The doorman looked so cold and unhappy when he held the door for her that Erin tipped him an extra fiver. He gave her a smile of pathetic gratitude. She knew the doorman worked for Evan. So did the security guard. There'd be two more guys at the top of the elevator, both armed. This wasn't an apartment; it was a fortress. Erin took it all in stride. After all, she belonged there. She was an O'Malley, too.

It wasn't until the elevator was halfway to the top that the thought struck her: if Evan really had gone stark raving paranoid and was picking off cops, she wasn't safe here. If he was willing to have Phil Stachowski and Del Ames murdered, he certainly wouldn't hesitate to wipe her and Rolf off the street.

She shrugged off the thought and tried to shake some of the tension out of her neck and back. She'd dealt with these goons before. They were at least as scared of her as she was of them. But she still appreciated the familiar weight of her Glock on her hip and the sight of Rolf at her side.

The thugs who guarded the elevator were expecting her. They gave her a casual once-over and waved her through. Neither one even suggested searching her for weapons. Junkyard O'Reilly had a reputation and wasn't a woman to be screwed with.

A familiar face greeted her at Evan's door. It belonged to a pleasant-looking man with a nice smile.

"Miss O'Reilly," he said, grinning cheerfully. "Come on in!"

"Good to see you, P.R.," she said. Paddy Ryan was Evan's assistant, one of the more diplomatic gangsters. Erin would never turn her back on him, but she did like him.

"The boss is in the living room," Ryan said. "He's drinking with Cars and Finnegan."

"What about the Snake?" she asked.

"Oh, yeah. Him too," Ryan said, shifting uncomfortably. "But he's not drinking."

"And Evan is?"

Erin was just making conversation, but she could tell Ryan was nervous. The smile stayed on his face, but he kept shooting sidelong glances at her. She walked as confidently as she could, but she was getting that prickly feeling on the back of her neck again. She tried to ignore it, following Ryan to Evan's living room.

Evan was sitting in a dark red leather armchair, a glass of whiskey in his hand. To one side, on a matching couch, were Carlyle and Finnegan. Both men also held drinks. Gordon Pritchard stood by the window, his left hand cupped around his right elbow. He'd been watching the snow, but he turned as Ryan rapped on the open door. Evan's gas fireplace was lit; its golden flames kindled sparks in Pritchard's dark eyes. The scars on his cheek stood out in sharp relief in the dim light.

"Good evening," Evan said quietly.

Carlyle stood up, as he always did when a woman entered the room. Evan did likewise. Finnegan stayed sitting, but raised his glass to Erin in an ironic salute.

"I understand you're busy this evening," Evan said. "So I'm pleasantly surprised you've decided to join us. Will you have something to drink?"

I'm on duty, Erin thought. "If you've got Glen D, I'll take a glass," she said. This was no time to stand on Departmental rules.

"Mr. Ryan?" Evan said, nodding to the corner of the room, which contained a small but well-stocked bar. Ryan immediately walked over and poured a shot of whiskey, which he handed to Erin. Everyone sat down again, Carlyle subtly shifting toward the middle of the couch so Erin could have the end and wouldn't have to sit next to Finnegan.

"I was saddened to hear of the troubles your department's been having," Evan said. "I do hope Lieutenant Stachowski recovers."

"You're well-informed, sir," Erin said. She was speaking stiffly and knew it, but didn't know how to stop herself.

"People talk," Evan said.

"On rumor's tongue continual slanders ride," Finnegan said.

"What in God's name is going on?" Erin demanded.

Evan's face didn't twitch a muscle. "I beg your pardon?" he said softly.

"You sent me looking for Stachowski," she said. "I track him down, in the middle of a snowstorm, and when I find him, he's got a hole in his head! So I'm asking what you had to do with this."

"Mr. Ryan, this doesn't concern you," Evan said.

Ryan got the message and made himself scarce, closing the door on his way out.

"Miss O'Reilly," Evan said. "I hope you're not accusing me of attacking a member of your department."

Erin felt her cheeks flush from more than the heat of the fire. "Of course not," she said. "But—"

He raised one hand slightly, cutting her off. "Because I have several witnesses who can vouch for my whereabouts tonight," he said.

"Obviously," she said.

"I can also attest to the activities of my principal lieutenants," he said, indicating the other three men with a slight tilt of his head. "None of them, I assure you, has spent any of the past hours gallivanting through the snow, exchanging gunfire with law-enforcement officers."

Erin gritted her teeth. "Sir," she said slowly. "We both know your influence extends well beyond this room. I know I didn't personally shoot Lieutenant Stachowski and Detective Ames, and neither did any of these other guys."

She actually hadn't been sure about Pritchard. The Snake was definitely the sort of guy who might've gunned down a couple of cops.

"Then what, exactly, are you implying?" Evan inquired.

"I'm implying that Lieutenant Stachowski was shot by one of the O'Malleys," Erin said. "With or without your orders."

Evan didn't blink. "I had nothing to do with the incident," he said flatly. "I gave no orders, and had I been aware of any such planned action, I would have forbidden it on pain of my *extreme* displeasure."

Erin nodded. The last time one of Evan's underlings had gone behind his back, the woman responsible had paid with her own life.

"Still," Evan continued, "I can appreciate your concern. The timing is unfortunate."

"That's one word for it," she said.

"Have you discovered the chink in my organization's armor?"

"Not yet," Erin said. "And it's going to be harder to do with Stachowski out of commission. I don't know what he knows and I've got no way of finding out until he wakes up. *If* he wakes up."

"The man surely has files," Evan said. "And as investigating officer in the matter of his troubles, I imagine you will be granted access to some or all of those files."

"Not undercover assignments," she said.

"Nevertheless, you may find a trail of bread crumbs," Evan said. "I'm merely observing you have the perfect pretext for sniffing about the unfortunate Lieutenant Stachowski. I still anticipate results."

"This shooting is only making my job harder," she said, trying to keep to her role as Evan's pet detective. "I can't protect your organization if the NYPD thinks you've declared war on them."

"And I've already told you, I had nothing to do with it," Evan said.

"Nobody cares what actually happened," Erin said, quoting one of Carlyle's dictums. "What matters is how it looks, and right now it looks pretty goddamn bad."

"It looks bad to *you*," Evan said. "The rest of your Department is not privy to some of the knowledge in your possession."

Shit, Erin thought. That had been a misstep. Time to change the subject. "You're absolutely right, sir," she said. "But with Stachowski out of commission, what does it matter? Doesn't that remove the threat to your family?"

"Hardly," Evan replied. "There remains the matter of the traitor in our midst. I want a name, Miss O'Reilly. The right name. Even if it should happen to be one of the men in this very room."

Carlyle met Erin's look steadily. If she hadn't known he was a traitor to Evan, she would never have guessed it from his appearance. Finnegan just looked slightly confused, as he usually did. Pritchard's face was a scarred mask, revealing nothing.

"I'll expect prompt resolution of the situation," Evan said. "But for now, you'll be wanting to get home. The weather's turned somewhat nasty. You'll also be wanting your lad to accompany you, I imagine, so I won't detain him further. Good evening, Mr. Carlyle, Miss O'Reilly."

Carlyle didn't say a word as Paddy Ryan handed him his overcoat. He shared the elevator with Erin and Rolf in silence. They knew better than to speak as long as they were in Evan's building.

"Will you be coming home, then?" he finally asked, once the storm insulated them from inquisitive ears.

"I should," she said.

"But you won't?"

"I can't. Not yet. I need to solve this."

"Can you give me a lift to the Corner?"

"Sure. It'll be on my way. Where's the Mercedes?"

"Finnegan brought me here in some misbegotten rusty old thing. I imagine he nicked it from a scrapyard."

"That sounds like him." Erin led the way to the Charger and used the remote tab to unlock it.

"Take care, darling," Carlyle said. "There's something about this I don't like."

Erin opened Rolf's compartment. The K-9 planted his paws and vigorously shook himself, spraying snow and icy water in all directions. Erin and Carlyle stayed outside to finish their conversation.

"There's plenty I don't like," Erin retorted. "Like the fact somebody's hunting NYPD detectives, including a certain Lieutenant I know. This was an ambush. The bad guys knew he'd be in the middle of Central Park tonight."

"How did they know?" Carlyle asked.

"The same way they always do. Somebody talked."

"Half a moment, darling," he said. "Why was the lad in Central Park? It's no fit night to be walking under the open sky."

"He was meeting one of his team," she said. "To prep him for surveillance on Evan's people."

"How many of your folk would know the time and place?"

Erin frowned, squinting through the driving snow as she carefully steered down the Manhattan street. "Not many. Probably just the two of them."

"So either Lieutenant Stachowski or the other lad is a traitor," Carlyle said.

"It's not that simple," she said. "One or both of them might have been followed. Or one of them may have told somebody else where they'd be, in case of trouble."

"Which lad was he meeting?"

"Detective Ames."

"He told you this?"

"No, but Ames is the one who died there."

"And what's that to do with anything?" Carlyle asked.

"There's no other reason for him to be in the park!" she exclaimed.

"None?" he asked gently.

"Wait a second," she said. "You think *Ames* was a traitor?"

"It fits, doesn't it?" Carlyle said.

"Then why would the guys who shot Phil shoot him too?"

"You're assuming the bad lads shot him."

Erin opened her mouth. She closed it again. "Damn it," she muttered. "But they didn't find a gun on Ames. So he didn't shoot Phil, no matter what. And if he didn't, someone else did, which means even if Ames was one bad guy, another was there too. That's the punk who shot Phil. Hell, maybe he shot Ames, too. We have to find that other shooter."

"And how are you intending to do that?"

"The way your boss told me to."

"You're going to pry into the good Lieutenant's files?"

"Yeah."

"Will they let you do that?"

She gave him a look. "I'm going to do it," she said.

"Are you certain you're wanting to step outside the lines on this?" he asked. "If you're caught misbehaving—"

"No!" she snapped. "Don't start with that. This isn't kids screwing around on the playground. Phil's my friend. He's had my back through this whole mess, and now he may be dying. Even if he lives, his career's over. He'll never be able to put on a shield again, whatever happens. He's got a family! There's a good woman back at the hospital who's trying to hold herself together for the sake of her kids, and I'm going to get the evil bastard who did this to them! Whatever it takes!"

"Whatever?" he repeated.

"Remember what you told me once?" she asked. "When I asked where you drew the line? You said when it came to the people you loved..."

"There's no bloody line," he finished. "I understand, but it's dangerous."

"You think I give a damn?"

"You should," he said sharply. "Because your life isn't merely your own, Erin. I've a stake in it, too. When you pulled me out of the gutter, when you gave me something to live for, you took on a responsibility. And I'm not the only one who needs you. You're not allowed to throw your life away."

"Okay, fine," she said, hating the sulky sound of her own voice. "I'll be discreet."

"That's all I'm asking," he said. "And believe me, I'd like nothing more than to see these scunners get all they deserve. But let's try not to get dragged down with them, aye?"

"Copy that," she said. "And on that subject, what were you and Finnegan doing at Evan's in the first place?"

"I rather think Evan was seeking to learn whether one of us was betraying him," Carlyle said with perfect calm.

"And that doesn't bother you?" Erin exclaimed.

"The lad's always suspicious," he said. "It's just a matter of degree. It's nothing to fret over."

"What *do* you fret over?" she replied. "Because this is life-or-death shit."

"Only if Evan learns the truth," Carlyle said with a slight smile.

"You guys are all crazy," Erin muttered. She opened the driver's side door, climbed in, and slammed it behind her.

Chapter 10

Time had lost all meaning. The moon and stars were invisible. Erin drove through an endless night of spinning snowflakes and bitter cold. The police-band radio in her car was alive with the chatter of first responders, but the streets were dead. Manhattan had ground to a standstill.

She'd been sorely tempted to follow Carlyle into the Barley Corner. Warm, beckoning light shone from its windows. She could feel the comfort and heat in her bones. A bowl of Marian's famous Irish stew, a glass of Guinness, and a long, hot soak in the tub were just what she needed.

Instead, she dropped him off at the curb and kept going, making her slow, slipping, sliding way to Precinct Ten. She had to change routes twice. The first detour was necessitated by an embankment of snow that had been plowed up at an intersection. A couple of city plows were doing their best to clear it, but it'd take time, so she backed up and worked her way around. The second obstacle was a traffic jam in which a minivan had collided with a delivery truck and gotten so wedged in place that they'd need multiple tow trucks to shift them. Then a semi-trailer had jackknifed trying to stop, resulting in an entire block's worth of trapped cars. The drivers of these vehicles had simply abandoned them and hurried away on foot.

"Maybe the world's ending," Erin suggested.

Rolf cocked his head. He had no eschatological opinions. He didn't even know the word "eschatology." Erin wouldn't have either, except for a particularly odd Sunday-school teacher she'd had in her pre-teen years. He'd been big into apocalyptic philosophy and had liked to read to the kids out of the book of Revelations. The parents had gotten wind of it and he'd been packed off somewhere, never to be heard from again.

"I guess if it is the end, the cops will be the first to know," she said, shrugging. "What a mess, huh?"

Rolf lay down morosely in his compartment. His snout was cold, so he tucked it under his tail.

The Ten was remarkably quiet. Apparently even the criminals had decided to take the rest of the night off, and all the Patrol units were out looking for accidents and stranded motorists. There was plenty of room in the departmental garage. Erin parked and went in.

The desk sergeant was all alone. He gave her a bleak stare.

"Five below," he said. "That's below zero, not below freezing. You believe that? We got ten inches on the ground and more coming. They're saying we're gonna get more than twenty. It'll be like back in '06. Remember that?"

"Yeah," Erin said. "I'd only been on the Force a couple years. It was crazy."

"They've banned travel," the sergeant said. "City-wide."

"About time," she said. "I had a hell of a time getting here."

"What're you doing here, anyway?" he asked. "This isn't your house."

"O'Reilly, from the Eightball," she said, holding up her shield.

"And you made it all the way up here? You're braver than you look. What's so important it's got you shoving through the drifts?"

"I'm working the Stachowski and Ames shooting," she said.

"Oh," he said. "Shit. Hell of a thing."

"Yeah," she said.

"What do you need?" he asked. "We'll get you anything we can."

"I need to check Stachowski's office," she said. "One of his active cases might give us a clue who wanted to kill him."

"Absolutely," the sergeant said. "I'll call the Captain and tell him you're on your way up. Third floor."

Erin considered the elevator, but decided she could manage two flights of stairs. She led Rolf up to the third floor, where she found a big-bellied, heavy-jowled NYPD captain waiting for her.

"Evening, Detective," he said, extending a hand. "Orville Rydell."

"Erin O'Reilly," she said, shaking hands. He had a good grip in spite of his bulk. His eyes, sunk in his fat cheeks, were still keen and bright. He appeared wide awake and alert, though his uniform looked rumpled and she guessed he'd been up all day and all night. The hands on the clock over the door stood at five minutes to midnight.

"O'Reilly?" he said. "I've heard about you. Pleased to meet you. I'm glad Major Crimes is sending their best people on this one."

"We do what we can, sir," she said. "It's a major incident."

"You're right about that," he sighed. "One of mine dead, another circling the drain. The last I heard, Stachowski made it through his first surgery, but it's still touch and go. Fifty-fifty whether he makes it to morning."

Erin swallowed. "He's tougher than he looks," she said. "I'm betting he pulls through."

"You know him?" Rydell asked.

Erin cursed inwardly. "By reputation," she said.

"Well, you're right," Rydell said. "He's a damn good man. So was Ames. A real go-getter. That guy took down more street dealers than you could believe. He had a real sixth sense for them."

"Or really good street intel," she said.

Rydell smiled grimly. "That, too. So, what leads do you have?"

"None I'm prepared to talk about," she said. "But I do have a few questions, if you don't mind."

"Of course," he said. "Come into my office. I've got coffee. It tastes like paint thinner, but it's hot."

"Good enough for me," she said.

Rydell's office was cluttered but cozy. The coffee was no better than he promised, but Erin had tasted worse. He motioned her to a tattered faux-leather chair across from his desk, then sank down behind a parapet of paperwork.

"Now, Detective," he said. "How can I help?"

"How well do you know Lieutenant Stachowski?" she asked.

"I've known Phil for years," Rydell said. "He's a Number Ten lifer, just like me. Thank God he's got his pension locked in. Finished out his twenty just a couple months ago. That'll be a comfort for Cam and the kids, no matter what happens. Maybe he should've hung up his shield then."

"What does he carry?" she asked.

"How do you mean?"

"His sidearm."

Rydell laughed. "Sidearm!" he exclaimed. "His desk's the one in the back corner down the hall. You can unlock his drawer and check for yourself."

"You mean his gun's still in his desk?" Erin asked.

"That's affirmative," Rydell said. "He never liked hauling it around. Not even when he was working Patrol. He always said the London Bobbies had the right idea."

"London doesn't have nearly as many guns on the street as we do," Erin said.

"That's what I told him," Rydell said. "And he carried his regulation piece on patrol, just like everyone. But he practically never drew it. He said once that the problem with wearing a gun is, you mix it up with a perp and the next thing you know he's got your gun. Then he kills you with your own piece. He said it's better nineteen times out of twenty if nobody's bringing a gun to a fight, especially when things get up close and physical."

"Did that ever get him in trouble?" Erin asked.

"Not that I can recall," Rydell said. "You wouldn't think Phil could fight, but he could throw down with the best of them. People always underestimated him, since he didn't look like much. But he was smart and quick. You know he can do card tricks?"

"Card tricks?" she echoed.

"Yeah," Rydell said. "Stage magic. He says it's all misdirection."

"A magician shows you the wrong hand," Erin said, thinking of another case she'd worked.

"Exactly," Rydell said. "Anyway, once Phil started riding a desk, that's where he left the gun. Since he was working plainclothes, meeting other officers most of the time, he said he didn't need it and it'd just get in the way. I'm serious about checking it, by the way. I know you'll want to, just to be thorough. But I've got ten bucks says it's in his desk, not even loaded. Standard-issue Glock, only ever been fired on the range."

"Do you have any idea what he was working on?" she asked.

"You know what his assignments were?" Rydell replied.

"Undercovers."

He nodded. "I never wanted to know," he said. "I was afraid I'd let something slip. I always figure, the fewer guys who know about that sort of operation, the better."

"That's true enough," Erin said.

"I do know he was working something big," Rydell said thoughtfully. "He came to me last week about the duty rosters. Said he needed some extra bodies. He wanted only people he'd worked with before, personally, on undercover assignments. That meant mostly Narcs. I got him the guys he wanted."

"Was Ames one of them?"

"Yes, he was."

"Who were the rest?"

Rydell tapped his double chin. "Hmm, there'd be Katzenberg, Bowes, Carter, and Sanchez," he said. "I think that's it. Why?"

"There was a leak somewhere," she said.

"I thought so," he said. "It feels like a setup to me. But why take Phil out? He hasn't been on the sharp end of the spear for five or six years. He wasn't the one doing the infiltration."

"That's what I'm trying to figure out," Erin said.

"How's your coffee?" Rydell asked.

She gave a noncommittal shrug.

"It tastes better when you're at the end of an overtime shift," he said. "Ready to take a look at his desk now? I don't think he'd leave anything lying around, but maybe you'll spot some little detail. That's what breaks cases, right? The little things?"

"That's what my dad always says," Erin said.

"Was he a gold shield, too?"

"Career Patrolman, down in Queens. The 116. Sean O'Reilly."

"I'll bet he's proud of you," Rydell said.

"Most of the time," Erin said.

Phil had an office, technically. It was a little square of space, partitioned off from the rest of the floor by flimsy wood paneling and cheap plate glass. The door was labeled LT STACHOWSKI. Rydell unlocked it and swung it open.

"I'll wait here," he said. "Not sure we'd both fit."

Rydell was right; this was a one-person room. Phil's desktop was neat and tidy, but file cabinets took up most of the floor space. His desk sported his computer, a few ballpoint pens, a yellow legal pad, and two photographs. Erin saw with a pang that one was a picture of Camilla, the other of the whole family in front of a Christmas tree. Everyone was smiling and happy.

The computer screen was dark, the machine powered down. Erin poked the power button and tried the first desk drawer on the right. It slid open, revealing exactly what Rydell had predicted; a boxy black handgun, identical to Erin's own Glock 18. A box of bullets also sat there, but the ammo hadn't been opened. A layer of dust coated both gun and bullets.

"Didn't he have to qualify on the range?" she asked.

"Regulations say officers have to qualify twice a year," Rydell said. "As you ought to know, Detective."

"I go more often," Erin said. "At least once a month, usually more."

"Next qualification wasn't due until January," Rydell said. "I expect that thing's been sitting there ever since his last one."

Erin nodded and slid the drawer shut. It hitched slightly, a splinter of jagged wood catching against the desk's frame. She frowned and peered more closely.

"Everything okay, Detective?" Rydell asked.

"This thing's been forced," she said, recognizing the telltale splintering of wood around the lock. "It looks fresh, too. The wood's still bright where it came apart."

"You mean somebody broke into Stachowski's desk?" Rydell was trying to sound casual, but Erin could tell he was alarmed. "Anything missing?"

"I can't possibly know that," she said. But she noticed the computer was still dark. She bent over and peered at the tower. The hard drive was missing. Cursing quietly, she reached into her hip pocket and took a pair of disposable gloves off the roll she always carried. She quickly opened the rest of the drawers, scanning the contents.

"What can you tell?" Rydell asked.

"The files are messed up," she said, giving a stack of manila folders a riffle. "All out of order. And somebody's screwed with his computer. Did he strike you as the kind of guy who keeps a messy office?"

"No," Rydell said. "He never misplaces anything." He took out his phone.

"What're you doing, sir?"

"I'm calling IAB," the Captain said. "One of my people is the victim of a crime."

"Two crimes," Erin corrected him.

"You're right, of course," Rydell said. "That only makes it worse."

"Can you hold off a minute, sir?"

He hesitated. "Why?"

"Do you trust your IAB guy?"

Rydell's eyes were hard. "What the hell kind of question is that, Detective?"

"An important one," she said. "Listen, sir. This has to be an inside job. Someone in this office is trying to get at Lieutenant Stachowski's data. Until we know who, we need to be really careful."

"Do you know what this person is after?" Rydell asked.

It was Erin's turn to hesitate. Rydell caught the pause and understood what it meant.

"Detective O'Reilly," he said. "Why did two of my officers get shot tonight?"

"I'm not at liberty to say, sir."

"This is about Phil's big operation," he said. "Don't bother with the can-neither-confirm-nor-deny bullshit, I know it's true. I assume the targets of his op are the people who came after him. Why?"

"Because they don't know who their real target is," Erin said.

"That's nonsense," Rydell said. "Killing Phil would only insulate his undercover from discovery."

"Not if the intention wasn't to kill him," Erin said quietly.

"Shooting a man in the head isn't exactly a good way to *not* kill him," Rydell said.

Erin was shaking her head. "No," she said. "We've been looking at this all wrong. The point wasn't to kill him, sir. That was never their plan. That was *Phil's* plan."

"Suicide?" Rydell said doubtfully.

"No! This was an attempted kidnapping. Phil decided not to go quietly."

"Who in their right mind would try to kidnap an NYPD Lieutenant?"

"Someone who wanted to know what he knows," Erin said grimly. "They didn't want to shoot him, but he didn't give them any choice."

"So what does he know?" Rydell asked.

"That's not really the question right now," she said. "The question is, how else can they find it out? When they screwed up at Central Park, I think they came here next. But I don't know whether they found what they were looking for here."

"He wouldn't keep sensitive info about undercover assignments in his office," Rydell said. "He's way too careful for that. Too many people come through this building, and you saw for yourself how flimsy these locks are. If he's got anything written down, it'll be somewhere else."

"Where?" Erin asked.

"If I knew that, it wouldn't be a well-kept secret," Rydell said. "I know him pretty well, but I don't track his movements. You'd need to talk to somebody closer to him."

"A partner?" she asked.

"When he made Lieutenant, he stopped having one. The top of the pile is a lonely place to be. I should know."

"Then who?"

He shrugged. "You'd want to talk to his old lady, I guess. Cam probably knows as much about him as anyone. I'd guess she's at the hospital right now."

"Last I heard," Erin said. "Do you really think he'd share case info with her?"

"I doubt it," Rydell said. "But she'd be the one most likely to know where he keeps important papers. A safe-deposit box, maybe, or some sort of vault or safe in his house. How important is this information, Detective?"

"It seems it's worth killing for," she said. She looked around at the file cabinets. Now that she was looking for it, she could see the scratches and bent plates where the simple locks had been jimmied or forced. There was no point combing through these files. She didn't even know if the information had ever been there, and if it had, the bad guys had gotten to it first.

"I suppose you're going to ask about the security footage," Rydell said.

"You've got cameras on this office?" Erin asked eagerly.

"We do," he said heavily. "Unfortunately, the system went down earlier this evening. Some sort of technical glitch. We're missing the past few hours."

"And that didn't strike you as suspicious?" she demanded.

"Not until just now," Rydell sighed. "Internal Affairs is going to be so far up my ass, I'll be shitting red tape for a week."

"I guess I need to talk to Mrs. Stachowski again," she said. "Thanks for your help, Captain."

And then, maybe, she'd finally be able to get some rest.

Chapter 11

"Report," Webb said. He didn't sound more tired than usual, but that wasn't saying much.

"Are you still at the hospital, sir?" Erin asked. She had her phone on speaker so her hands were free to work the steering wheel. All the same, it felt more dangerous than normal. Road conditions had only gotten worse.

"Yes. It's looking like we may be stuck here overnight. Where are you?"

"On my way from the Ten. Is Camilla Stachowski still there?"

"No."

"Did they let her in to see Phil?"

"You misunderstood," he said. "She's gone."

"Where?"

"Home."

"Why?"

"Because they're locking the city down," Webb said. "They're closing all the bridges, all the ferries, the works."

"What about the tunnels? Those won't be snowed in."

"Everything, O'Reilly. Governor's orders."

"But what about her husband?"

"Her husband's in a coma," Webb said grimly. "The brain surgeon's still working on him, and will be all night I expect. She can't do a thing for him, so she's gone to take care of her children while she still can. If she'd waited any longer, she wouldn't have been able to make it to Jersey."

"When did she leave?" Erin asked.

"Not too long after you did. And unless you've got a good reason to come here, don't. Go home, or back to the Eightball if you really want to. It's getting bad. Neshenko's helping the staff set up emergency logistics here. They're getting their backup generator online and he's scrounging blankets and food. He keeps saying something about General Winter being in command now. I think that's some sort of Russian thing."

"Copy that," she said. "How long until they close the tunnels?"

"One o'clock."

Erin glanced at the clock and considered her position. "I might make it," she said.

"Make it where?" Webb asked sharply.

"Jersey."

"O'Reilly, you're not listening to me."

"I heard what you said, sir. But I think there's something at the Stachowski house, or something Mrs. Stachowski can tell me."

"You'd better tell me what you found out first," he said.

Erin's explanation took her most of the way to the Holland Tunnel. She'd never seen less traffic on the Manhattan streets, and never been less happy about it.

"So you think somebody ransacked his office after he was shot?" Webb asked. "Or maybe before?"

She hadn't considered that. "One or the other," she said. "I hope it was before."

"Why?"

"Because that'd mean they didn't get what they were looking for. Otherwise they wouldn't have needed to try for Phil."

"And that's your theory? Perps couldn't find their answer, so they tried to interrogate him and botched the job?"

"That's my best guess."

"O'Reilly, why do you need his files?" Webb asked. "You already know what they're looking for."

"I need to know if they've got it or not," she said. "Damn it, I need Phil to wake up so he can tell me what they might have found."

"You do know, even if he wakes up, he may not remember his own name, let alone anything else," Webb said.

She closed her eyes for a moment and gripped the wheel. "Yeah, I know. Hey, can you do me a favor, sir?"

His sigh was clearly audible, even over the road noise. "What?"

"There's a squad of Narcotics guys hanging around the hospital. Katz, Mingo, Bowes, and Carter. Can you keep tabs on them?"

"Those are the people Stachowski was bringing into the case," Webb said.

"Exactly."

"You think one of them is a mole."

"They're my top suspects."

"Okay, I'll make sure I know where they are and what they're doing. And they won't get in to see Stachowski, I can guarantee that. Like I said, he's in surgery now, and he'll be in intensive care after that, assuming he survives. They won't even let family in. I'll have guards on his door, reliable people."

"Thank you, sir."

"And O'Reilly?"

"Sir?"

"Watch where you're driving. If I find out you've spun your car into the Hudson, I'm going to be very disappointed in you. Do that, and you'll be better off swimming the rest of the way to New Jersey than facing me in the morning."

"Copy that, sir."

Erin was driving carefully, so she was able to bring the Charger slewing to a stop at the tunnel entrance. The road was blocked by a row of NYPD blue-and-whites manned by unhappy, stubborn Patrol officers. Her credentials left them unimpressed.

"Look, lady, you could be the Mayor and I'd tell you the same thing," the sergeant in charge said. "Hell, you could be the Pope. I don't make the orders and I don't control the weather. Orders are, nobody gets through except in life-or-death emergencies, and the weather's gonna make damn sure it don't happen. You think you can wave your shiny gold shield and the snow's gonna part for you, like Moses crossing the Delaware?"

There was a moment of confused silence.

"This is life or death," Erin said, bending the truth as much as she dared. "I've got a cop in the hospital, hanging by a thread. I need to get through to his wife."

"She pregnant?" the sergeant asked sarcastically. "How about sick? She got cancer? What is this, a damn Hallmark holiday special?"

"If it is, do you really want to be playing Scrooge?" Erin replied. "Listen, this is about Lieutenant Stachowski. You must've heard about him. It's been all over the radio tonight."

"That thing in Central Park?" one of the other cops said. "Hell yes, we know about it. You're going after the bastards who shot our guys?"

"Yeah," Erin said. "And the road leading to them runs through this tunnel."

"You gonna get them?" another cop asked.

"I'll slap the cuffs on the sons of bitches, read them their rights, and teach them the true meaning of Christmas," she promised.

"Sarge, you really think our orders apply here?" the first uniform asked.

The sergeant considered. "Okay," he said. "I oughta make you sign, like, a liability waiver."

"Your body cams turned on, guys?" Erin asked the uniforms.

"Mine is now," one said, clicking a button on the camera stuck to his chest.

"Then this is me, Detective Erin O'Reilly, promising not to sue the NYPD, or the Highway Department, or anybody else, over whatever stupid shit I get into on the road, here or across the river in Jersey. I absolve the City. You got that? *Now* will you move that damn Patrol unit out of the way?"

Two minutes later, the tires of Erin's Charger were humming on dry concrete under the Hudson and she was on her way to New Jersey.

*   *   *

"What's happened?" Camilla Stachowski asked when she opened the door to Erin.

"He's still in surgery," Erin said quickly. "And that's the best news we can have right now. They'll call you as soon as there's anything to report."

"Then what are you doing here?" Camilla asked. "I only got home a few minutes ago myself. You must have had a terrible time on the roads."

"May I come in?"

"Of course."

Camilla ushered her into the living room. Another woman sat on the couch. She was a little shorter and stouter than Camilla, but showed a strong family resemblance.

"This is my sister, Moira," Camilla said.

"Detective Erin O'Reilly, ma'am," Erin said. "And this is my K-9, Rolf."

"Detective O'Reilly is working Phil's case," Camilla explained.

"I'm sorry for your family's troubles," Erin said, realizing as the words left her mouth that they were exactly what Carlyle would have said.

"Thank you," Moira said. "It's really awful. Anything I can do to help Cam, I will."

"I'm sure," Erin said. "Thanks for looking after her kids."

"Absolutely," Moira said. "That's what family is for. I'm staying over tonight, and for as long as she needs me."

"But it's been a very long day," Camilla said. "And we're all tired. Do you work the night shift, Detective?"

"Not usually," Erin said.

"Then you must be exhausted, too. Are you driving back to Manhattan tonight?"

"After I'm done here, yeah. I'll have to."

"Then we'd better take care of things quickly," Camilla said briskly. "Otherwise you may not be able to get through. What do you need?"

"Where are the kids?" Erin asked.

"Upstairs, in bed," Moira said. "I finally got them to go to sleep about half an hour ago. I read them five chapters of *The Lion, The Witch, and the Wardrobe* before they nodded off. It seemed appropriate, since we're so close to Christmas and it's snowing."

"Is there somewhere we can talk?" Erin asked Camilla, giving Moira a sidelong glance.

"We'll go to the kitchen," Camilla said, understanding. "I'll get you something hot to drink. Moira, why don't you go on up to bed? I'll be along shortly."

In the kitchen, Camilla busied herself getting coffee. The pot was already half full; Erin saw used cups by the sink and reckoned the household was running on caffeine and fumes.

"We think the person who shot Phil was looking for information he had," Erin said.

"What sort of information?" Camilla asked.

"We don't know," Erin said. "But I think it was something to do with one of his undercover officers."

Camilla shook her head and handed Erin a steaming cup of coffee. "Phil would never give up one of his people. Never. He'd rather die."

"I know," Erin said quietly. "I think that's more or less what happened."

"Oh, God," Camilla whispered. "You think someone tried to get him to rat out another officer and he refused?"

"Phil wasn't carrying his gun," Erin said. "I think he grabbed a weapon away from one of the guys who was holding him. That's why they shot him."

Camilla didn't say anything, but her eyes filled with tears. She clenched her jaw and swallowed.

"I don't think he talked," Erin said. "But the bad guys got into his desk at the Ten. I don't know what they found there. What I need to know is whether he ever brought paperwork home with him."

"Sometimes," Camilla said. "But he wouldn't just leave it lying around."

"Where does he keep it?" Erin asked. "Is it secure?"

"There's a safe in the basement," Camilla said. "I'll show you."

Erin and Rolf followed her down to the cellar. It was unfinished; just plain cinderblocks. The air was cold and there was a musty, earthy smell. Camilla pulled a cord, turning on a bare bulb that hung from the ceiling.

"There's the safe," she said, pointing to the corner.

"Wow," Erin said. "That looks like something out of an old bank."

"It is," Camilla said. "Phil bought it at auction when the bank down the street closed. It didn't cost all that much, but moving it was a terrible job. I didn't think we'd ever get it down the stairs. If we sell the house, it's staying here."

Erin approached the squat, olive-green block of metal. It was icy cold to the touch and felt very heavy and solid. "You'd need a team of engineers and a lot of heavy equipment to even put a dent in this thing," she said.

"We've got our keepsakes in there," Camilla said. "Our marriage license, the kids' birth certificates, all the stuff people usually keep in safe-deposit boxes. This is just as good. It's fireproof, waterproof, and bulletproof."

"Hold on," Erin said. "If this has important family papers in it, you must know the combination, too."

"Of course," Camilla said. "And I guess that's a good thing, in case..."

She didn't finish the sentence. She didn't have to.

"Camilla," Erin said, deliberately using the woman's first name. "I have to know if Phil's got anything written down about his current cases. This is really important. Can you open that for me?"

Camilla hesitated. Sudden doubt was in her face. "How do I know you're who you say you are?" she asked suddenly.

Erin felt a flash of indignation, but quickly smothered it. The other woman actually had an excellent point, though it was a little late to be bringing it up. After all, she was Junkyard

O'Reilly, mob cop and contract killer, though she really hoped Camilla didn't know that.

"Phil's my friend," she said. "I've trusted him with my life. If I don't figure out what happened to him and why, more cops are going to be in danger. I'm sorry I didn't tell you that before. I've got my reasons, and I can't tell you all of them. I can't make you trust me. But I'm on your side. If I could've stepped between him and that bullet, I would've done it. I feel like some of what happened is on me, and maybe I can't make it right, but I'm going to do everything I can to try."

Camilla bit her lip and nodded. "Okay," she said. "I believe you."

She walked to the safe and, screening the dial with her body, spun it quickly left, right, left. The tumblers thudded into place one after another. The door swung open.

"There," she said, stepping back and rubbing her arms. "Take a look around. Brr! It's so cold down here. I'm going upstairs. When you're done, please put everything you don't need back in the safe and lock it."

"Copy that," Erin said. She understood why Camilla didn't want to hang around. The basement was an unpleasant place, and it really was cold. She half expected her fingertips to freeze to the metal. And there was a fair amount of stuff in the safe. A family generated a lot of important paperwork over the years, and it would take time to wade through it.

Erin found a battered metal folding chair in the corner. She unfolded it and sat down, flinching at the icy touch of the metal through her clothes. Rolf stood beside her, head cocked quizzically. She pulled out her pocket flashlight for extra illumination and got to work.

Phil was organized and tidy, which was a very good thing. Erin was able to weed out the family files pretty quickly, setting them aside on the floor. She found an album that proved to contain wedding photos, which made her want to bury her head in her hands and cry. But she didn't have time for that, so she put it with the other family papers. Then there were certificates of insurance for the house and all the people in the family, the titles on two cars, the car insurance, a few savings bonds that would mature in another decade, and all the other paper flotsam of an ordinary American middle-class life.

But she didn't find any police files. She didn't know what she'd been expecting; it wasn't like Phil would have Erin O'Reilly's personnel jacket sitting there with "Undercover Officer" stamped in red ink on the cover. He wasn't a moron. But the absence of evidence did not equate to evidence of absence. That was one of the first things a detective learned about crime scenes. Just because it wasn't there didn't mean it hadn't happened, and didn't mean there wasn't evidence *somewhere*. But where?

Erin sat back with a groan. Her hands had gone numb again. She sighed and realized she could actually see her breath. How cold was it down here? Forty degrees? Colder?

"I'm going to get frostbite," she muttered to Rolf. "The Department's going to see a disability claim because I left my fingers down in this godforsaken basement. You think they'll accept it as a line-of-duty injury?"

Rolf extended his snout, opened his mouth, and gently licked her fingers.

"Yeah, those," she said, smiling at him. "How'd you know? You're a pretty smart boy, you know that, kiddo?"

Rolf wagged his tail. He was well aware.

A muffled, almost musical tinkling sound came faintly from upstairs. It had a holiday ring to it, like sleigh bells, or maybe icicles falling off the roof. She might not even have noticed it, but it was after two in the morning and the house was very quiet.

Erin stood up, stretching her stiff muscles. "What was that?" she asked, not expecting an answer.

Camilla's voice filtered down from somewhere overhead. Erin couldn't make out her words, but the woman sounded frightened and angry. Who was she talking to?

Erin started for the stairs. Then a distinctly male voice she didn't know said, very clearly, "Shut up, bitch!"

Oh, shit, Erin thought. She started running up the stairs, fumbling at her belt with numbed fingers for the grip of her Glock.

She was just two steps from the top when the shotgun fired.

Chapter 12

The two blasts overlapped one another, coming so fast they had to be from more than one gun barrel. Before the echoes had time to die, a body thudded to the floor. Erin whipped out her Glock, heart hammering, and leaned around the doorframe, dreading what she'd find.

She saw the legs and feet of a downed human protruding from the kitchen doorway. They lay perfectly still, not even a quiver of life in them. But the legs belonged to a man. The shoes were old, battered, and way too big to be Camilla's.

Somebody, another man, screamed in terror or pain. Erin pivoted around the doorway, bringing the Glock in line. She saw a man's back as he dashed out the back door of the Stachowski house and into their little postage stamp of yard. Erin also saw the revolver in his hand.

"Drop it!" she shouted. "NYPD!"

The running man thrust his gun-hand around his body and fired twice, blindly, in Erin's general direction. One bullet whined past her ear like a malevolent hornet. The other missed by a larger margin.

Erin squeezed off two shots at the man's center of mass. He stumbled and floundered into the snow, disappearing from view. But he was still up and still armed.

"Rolf! *Fass!*" she snapped, dropping the K-9's leash.

That was all Rolf needed. He was out the door in less than two seconds, bounding into the snow with a speed and enthusiasm Santa's reindeer might have envied.

Erin risked a quick glance over her shoulder to make sure nothing was coming at her from behind. The door to the front hall closet stood open. Next to the door, face very pale, Camilla Stachowski stood with a double-barreled shotgun in her hands. Wisps of blue-gray smoke drifted from both barrels.

Camilla, moving with slow, mechanical motions, broke the shotgun open and ejected the empty shells. She reached into the closet. Her hand came back into view with a fresh pair of crimped twelve-gauge shells, which she inserted into the gun and snapped it closed again.

"Stay there!" Erin ordered her. "Call 911!" Then she was running after her dog. She passed the body in the kitchen, recognizing almost instantly that it posed no threat. The guy had taken a double blast of buckshot point-blank to the face and upper body, neither of which remained recognizably human.

Sounds of a struggle came from the yard. Erin plunged out into the snow, not bothering to pull on her gloves. She hadn't heard another gunshot, so Rolf was probably okay, but there was no way she'd leave her partner to fight an armed opponent alone.

The Stachowski yard was ringed by a six-foot privacy fence. The man had tried to get over it, but the snow had slowed him down and Rolf had gotten to him before he'd made it. Not that he would've gotten far even if he'd cleared the fence. Erin had seen Rolf scramble over obstacles that tall plenty of times. He could do it faster than most humans.

Man and dog were struggling in a snowdrift, clouds of white powder flying. Rolf was snarling excitedly and Erin could see the tip of his tail whipping back and forth. He was definitely getting the better end of the conflict. The man was almost completely buried by the snow and the exuberantly vicious dog. He had his hands over his head and was trying to curl into a ball; the smartest thing he could do under the circumstances.

"Stop fighting my dog!" Erin shouted, wading through the snow toward them.

The man didn't answer, except in a series of sounds somewhere between screams and whimpers. In truth, what he was doing couldn't really be described as fighting. He was just trying to keep anything sensitive or important out of Rolf's jaws. Rolf, for his part, had finally gotten a good grip on the man's right arm. The dog started tugging, planting his paws and giving short, sharp jerks with his powerful neck and back muscles. However, he couldn't get a good purchase in the snow, so his back legs were flailing and kicking.

Erin finally got there and took a second trying to figure the situation out. The man's hands were empty now, so wherever his gun was, he wasn't holding it. He'd dropped it, either on the far side of the fence or when Rolf had grabbed him. She'd worry about that later.

"Rolf, *pust!*" she ordered. Rolf immediately released the man. The Shepherd bounded back a couple of feet and pranced excitedly, mouth open, tongue hanging out. This was turning out to be a much better evening than he'd expected.

Erin kept her gun trained on the man at her feet. "Get on your belly!" she snapped. "Spread your arms and legs! Do it now!"

The man slowly uncurled himself. He was a little guy, not much more than Erin's height, and even with a jacket on, he looked scrawny. Erin didn't relax her guard. The little perps could be the most dangerous ones; unable to rely on brute force, they tended to fight dirty.

She got out her cuffs. "Cross your hands behind your back," she told him. She kicked his feet a little further apart, to make sure he couldn't get up fast. Then she holstered her Glock and cuffed him with the smooth speed that came with long experience. The man didn't resist. He was moaning softly, a sound of pain almost impossible to fake.

"Are you shot?" she asked.

He mumbled something unintelligible. He was starting to shiver violently from a mix of cold and shock.

"Damn," Erin muttered. She grabbed him by the cuffed wrists and hauled him up, thanking her stars he wasn't any bigger. He wasn't much help, but she manhandled him back into the Stachowskis' kitchen, Rolf dancing beside her the whole way. The K-9 was really hoping she wouldn't forget to give him his rubber Kong ball. He was sure he'd earned it.

She kicked the door shut behind her, noticing broken glass on the kitchen floor as she did so. The window in the door had been shattered; that must have been the sound she'd heard.

A figure carrying a gun came into the kitchen. Erin's head came around and her adrenaline spiked, but it was just Camilla, still carrying the shotgun.

"The police are on their way," Camilla said, her voice remarkably steady.

"Good," Erin said. She was looking at the man she'd handcuffed. His jacket showed a puff of down near the shoulder and was soaked with blood. He'd taken a bullet square on the shoulder blade. The bone was probably cracked, and he might have internal damage. She grabbed a nearby dish towel and applied pressure. The man groaned and shifted, but lacked the strength to struggle much.

"Cam?" Moira called from the living room. "What was that noise? It sounded almost like... oh my God! Is that man..."

"Moira, go upstairs," Erin said. "Don't touch anything. Not a thing, you understand? Everything's going to be fine. You need to take care of the kids. Don't let them come down here. Go."

Every cop learned to use a voice which conveyed the full weight of authority. Most civilians would obey it without question. Moira was no exception. The woman retreated without another word.

"He's dead, isn't he," Camilla said. She sounded almost thoughtful. "And I shot him."

"Yeah," Erin said, meeting honesty with honesty. She absently fished Rolf's toy out of her pocket and tossed it to him. The rubber ball didn't have a chance to hit the ground. Rolf's jaws clamped shut and the chewing and wagging began.

"They came in the back way," Camilla said, still speaking with unnatural calmness. "I heard the window break, and I saw two men on their way in. The gun safe is in the front closet. We always keep it locked. That way we can keep the shotgun loaded. I got the safe open and told them to leave. I said I'd shoot. I guess they didn't believe me."

"I guess not," Erin said. "Did you see weapons?"

"The man I shot had a knife," Camilla said. "It's still in his hand. Look."

Erin glanced at the body. Sure enough, the dead man was still holding a cheap folding knife.

"They were going to hurt my family," Camilla said. "I'm not sorry I did it. I'd do it again."

"I understand," Erin said. "Right now, though, I need you to take the shells out of that gun and put it on the counter."

"I didn't have a choice," Camilla said, and Erin could see she wasn't nearly as calm as she sounded. The truth of what had just happened was sinking in. Another few minutes, Erin figured, and she'd either withdraw into herself or fall apart. But for the moment, Camilla retained her faculties. The woman opened the shotgun and extracted the live shells. Then she set the gun down, just like Erin had told her.

"I know," Erin said. "This was clear-cut self-defense. You've got the right to protect your family. You're not going to get in any trouble."

"Trouble?" Camilla repeated. She gave a short, sharp, incredulous laugh. "I'm not worried about *that*."

You should be, Erin thought but didn't say. Murder was murder, and lots of people who thought they were defending themselves ended up doing time for manslaughter. She didn't think Camilla would be one of them, but life wasn't fair and you never knew. It was a damned good thing Erin and Moira had been in the house when it had happened. The more witnesses that could support Mrs. Stachowski, the better. And where were the damn Hoboken cops? She ought to be hearing sirens by now. It was the storm causing the delay; it had to be.

Erin took out her phone, dialing 911 with one hand while keeping up pressure on the man's bullet wound with the other. "We need an ambulance," she said.

"For that piece of trash?" Camilla said with a coldness that chilled Erin worse than the blizzard. "You should have shot him in the head."

"Maybe," Erin agreed. "But I didn't."

"I'm not sorry," Camilla said again, more fiercely.

Erin considered the bleeding man and his dead companion. Their clothes were tattered and dirty. The wounded guy was unshaven. Both were unkempt, and even over the strong odors of gunpowder and fresh blood, Erin could tell they didn't smell so good. These weren't professional assassins. They seemed like they were one step up from homeless bums.

"Who the hell are you guys?" she asked. But the wounded man was in too much pain and shock to answer, and his buddy was even less help.

Erin finally heard sirens, but they were distant. It'd be a couple minutes before they arrived. She'd wait until local law took over the scene. Then she'd need to call Lieutenant Webb. This had happened just over the Jersey border, which would complicate things. Webb, Captain Holliday, and probably the Commissioner himself were all about to lose what was left of their night's sleep.

*   *   *

The Hoboken cops took Erin and Camilla downtown, along with Rolf. There was an unspoken understanding that Camilla wasn't under arrest, at least as long as she didn't try to leave. Moira took the Stachowski kids to her own house, recognizing nobody would be getting any peace with the CSU guys tramping all over Phil and Camilla's place. Then there was also the small matter of the dead guy in the kitchen doorway. All things considered, it was better for the children to be somewhere else.

Now Erin sat in an interrogation room, opposite Captain Halverson of the Hoboken PD. She'd handed over her Glock as part of the standard officer-involved-shooting protocol, and given her backup revolver to the cops who'd brought her in, but they'd let Rolf stay with her, mainly because nobody else knew quite what to do with him. The K-9 lay under the table at her feet, placidly gnawing his rubber toy. He was the only one having a good night.

"Your Lieutenant is on his way," Halverson said. "Your Captain, too. But God only knows when they'll get here, or how. I'm amazed you got this far yourself. These are the worst road conditions I can remember."

"It's not so bad once you get moving," Erin said. "Where's Mrs. Stachowski?"

"She's giving her own statement down the hall," Halverson said. "You understand, of course, why we need the two of you to provide independent narratives."

"So we don't make up a bunch of bullshit, sir?" Erin asked with mock sincerity. Normally she'd be more polite to a high-ranking cop from another city, but it had been a really difficult night.

"Precisely," Halverson said, smiling thinly. "You may, of course, request a representative from your union to be present."

"And how would he get here?" Erin retorted.

"That's a good question," Halverson admitted. "All the bridges and tunnels are closed. Your Captain might take a helicopter, but I'm not even sure a chopper can fly in this. They may not be here until morning, if then."

"I'm good without the union rep, thanks," Erin said. "Hell, I didn't kill anyone."

"So I understand," Halverson said. "Now, just so we're clear, you told the responding officers you did not directly witness the fatal shooting. Is that correct?"

"That's right. I was in the basement. I ran upstairs when I heard the confrontation, but the shots were fired before I got there."

"How long after the gunshot did you enter the scene?"

"Three or four seconds, tops."

"Please describe what you saw."

They went over the events step by step, piece by piece. It took almost an hour. Erin held her impatience in check.

Halverson was just doing his job, the same as Webb or Holliday would've done in his place. Everything seemed clear-cut to her, but the other cops hadn't been there. They needed to get it all laid out, plain and straightforward. A little trouble now could save a whole lot more after the lawyers got involved.

"Did you recognize either of the intruders?" Halverson asked.

"I'd never seen the wounded guy before," Erin said. "The other one... I couldn't say. I only saw him after he got hit, and he could've been almost anybody. The buckshot really messed up his face."

Halverson nodded. "Okay," he said, standing up. "I think we're done here. You're good to go, Detective. Not that you'll get far if you step out the front door. We've got better than thirteen inches of accumulation, and more on the way."

"I'd like to check on Mrs. Stachowski," Erin said. "If that's okay."

"It shouldn't be a problem," Halverson said, leading the way into the hallway. "You're in the clear now. Like you said, you didn't kill anyone. We've got a positive ID on one of the perps, too."

"Who is he?" Erin asked, a little too eagerly.

"Ozzie Cowan," Halverson said. "He's gutter trash. Repeat offender, small-time drug dealer and strong-arm thug. Good guy to throw some lead into, if you want my opinion. This is looking like a home invasion gone bad, a couple junkies looking to score some pills. They just picked the wrong house this time."

"That's for sure," Erin said. "Where's this guy from?"

"Your stomping grounds," Halverson said. "The Big Apple, Hell's Kitchen."

"What was a New Yorker doing in Hoboken on a night like this?" she wondered.

Halverson shrugged. "Who knows? Who cares? We've got him on B&E, together with possession of an unregistered firearm and attempted murder, of a cop no less. With a rap sheet like his, this boy's going down hard. The next time he hits the street, he'll be old enough to collect Social Security."

"And the other perp?" she asked.

"We're running his prints," Halverson said. "It's not like we can do facial recognition, or even dental records. That lady knew what she was doing with that shotgun. Dumb bastard probably never even knew what hit him."

Halverson stopped in front of the lounge. Inside, Camilla Stachowski was sitting on a sofa that was a near-twin of the disreputable couch in the Major Crimes break room. She had the inevitable cup of coffee in her hands. A female detective was sitting in a beat-up old chair opposite her.

"You get what you need, Mueller?" Halverson asked.

"Yes, sir," Mueller said. "We're still waiting on her bloodwork."

"I'm not on any medications," Camilla said. "I don't even drink."

"Here's her statement," Mueller said, handing her notepad to the Captain. "I don't see any problems. She told him to stop, threatened to shoot, and he advanced on her with a weapon. It doesn't get more cut-and-dried than that."

"Good," Halverson said. "How are you feeling, Mrs. Stachowski?"

"I feel fine," Camilla said quietly. "I thought I'd feel terrible, but it doesn't bother me, not at all. I'm bothered that I'm not more bothered. Does that make sense?"

"Yeah," Erin said.

"Taking a life is a big deal," Camilla said. "It ought to stay with a good person, haunt her. But I'm *glad* I shot him. What does that say about me?"

"It says you're a brave woman who wasn't about to let a couple low-life junkies threaten her or her family," Erin said. "You did what you had to do."

"It's still early," Halverson added. "You may find you feel different after a day or two. Often, when an officer has a critical incident like this, the full impact doesn't hit them right away."

"I suppose," Camilla said doubtfully. "Have either of you ever shot anyone?"

"I just shot a guy in your backyard," Erin said.

"Killed them, I mean," Camilla said.

"I haven't," Halverson said.

"I have," Erin said.

"How do you feel about it?" Camilla asked.

"I didn't like it," Erin said. "But I don't regret it. Every time, it was necessary. I do have bad dreams sometimes. That may happen to you. It's nothing to be ashamed of; it's totally normal."

"I don't think so," Camilla said. "I don't feel anything toward that man. I feel numb, sort of frozen on the inside. Does that make me a bad person?"

"No!" Erin and Halverson said in unison.

"It made you a damn good shot," Erin said.

"Phil said a shotgun was the best weapon for home defense," Camilla said. "The pellets won't penetrate more than one wall, and the spread makes it hard to miss. I should've only fired one barrel and saved the other for the second man. That was careless and stupid."

"It worked out okay," Erin said. "I got the other guy."

"I would have killed him, too."

"Camilla," Erin said, laying a hand on the other woman's shoulder. "It's okay."

Camilla nodded, but she clearly didn't believe her.

"Can she go home?" Erin asked Halverson.

"Not right away," he said. "They're not done collecting evidence. The house is still an active crime scene. But she can go to her sister's and see her kids, if she wants."

"I'd like that," Camilla said.

"I'll detail a Patrol unit to get you there," Halverson said.

"Detective O'Reilly?" Camilla said. "Thank you. I think you saved my life."

"You saved yourself," Erin said. "I was just there to pick up the pieces. It's the least I could do."

"I just wish you'd been with Phil tonight," Camilla said softly. "He needed a friend as much as I did."

"Me, too," Erin said. "Take care of yourself, ma'am."

Chapter 13

During a blizzard, sensible people stayed indoors. They built a fire, wrapped themselves in blankets, and sipped cocoa. They didn't drive around a snowbound city getting in gunfights, and they absolutely did not wander into the parking lot of the local police station to flag down a helicopter.

Being sensible apparently wasn't a requisite to be an NYPD detective. Erin found herself helping shovel snow off the helipad, assisting a handful of Hoboken cops. The big city plows were all busy trying to keep the streets open, so they were down to hand shovels and a single sorry excuse for a snowblower. It was cold, backbreaking work, illuminated by cold halogen floodlights.

Just a minute or two after they'd finally scraped the big H clear, the running lights of a helicopter emerged from the storm. Its rotors whipped the flurries into a maelstrom of white. Erin flung an arm across her face and crouched down, scurrying into the shelter of the doorway.

The chopper pilot knew his business. He set his bird down as neatly as if it had been broad daylight on a still summer afternoon. A pair of men tumbled out of the passenger compartment and were nearly flattened by the rotor wash as they struggled toward the building. Erin waved to them and received a cursory gesture in return.

A minute later, Captain Holliday and Lieutenant Webb joined her inside, stamping snow from their shoes. The tips of Holliday's mustache were white with frost. Neither man looked happy. The pilot peeled off the moment he was in the door and made for the nearest coffee machine.

"Don't you have a warmer coat, sir?" Erin asked Webb, who was still clad in his customary threadbare trench coat.

"I'm from southern California," Webb said bitterly. "And I never thought I'd say this, but when I retire, I swear to God, I'm going back. But I've got a better coat; it's hanging warm and snug in my closet, a very long way from here. Thank you for reminding me."

Captain Halverson extended a hand. "Dan Halverson," he said.

"Fenton Holliday," Holliday replied, shaking. "Thanks for having us out here."

"If I can play nice when the Feebies come to town, the least I can do is offer the same courtesy to you big-city folks across the river," Halverson said. "Stachowski is one of yours, and one of your detectives was involved. You'd do the same for me."

"You all right, O'Reilly?" Webb asked.

"I'm fine," she said, and for once she almost meant it. "I didn't get a scratch. Rolf mixed it up with one of the perps, but he came out of it okay."

Rolf let his jaws fall open. His tongue rolled out in a smile that was only a little smug.

"We'll talk in the lounge," Halverson said. "My office is a little small for all of us, particularly when one of us smells like a wet dog."

"He didn't mean that," Erin told Rolf.

"I think he did," Webb said. "You probably don't notice it anymore."

"It's better than Vic's cologne," Erin said.

Webb considered this. "You've got a point," he said. "But that's faint praise."

"The lesser of two evils is still evil," Holliday remarked.

In the lounge, Erin carefully perched on the edge of the couch. Webb sat next to her, Holliday on the far end. All of them accepted Halverson's offer of coffee. How many cups had Erin drunk in the past few hours? She wondered how much damage all the caffeine was doing to her system and decided she didn't care. She'd do whatever it took to get through this endless, freezing night.

"In the past eight hours," Holliday said, "we've had one NYPD detective murdered, another critically wounded, and the wounded officer's family attacked. We know the two officer shootings are related; they're part of the same incident. What we need to know is what this has to do with the second attack."

"Probably nothing," Halverson said. "We've identified one of the intruders as a small-time hood. But we did recover a gun from the yard. Do you know what sort of weapon was used in your shooting?"

"Nine-millimeter automatic," Holliday said. "Our CSU techs recovered three casings from the scene. Two appear to have come from Detective Ames's sidearm; the other is from another weapon, which has not yet been located."

"That's not the same gun as the one we recovered," Halverson said. "Our boy used a .38 revolver. The second perp, the one Mrs. Stachowski blasted, only had a knife."

"He could've ditched the gun," Webb said doubtfully.

All the others shook their heads.

"Not likely," Holliday said, voicing their thoughts. "A smart perp would get rid of a gun he'd used to kill a cop, I agree, but not if he was on his way to commit another crime. He would've kept the pistol until he was done."

"Anyway, Cowan wasn't a very good shot," Erin said. "He sent a couple rounds my way, but he didn't even bother to aim. He's not trained. I can't see him landing headshots unless he was damned lucky."

"Then what's going on?" Halverson demanded. "Did these detectives piss off some South American drug lords or something? Is there an open bounty on them and their families?"

"That's what we're here to figure out," Holliday said. "We need to talk to this Cowan character."

"He's at the hospital," Halverson said. "Thanks to the somewhat better marksmanship of your detective."

"I only winged him," Erin said.

"It's still a bullet," Halverson said. "But he'll pull through just fine."

"Is he up for answering questions?" Holliday asked.

"You'd have to ask his doctor," Halverson said.

"Then we'd better go to the hospital," Holliday said. "Until we can pin down a motive, we can't even speculate as to what's going on."

"The motive was robbery," Halverson said.

"That's one theory, yes," Holliday said mildly.

"It won't be easy getting to the hospital," Halverson warned.

"It can't be more than a few blocks," Erin protested.

"That'll take a long time, the way this night is shaping up," Webb said.

"The sooner we start, the sooner we'll get there," Holliday said. "You've got your car here, don't you, O'Reilly?"

"Yes, sir. But it'll only seat one other human plus Rolf, unless someone wants to squeeze into his compartment with him."

"You can borrow one of my Patrol units," Halverson said. "In fact, I'll come with you. Remember, this is a Hoboken case, whatever you Big Apple boys want to think."

"We'll keep that in mind," Holliday said, smiling. "I appreciate this."

*   *   *

The plows had made a pass down the streets in question, and most of Hoboken's residents were home and in bed, so the drive took just fifteen minutes. Their little caravan pulled into the second hospital Erin had visited that night. All the sterile, coldly-lit hallways were starting to blur together in her fatigue-addled brain. For a second, she thought she was back in Bellevue.

"What's Phil's condition?" she asked Webb.

"Still in surgery," Webb said. "It'll be hours yet."

"Jesus," she murmured. "Poor Camilla."

"Did she really blow a guy away with a shotgun?"

"Absolutely," Erin said. "The range couldn't have been more than ten feet. Gave him both barrels and turned him into hamburger."

"Good for her," Webb said.

Halverson presented his shield to the ER nurse, who had a colleague lead the cops down a hallway. They found a bored-looking cop sitting outside the room in which Ozzie Cowan lay. Cowan had a sling on one arm and a handcuff attaching the other to the bed railing. He looked awake and reasonably alert.

"He's on a morphine drip," the nurse said. "He may be a little foggy."

"That's fine," Halverson said. "We just need to ask him some questions."

"Didn't he lawyer up?" Holliday asked.

"Nope," the cop at the door said. "He was pretty out of it when they brought him in, and nobody's asked him any questions yet."

"I'll bet 'lawyer' is the first word out of his mouth," Halverson said.

"I'm not a gambling man," Holliday said.

"Wasn't Doc Holliday a professional card player?" Halverson asked.

Holliday's smile was as thin and brittle as new ice. "So I've been told," he said. "But the name and the mustache are all we have in common."

Halverson looked at the detectives. "We could fight over this guy," he said. "His crime is in my jurisdiction, but he attacked the family of an NYPD officer. But it's late and I'm too tired to pick fights. Besides, we don't need a confession from this jerk. We've got him dead to rights. So you can ask him whatever you want. Just don't jeopardize my case and we'll all still be friends. I'll be in the room, but I won't say anything."

"Fair enough," Holliday said. "Lieutenant, I think this is your show."

Webb nodded. "You and me, O'Reilly," he said. "I'll take lead."

"Rolf, *sitz*," Erin said, pointing next to the guard. "*Bleib.*"

Rolf sat and stayed. Webb, Holliday, Halverson, and Erin went inside.

"Hey Ozzie," Webb said. "How're you feeling?"

Cowan stared at him for a moment. Then his lips curled into a slow, dreamy smile.

"Pretty solid, bro," he said. "This hospital shit ain't half bad."

Erin blinked. She'd never heard anyone call Webb "bro" before. It must be the morphine talking.

"That's good," Webb said, falling effortlessly into the "good cop" persona he liked to use for interrogations. "Is there anything you need?"

Cowan considered. "Nah," he said. "I'm good."

"Do you know what you're doing here?" Webb asked.

"Getting well," Cowan said, still smiling. "Got shot, bro."

"Do you remember how that happened?"

Cowan's smile faltered. "Uh... not really," he said.

"You were shooting at me, buddy," Erin growled. If Webb was going to be good cop, that left her playing bad cop, and that was fine by her. "That's why I put a round in you."

"That wasn't very nice," Cowan said. "Your dog jumped me, too. That's, like, police brutality."

"You were wearing two layers of clothes," Erin said. "He didn't even break the skin. You want to see some brutality, I can arrange that."

"Take it easy, O'Reilly," Webb said. "Maybe this is all a big misunderstanding. Ozzie, why don't you tell me what you were doing in Mrs. Stachowski's house?"

"Me and Iggy was just looking for something," Cowan said, a little sullenly. "We didn't want no trouble."

Erin silently applauded Webb. He'd just gotten Cowan to admit to breaking into the Stachowski house, with an accomplice. Since the man had been carrying a gun, that made a slam-dunk case for armed robbery and hope invasion. He'd also gotten the name of the other man.

"Was Iggy a friend of yours?" Webb asked.

"Yeah," Cowan said. "It wasn't right, what that bitch did to him."

Erin fumed inwardly, but knew better than to butt in. Webb was getting results; that was the important thing.

"What were you looking for?" Webb asked.

"Hey, it wasn't even for me, y'know?" Cowan said, as if that would help his case. "I mean, I guess we would've grabbed some pills if we'd seen them lying around, but that wasn't why we was there."

"Ozzie," Webb said with kindly patience. "You're in a lot of trouble right now. I want to help you, but you need to give me something to work with. First, I want you to tell me about Iggy. He's dead, he can't get hurt anymore, so what's the harm? What's Iggy's full name?"

"Iggy Dutton," Cowan said. "I think it's short for, like, Ignatius or something."

The police might already know this. Halverson's people had been running the dead guy's prints, and he was almost certain to have a record. But the main purpose of Webb's question was to grease the wheels of the conversation. Once a perp started admitting things, it was a lot easier to keep him confessing. It was a momentum thing.

"And you said he was your friend?" Webb asked.

"Yeah," Cowan said. "When we'd score some stuff, we'd get happy together."

"But you weren't there to score dope, you told me that."

Cowan shook his head slowly. "Hey," he said. "You think they'd give me more of that good shit? I been pushing this button but it don't do nothing."

"Maybe in a little while," Webb said. "They don't want to give you too much. So what were you looking for?"

"Just some papers, bro. Nothing important."

"What papers?"

"I dunno."

"Ozzie," Webb said, shaking his head in paternal disapproval. "You're smarter than that."

Erin doubted this, but kept her mouth shut.

"How would you know you had the right ones?" Webb asked. "There's all sorts of papers."

"Iggy knew all about that," Cowan said. "He was gonna ask the chick."

"The chick?" Webb asked.

"Yeah, the lady with the shotgun. But we didn't know about the gun, no shit. The guy said she was just, like, some hot chick. A real MILF, know what I mean?"

Cowan leered. Webb blinked, but his expression didn't change. Either he didn't know the term, which was possible, or he hadn't made the connection to what the junkies had been intending to do to Camilla, which was less likely. Maybe he just had really good self-control.

Erin, who had somewhat less self-control than her Lieutenant, and was female into the bargain, felt her hands curl into fists. The acronym stood for Mother I'd Like to Fuck, and in this context, it was only too clear what these bastards had meant to do. They'd had more than robbery on their minds. Erin was feeling less sorry for the late Iggy Dutton by the second, and was starting to wish she'd shot Ozzie more than once.

"What were you getting for this?" Webb asked with glacial calm. "Besides the hot chick, that is."

"Five hundred," Cowan said proudly. "Each. And we wouldn't take the fall for the charges."

"Of course not," Webb said. "You weren't planning on getting caught."

"Not those charges," Cowan said, laughing like Webb had told an excellent joke. "The other charges!"

Erin and Webb shot one another a baffled glance. The unspoken question jumped between them, *what the hell is this guy talking about?*

"Did you get busted for something else?" Erin demanded.

Cowan laughed harder. "You're the cops," he said. "Don't you know this shit already?"

"How could this guy make the charges go away?" Webb asked.

"Because he's the dude who stuck us with them in the first place," Cowan snorted. He looked down at the button attached to his morphine drip. "I think this thing's broken. I been clicking it and clicking it and nothing's happening."

"It's limited," Webb said absently. "So you don't kill yourself with an overdose. Does this guy have a name?"

"Course he does," Cowan said. "Be pretty stupid if he didn't. Everybody's got a name."

"What is it?" Webb asked.

"Dunno. Can I have some more shit now?"

"In a minute," Webb said. "Was this guy a cop?"

"Yeah," Cowan said. His smile broadened as a thought slowly caught up with him. "Hey, does that make this whole thing, like, legal?"

"No, it does not," Webb said. "What did he look like?"

"Iggy talked to him, not me," Cowan said. "This whole thing was Iggy's idea."

"Of course it was," Webb said dryly. Trying to pass the blame on to a dead accomplice was one of the oldest tricks in the book.

"Bullshit," Erin said. "I think you're lying, Ozzie. If you got busted by this guy, you must've seen his face. So describe him."

"I'm telling the truth," Cowan said. "Hey, you're kind of a babe, you know that?"

"I'm the babe who shot you," she said grimly. "And I'd be happy to do it again. You don't want to yank me around. What'd he look like?"

"When we got busted, there wasn't just the one guy, okay?" Cowan said. "It was, like, a whole team of guys. Four... no, five of them. And one was this great big dude."

"And you didn't get any of their names?" Webb asked.

"Bro, I was so high that night, I didn't hardly know where I was," Cowan said, grinning at the memory. "I didn't even mind getting busted so much."

"Names will be on the arrest report," Erin said quietly to Webb, who nodded.

"The papers," Webb said. "What was Iggy expecting the lady to tell him?"

"He was gonna ask her about her husband's stuff," Cowan said. "Like, secret-agent shit. I didn't really get it. Iggy knew all that stuff. Why don't you ask him?"

We can't ask him because his brain's all over the Stachowskis' kitchen floor, dumbass, Erin thought. "Iggy's dead, remember?" was what she said.

"Oh, yeah. Right." Cowan appeared to have genuinely forgotten this. "Bummer. Hey, can I get some more happy juice?"

"I'll ask the nurse," Webb said. "I think we're done here."

Chapter 14

"This is serious," Halverson said.

"No shit," Erin said over her shoulder. "Sir." She was on her way to her car and the onboard computer attached to its dashboard.

"What Detective O'Reilly means is that the situation was already serious, given that it involves the death or wounding of two detectives and an assault on a policeman's family," Holliday said diplomatically, demonstrating why he'd been made a captain and Erin probably wouldn't be.

"I know," Halverson said, hurrying to keep up with the NYPD cops. "But this is an allegation against a serving officer."

"Don't get too excited, Captain," Webb said. "So far it's just the word of a junkie; a stoned junkie, come to that. It won't stand up in court, even if it's true."

"I'm not talking about court," Halverson said. "I'm talking about systemic corruption."

"Then you can be grateful it's not your system, Captain," Holliday said. "We're talking about the NYPD. I'm fully apprised of the potential implications. This isn't the first time we've had officers disgrace the shield. We're aware of the situation now and we're going to handle it."

"Of course," Halverson said. "It would help if we had the name of the alleged officer."

"Which is why I'm going to look up Cowan's arrest records right now," Erin said. She hesitated only a moment as the hospital's doors slid open, letting in a blast of arctic air. Then she lowered her head and pushed out into the storm. Rolf flattened his ears, but he went with her without complaint.

Webb was the only human who followed. The two Captains stayed in the lobby. That made sense. As the acronym went, RHIP: Rank Hath Its Privileges. Besides, there wasn't room for all of them in her car. Erin let Rolf into the back and slid into the driver's seat, while Webb squeezed himself into the passenger side next to the computer.

"I suppose you don't want me to smoke in here," he said without much hope.

"Please don't, sir," Erin said. "I practically live in this car sometimes, and I don't want Rolf getting cancer."

"You really should take up smoking," Webb said. "It's remarkably calming to the nerves."

"So is alcohol," Erin said as she brought up the departmental database and started typing. "I've only got room in my life for one terrible habit and I like booze too much to quit. Speaking of terrible habits, you got great results from that interrogation. I think we ought to consider doping up the perps back at the Eightball before we talk to them."

"You know we can't do that," Webb said. "Unfortunately."

"Oswald Cowan," she read off her computer screen. "Twenty-four years old, resident of Manhattan. Numerous drug collars, nothing too heavy. But we've got an assault beef and one count of attempted rape."

"This is strictly off the record," Webb said, "and I'll deny saying it, but it's too bad you didn't hit him about six inches over and three down from where you did."

"If I had, the world would be a better place, but we wouldn't have this lead," she said. "Okay, here we are. His most recent arrest was last week. He got grabbed with felony weight of fentanyl. He said he wasn't planning to deal it, but the DA didn't buy it."

"Then what's he doing on the street?" Webb asked.

Erin shrugged. "He made bail. Who knows where the bond came from? It's through a bail bondsman. I guess we could ask him, but I don't know that we have to. The arresting officers were detectives Ames, Bowes, Sanchez, Carter, and Katzenberg."

"Our dead narcotics detective is named Ames," Webb observed.

"The same," Erin said. "Delbert Ames. And I met the rest of those guys at the hospital."

"Really?" Webb asked, raising his eyebrows.

"Yeah. They came to check on Phil, said they were worried about him. They've all worked undercover for him."

"Interesting," Webb said. "One member of the squad killed, the others hanging around our critically-wounded officer. A suspicious man might think that was worth looking into. Is this why you said our perp might be wearing a shield?"

"Yeah," Erin said. "That whole Narcotics squad could be dirty. But we don't know which one approached Dutton."

"And why," Webb said. "What does he want?"

"He wants the O'Malley mole," Erin said.

Webb gave her a slow, considering look. "Ah," he said.

"Let's go back inside and talk about it," she said. She'd had sensitive conversations in her car, and it was probably secure, but she was never a hundred percent sure it was safe.

Back in the hospital, they excused themselves from Captain Halverson's company and found a secluded alcove. Holliday positioned himself where he could watch all approaches and give warning if anyone was coming.

"At least one of Ames's squad is working for someone in the O'Malleys," Erin said.

"Other than Ames himself?" Holliday asked.

"Stachowski was found with Ames's gun next to his hand," Webb said. "According to CSU, that gun was fired twice. I expect ballistics to match those bullets with the ones in Ames, which means Stachowski probably shot him. I'm guessing someone else shot Stachowski, but that wouldn't have to be a cop."

"Another one of the squad has to be in on it," Erin argued. "They wouldn't have risked going after Phil's family until they knew they couldn't get anything out of him. They must've contacted Dutton right after the Central Park shootout and told him to go straight to the Stachowski house. They wouldn't have had time to search Phil's office, too, so they must've done that beforehand."

"That makes sense," Holliday said. "Making a move on Lieutenant Stachowski is a desperation play, and so is attacking his wife. They probably tried ransacking his office first. Do you think it's the whole squad?"

"I have no idea," Erin said. "But if two of them are dirty, I have to assume the rest are compromised, too. What can we do to them?"

"I can contact Internal Affairs," Holliday said. "I'll put Lieutenant Keane in touch with the Ten's IAB team. They can take it from there."

"Not good enough, sir," Erin said. "Who knows how long that'll take? Days? Weeks? These guys are moving *now*. They're coming after us. They're coming after *me*."

"I know that, O'Reilly," Holliday sighed. "But we have protocols for a reason. This isn't the first time you've butted heads with other NYPD officers. I'm worried about your reputation."

"Maybe we should be more worried about her physical safety, sir," Webb put in.

"I appreciate your concern, sir," Erin said to Holliday. "Really. But we've got to shut this shit down fast."

"We don't have jurisdiction over the home invasion," Holliday reminded her. "And if we believe our officers were shot by other officers, that is a textbook IAB situation. They won't like being kept in the dark, particularly after the incident with the Organized Crime Task Force."

"That was SNEU," Erin said. "Not Major Crimes."

"Along with you and Detective Neshenko," Holliday said. "Do you really think they're going to be disposed to split hairs? O'Reilly, do you *want* to work Internal Affairs? Because a transfer could be arranged."

"I'd rather have my molars pulled, sir," she said. "Without anesthetic."

"Then maybe you should stop acting like an IAB cop," Holliday said gently. "Between the Maxwell incident and that other thing with Officer Michaelson, a pattern is emerging."

"Michaelson wasn't my fault," Erin said, recognizing the same sulky tone in her voice that Vic sometimes used. "He was dirty before I even put on my Patrol shoes for the first time. And he was going to shoot himself. What was I supposed to do? He murdered a couple of guys for the Mob. He had to go to jail. And Maxwell was trying to kill Officer Firelli and his wife. Besides, Firelli's the one who took Maxwell down, if you recall."

"Nobody's faulting your results," Holliday said. "But if you bring one or more of these guys in, it's going to become an IAB matter regardless."

"Phil's my friend," she said stubbornly. "I want to get the guys who shot him."

"All right," Holliday said. "I'll have to inform IAB, of course, but the storm has stretched everyone's resources thin. I see no reason we can't hold off on reporting to them until the weather clears."

He said it with a straight face. His mustache didn't even twitch. Erin gave him a grateful smile.

"Thank you, sir," she said.

"What's your next move?" Holliday asked.

"We dig into their financials," Webb said. "I'll have Piekarski start looking into it. And I'll get a warrant to check their phone records."

"They'll have burners," Erin predicted.

"It's still worth a look," Webb said. He checked his watch. "I didn't realize it was so late. I doubt even Judge Ferris will still be awake."

"There's a night judge," Holliday said. "For just such situations."

"I'd rather work through Ferris," Webb said. "He's discreet and reliable."

Holliday smiled knowingly. "And your squad saved his life a short while ago."

"That, too," Webb said. "As it stands, we don't have enough to pin anything on any of them, but if our records search turns up anything, that may change."

"If you start questioning them, it'll tip them off that you're on to them," Holliday warned. "Does anyone know where they are right now?"

"If the bad guys couldn't get to Phil at the hospital, they could be anywhere," Erin said.

"We can always hope Stachowski wakes up," Holliday said. "If he does, and if he remembers anything, he'll be able to identify his attackers."

"Respectfully, sir, hope isn't a plan," Erin said.

"No, it's not," Holliday sighed. "Well, I have to get back to Manhattan. I shouldn't have left the station, not in the middle of this weather, but it was an unusual situation. The chopper should be waiting at the Hoboken PD. Want to hitch a flight back to the island?"

"Sounds like fun, sir," Erin said. "But I've got my car."

Webb shook his head. "The car's staying in Jersey until this whole thing blows over," he said.

"And so are my guns," Erin said gloomily. "They'll keep my Glock until the shooting's officially cleared, and they forgot to give me back my .38."

"Fortunately, we're going to a police station," Holliday said dryly. "I suspect you'll be able to acquire another firearm."

"I'd be more worried about the snow," Webb said. "The flight out was hairy. The one back might be worse. Do you get airsick?"

"No," Erin said.

"First time for everything," Webb said with a sour smile.

*   *   *

Erin had been up in helicopters, but not often, and never in conditions like these. The pilot had said some things about ice on the rotors, which made her nervous, but he'd knocked some chunks loose and seemed unconcerned, so she pretended to feel the same. The snow presented no real problems, but the gusts of wind were terrifying. The chopper lurched to and fro, sometimes dropping sickeningly.

Holliday didn't seem worried. Erin found herself wondering whether men grew mustaches in order to hide their emotions behind a mask of facial hair. It was unfair that women didn't have that option. She'd have to ask her dad about it, if she survived the flight.

Webb clutched the handhold next to the helicopter's door, looking like he was about to throw up. He kept muttering to himself, like a mantra, "Five years to retirement. Five years to retirement."

The only passenger who was enjoying himself was Rolf. The K-9 hadn't been in a chopper since his early training days. He ought to have been nervous, but he was excited. He liked the exhilarating speed of the vehicle. He sat next to Erin, tongue hanging out, a big grin on his furry face. He only wished they would open a window so he could stick his head out. There must be all kinds of amazing smells swirling past them.

"This isn't so bad," the pilot called over the intercom. "I was up during Hurricane Sandy, helping the Coast Guard. Now *that* was some wind. And it was raining so hard it was like flying through a car wash. We're talking instruments only. You try doing a blind landing with sustained hundred-plus windspeed, that'll strip years off your life."

"Hey, buddy?" Webb called.

"Yeah?" the pilot replied.

"Stop cheering us up."

"Ladies and gentlemen," the pilot said cheerfully. "The captain has turned on the 'fasten seat belt' light. Please remain in your seats, as we are experiencing some mild turbulence. In the quite likely event of a water landing, your fellow passengers may be used as personal flotation devices."

"O'Reilly, would you please shoot him?" Webb said.

"Then who'd fly the chopper, sir?" Erin replied, trying not to think about crash landings.

"Damn," Webb said.

"Besides, I don't have my guns," she reminded him.

"That reminds me of something I heard from a guy who was flying Apache gunships during Desert Storm," the pilot said. "This is good. Listen..."

Erin tuned him out. She wished she had some rosary beads. It'd give her something to do, and if they did crash and die, it might score her some points in the afterlife.

As if in answer, the helicopter lurched into a sidelong descent.

"We'll be landing in five," the pilot said, more serious now. "Everybody got your belts buckled?"

"Hell yes," Webb muttered. "I just wish I had more belts. I'd turn myself into a nylon-strap mummy if I could."

"It's only a short flight," Holliday said. His voice was as cool as the December morning. Erin envied him.

The chopper's nose suddenly angled sharply up. The forward motion stopped so fast, the momentum rammed Erin against her harness. Rolf scrabbled with his paws, but she'd fastened a restraint across his chest and he stayed in his seat. Then the helicopter dropped straight out of the sky.

Erin was conscious of a sensation of free-falling, like being in the world's fastest elevator. Her stomach remained somewhere behind and above them. Bile tried to climb out her throat along with her heart. She swallowed it down with a desperate gulp, tried to remember the words of the Hail Mary, and got stuck on "full of grace."

The chopper came to an abrupt halt, hovering. Then it went down another foot or two and the skids thumped to the pavement.

"Ladies and gentlemen, we've landed in Manhattan," the pilot said. "Local time is 3:43AM, temperature is minus five degrees. Thank you for not smoking, and please recommend us to your friends."

"Or enemies," Webb said darkly. "If it wouldn't violate the Eighth Amendment, I'd recommend this for prisoner transport."

Erin stuck her head forward into the cockpit. "Thanks," she said to the pilot. "I know that wasn't as easy as you made it look."

"Forget about it," the pilot said. "I only thought we might die for a couple seconds there. You have a good night, Detective. But if you want to go somewhere else, you're gonna need another pilot. I'm packing it in until the sun comes out and this wind dies down."

The Eightball's helipad was on the roof of the station. It was one of the shorter buildings in the area, which should have meant the skyscrapers shielded it from the full force of the wind, but it wasn't working that way. The tall buildings channeled the air, creating a wind tunnel that ripped at Erin's face and clothes. Little splinters of ice buried themselves in her cheeks as she got out of the chopper and stumbled toward the stairwell entrance. She, Webb, Holliday, and Rolf forced their way into the teeth of the wind. Finally, Erin grabbed the doorknob, got it open somehow, and staggered inside.

Holliday came last, dragging the door shut. The howl of the wind dropped to a muffled, bearable groan. The Captain took off his hat and knocked snow off the brim. His mustache had collected so much snow during the short trip across the roof that it looked like his upper lip was dangling a matching pair of icicles on either side of his mouth.

"Did you enjoy your little trip to New Jersey, O'Reilly?" Webb asked.

Erin shook her head. "Nobody goes to Jersey for fun, sir," she said. Her face felt like it had been sandblasted. Little drops of water dripped from her hair and ran down the back of her collar.

Rolf braced his paws and tensed.

"Oh, no," was all Erin had time to say before the dog started shaking himself. Snow and slush flew in every direction, spattering all three cops.

There was a momentary pause. Then Holliday began to chuckle. The other two joined in. It felt slightly hysterical, but also good.

Chapter 15

"You want me to do *what?*"

Zofia Piekarski couldn't believe it. She was tired, grumpy, and very much wanted to be somewhere else.

Erin was only half listening. She was checking the Glock 18 she'd gotten from the armory. It ought to be identical to her usual sidearm, but only an idiot trusted a weapon they hadn't personally examined. She slid the magazine out of the gun, reloaded it, and racked the slide to chamber a round. It worked smoothly and perfectly.

"You heard me," Webb said. "Start checking these officers' financials for irregularities."

"These are Narcotics detectives!" Piekarski exclaimed.

"And?" Webb said.

"I'm a Narc!"

"You *were* a Narc," Webb corrected her. "Now you're detailed to Major Crimes. And if you're suggesting that you wouldn't have reported criminal behavior by a fellow SNEU officer back when you were working with them..."

"That's not what I meant," Piekarski said. "But there's a big difference between reporting something sketchy when you see it, and prying into other cops' business looking for trouble."

"If they're innocent, they've got nothing to hide," Webb said blandly.

"I'm not a civilian, sir!" she spat. "Don't talk to me like one. Everybody's got things to hide and you know it. Nobody's squeaky clean, and I'm not going to get a basically good cop in trouble."

"We're talking about corruption and murder, Piekarski," Webb said. "This is the Job."

"I didn't sign up to be an IAB rat," Piekarski said stubbornly. "Vic would agree with me."

"Neshenko's still at the hospital," Webb said. "I'm not going to bother him. He's busy helping out and standing guard over our barely-living victim. Our victim who is also, need I remind you, a cop, and at least as worthy of your protection as the scumbags who shot him. Furthermore, *Detective Third Grade* Neshenko is three rungs down the ladder of command from me, so I don't have to get him to agree with me. Nor do I have to explain my orders to you, *Officer* Piekarski."

"Drop it, Zofia," Erin advised. "The Lieutenant gets really grouchy when he's short on sleep."

"He's got no excuse," Piekarski said. "At least he's not pregnant. Well, not exactly."

"Was that a crack about my weight, Officer?" Webb demanded.

"Just the hormones talking, sir," Piekarski said.

"Anything else they'd like to add?"

"No, sir. Just getting started looking over these financial records."

"Glad to hear it." Webb shuffled into the break room and emerged a minute later with his latest cup of coffee.

"Heard you were in another gunfight," Piekarski said to Erin. "And you didn't bring me along."

"It wasn't much of a gunfight," Erin said. "The bad guy couldn't shoot for shit and he was mostly just trying to get away. The other one was dead by the time I got into the room."

"Really? I didn't hear that part." Piekarski perked up a little at the prospect of action, even second-hand and after the fact.

"Yeah. Camilla Stachowski wasted him with both barrels of a twelve-gauge hunting gun."

"Damn." Piekarski was impressed. "You know, for all the times I've drawn my gun, I've never killed anyone. That lady's never even put on a shield and she bags a perp in her own home?"

"You're lucky," Erin said. "She wasn't. She thinks she's fine, but she's not. When you put someone down, even a bad guy, it stays with you."

"How many?"

"How many what?"

"Bad guys. How many have you dropped?"

Erin shook her head. "It's not a scoreboard."

"I know that!" Piekarski retorted. "I'd just like to know where you're coming from."

"I got one Russian Mob guy last year," Erin said. "Maybe two, but I'm only sure of the one. Then there was that German terrorist, and Siobhan Finneran. Plus Mickey Connor, of course. That makes four."

"Do you feel bad about any of them?"

"Yes and no," Erin said quietly. "I didn't feel like I had a choice at the time. If I had, I wouldn't have done it. But I still have bad dreams about them sometimes, even though they were lousy human beings. Killing's a weight you carry around with you, and you can't put it down. It's easier to do than to live with."

"How come it doesn't bother the bad guys?" Piekarski wondered. "They can't all be psychopaths."

"It does bother them," Webb interjected. "You wouldn't believe how many perps turn themselves in, full of remorse, before we get the chance to run them down."

"And a lot of the rest use a shit-load of drugs and booze to numb themselves," Erin added.

"Good thing we don't do that," Webb said, deadpan. "I want you looking at arrest records, O'Reilly. If our guy offered to get a perp off the hook in exchange for doing a job, this probably isn't the first time he's done it. Look for sure-thing charges getting inexplicably dropped. And try to stay awake while you're looking."

"I'm definitely going to need more coffee," Erin said, heading to the break room.

*   *   *

Erin guessed her BCL, Blood Caffeine Level, would be around .28, if that was a thing cops measured. With booze, that sort of concentration was more than enough to get you hauled off to jail if a cop pulled you over—assuming you were conscious enough to get arrested. She ought to have been wide awake, bouncing off the walls.

But on the other side of the equation was a long, sleepless night, during which she'd had more than one serious adrenaline spike. When the body's fight-or-flight juice drained away, it left utter exhaustion in its wake. And that was without taking into account her current activity, scanning old arrest reports. At the best of times, that was a sure cure for insomnia.

Erin worked her way methodically through the Narcotics squad's case history, starting with the most recent ones. She noted they'd been operating in the Hell's Kitchen area, which was O'Malley territory. The squad had worked together for better than three years and had received numerous commendations. Carter had killed a dealer in a gunfight. Katz had been wounded twice in the line of duty, and had been singled out for shielding a wounded civilian with his own body during a shootout between rival pushers.

There were guys they'd busted who'd been released later, charges dropped. That was part of the Job. Not every perp was brought to justice. Sometimes bad guys walked. But maybe there was a pattern somewhere. Erin tried to concentrate, to drill down to the cold, hard facts. Her eyes were a little blurry, and her head was heavy, but she felt pretty good, considering. She just wished she didn't have to keep re-reading the same sentences in the reports. The words weren't sticking together like they should. Maybe she ought to get another cup of coffee, or stand up and stretch her legs.

Somebody was shaking her shoulder. Erin jerked awake. She hadn't even felt herself falling asleep. Piekarski's hand jostled her back to reality.

"Huh?" Erin said. She was aware she'd had her head on her desk, next to her keyboard. A little saliva had trickled out of the corner of her mouth. She wiped it away with the back of her hand as she sat up, thinking she was becoming more like her K-9 every day.

"We've got visitors," Piekarski said.

Erin rubbed her eyes and tried to figure out what time it was and what the hell was going on. The hands on the clock over the stairwell indicated it was six thirty-five. Was that AM or PM? She had no idea.

Under the clock, Lieutenant Webb was standing talking to a trio of snow-covered men. One of them was very big and broad-shouldered, built like Vic. One of the others had a round, soft-looking baby face. The third had Hispanic features.

"That's... what's-their-names," Erin said groggily, not making the connection with what she'd been doing. "The Narcotics guys. The big one's Katz, right?"

"The other two are Carter and Mingo," Piekarski confirmed. She lowered her voice. "The ones we've been looking at."

"Right." Erin shook her head to clear it, and only succeeded in giving herself a throbbing headache. She quickly closed her database. "What're they doing here?"

"They just arrived," Piekarski said. "I don't know what they want."

Erin stood up. "Let's find out," she said.

Rolf had also been asleep, but the rumble of Erin's chair wheels on the floor roused him. He scrambled to his paws, stretched, yawned hugely, and trotted after her.

Webb turned toward the two women and the dog. "I think you already know these gentlemen," he said. "They've come to offer their assistance."

"We want to do anything we can," Katz said. "Del and Phil are our buddies. I want to get the bastards who did this."

I'll just bet you do, Erin thought grimly. All three men were prime suspects in her book, and what better way to find out if they were in trouble than to stick close to the investigation? She hoped none of this was showing on her face.

"I hear you," Piekarski said, speaking with no hint of irony. "I just came over from SNEU. One of my old team caught a bullet in a bust that went sideways. I would've kicked down Hell's front door if it meant taking out the SOBs who shot him."

"Hundred percent," Mingo said. He was a slender, olive-skinned guy who looked to be about Erin's own age. His eyes were very dark, reminding her of Snake Pritchard, and he had a neatly trimmed goatee and mustache.

"What can we do?" Carter asked.

"That depends," Webb said. "I assume your CO's signed off on this?"

"That'd be Lieutenant Bowes," Carter said. "He's sorry he's not here himself. He's gone to talk to Del's wife. Widow, I guess she is now. And he's got all the housekeeping and paperwork stuff to do, but he says we're free to do whatever you need."

"Had a hell of a time getting here," Katz said. "The streets are practically blocked. If this keeps up, we're gonna need the National friggin' Guard."

"Which one of you is senior?" Webb asked.

"I'm a Second Grade," Mingo said. "I guess that puts me in charge of these newbies."

"I got ten years on the Job," Katz said indignantly. "And you only got nine. Plus, I can kick your ass on the range or in the ring. So don't be calling me a newbie just 'cause you got rank on me. You just knew the right guy to jerk off. I was never no good at that game."

"What's the scoop?" Mingo asked Webb, ignoring Katz. "Do we have any suspects?"

"What we've got is a mess," Webb said. "Have any of you ever been to Stachowski's house?"

Mingo blinked. "What's that got to do with anything?" he asked. "Phil got shot in the park, not at home."

"I don't think any of us have ever been there," Carter said. "We'd have no reason to go. Stachowski's never been to my place, either. He liked to keep work and home separated."

"Hey," Katz said. "Don't go talking past tense. He ain't dead yet. I'm still betting he pulls through."

"If you say so," Carter said, shaking his head.

"Why're you asking about Phil's house?" Mingo pressed.

"Because a couple of lowlifes broke in a few hours ago," Webb said.

"Oh, shit," Katz said, his eyes going wide. "What about Cam? Is she okay?"

"I thought you'd heard," Webb said, but Erin knew better. He'd been angling for a reaction, and she'd been watching them. All she'd seen was mild interest from Carter and confusion and concern from the other two. If they were acting, they were good at it.

"Mrs. Stachowski wasn't hurt," Erin said. "It turns out, she's more than capable of looking after herself. She got her husband's shotgun and took care of business. Both bad guys got shot."

"Good for her," Mingo said. "Who were they?"

Webb shrugged. "Just street trash looking for an easy score," he lied. "It looks like a coincidence."

"That's some shit luck," Katz said. "Poor lady. Her husband's in the hospital and then this happens? I think we oughta go check on her."

"Nobody's getting to Jersey right now," Webb said. "Everything's closed down until the storm's over. I'm surprised you guys made it all the way here from Bellevue."

"It wasn't easy," Mingo said. "So you don't think the guys who broke into Stachowski's house are the same ones who shot him and Ames? That's one hell of a coincidence all right."

"It's too early to tell," Webb said. "But if I had to guess, I'd say the Central Park shooting had all the hallmarks of an organized crime hit. It could be retaliation for one of Stachowski's old operations."

"Mob guys aren't going to hit a cop," Carter said. "Too much blowback."

"Are you an authority on this, Detective?" Webb asked.

"Well, not exactly," Carter said. "I'm just saying—"

"Then maybe we shouldn't rule anything out just yet," Webb said. "If you want to be helpful, we've got a workstation available. Detective Neshenko is otherwise occupied right now, so you can use his computer. Look into major operations Stachowski's overseen in the past. I want a list of underworld figures who might have a beef with him."

"Paperwork?" Katz said, sounding both outraged and disgusted. "We came all this way for paperwork?"

"If solving this was as simple as kicking down doors and cuffing perps, we'd already be doing it," Webb said dryly. "This is detective work, gentlemen. If you don't like it, remember you volunteered."

"Can I talk to you for a second, sir?" Erin said as the Narcotics cops headed to Vic's desk.

"Sure," Webb said. "I was just on my way downstairs to see if the machines have anything that might pass for breakfast. Walk with me."

At least that told Erin what time it was.

On the stairs, out of earshot of Major Crimes, Erin started talking. "What gives?" she demanded, keeping her voice down. "We're investigating these jerks, and you just gave them the keys to the office!"

"Relax, O'Reilly," Webb said. "Neshenko's computer doesn't have anything on it. Besides, his personal files are under his login. They won't be able to access them without his passwords."

"That's not the point! One of those assholes shot Phil! Maybe all of them!"

"We don't know that," Webb said sharply. "Those assholes, as you call them, are members of the NYPD, the same as you and me."

"Okay, assholes with shields," she said. "They're not the first."

Webb smiled faintly and stopped in front of the vending machines. His smile faded as he considered the offerings. "This gives us a perfect opportunity to study them up close," he said. "There's an excellent chance someone will let something slip."

"They've also shown they're ready and willing to kill other cops," she reminded him. "This is dangerous."

"Haven't you ever heard the saying, 'Keep your friends close and your enemies closer?'" Webb replied, feeding a dollar bill into the machine and pushing a number. A Hostess apple pie slid out of its position and fell into the dispensing trough.

"Of course I have," she said. "It's from *The Godfather*."

"It's *The Godfather Part Two*, actually," Webb said.

"Same thing! That's like getting advice from a fortune cookie!"

"It's also attributed to Sun Tzu," Webb said. "So you're more right than you realize, if unintentionally racist."

Erin spluttered indignantly.

"I'd think you would understand the value of being close to potential enemies," Webb added quietly.

He turned the pie over and examined the wrapper. "This expiration date isn't until next year," he remarked. "That's a little unsettling."

"You're right, sir," Erin said.

"About the pie?"

"No. Well, yes. But about the other thing, too."

"I'm glad you agree," he said. "I'm counting on you to keep an eye on them. As you said, at least one of these guys is probably the man we're looking for. Shall we go back and see what they're up to?"

Chapter 16

Back upstairs, Erin tried to organize her thoughts. Webb put his apple pie in the microwave in an attempt to improve the flavor, but succeeded only in burning his mouth. Carter sat at Vic's computer, sifting data. Mingo talked with Piekarski, discussing narcotics operations. Katzenberg wore grooves in the floor with his constant pacing in front of the windows. Rolf snoozed.

When Erin went to the break room for yet another cup of coffee, Katz followed her in. The big man filled the doorway behind her, glowering down at her. She wasn't nervous, not even when he shouldered the door shut. This was her house. She'd taken a perp down in this very room.

"Got a problem?" she asked.

"Depends," he said.

Erin flexed her legs, balancing on the balls of her feet. She was holding a cup of scalding coffee. If he went for her, she decided, it was going in his face. Then her knee was going in his crotch.

"On what?" she asked.

"On you."

"Katz, I'm tired," she said. "It's been a long, lousy night. I don't want to play games. Speak plainly, or shut up."

"I've heard of you," Katz said. "You're supposed to be a serious lady, a real tough cop. I mean, you blew Mickey Connor away, right? And that terrorist last year."

"I'm still waiting for you to get to the point," she said.

"So how serious are you? About getting the assholes who nailed Phil and Del?"

"Deadly," she said levelly, meeting his eyes.

"Okay, so who're our suspects?"

"We're still collecting information."

"Wrong answer." Katz shook his head emphatically. "Don't bullshit me, O'Reilly. And don't shut me and my guys out of the loop. Piekarski out there, she lost a teammate, so she knows what's up. But what about you? I know Phil don't mean nothing to you, but he means a lot to me, okay? He saved my life once."

"He did?" Erin was surprised and too tired to hide it. "How? When?"

"When I was undercover," he said. "Three years back, working this crew of meth cookers in the Kitchen. They was posing as a work crew, upgrading wiring. They'd set up their labs in maintenance rooms in these old buildings that were being renovated. They'd move the shit every couple months, so it was real hard to pin them down. It took two months, but I got inside. But they got suspicious. One night they take me to this vacant lot and they shove a revolver in my face. But I remember Phil, and the stuff he taught me, and I don't lose my cool. I play it out and stall them, giving them all this bullshit about how I'm a stand-up guy and I can't believe they'd think I'm NYPD."

"Good for you," Erin said. "But—"

"Phil's down the block," Katz interrupted. "In a van with all the surveillance gear, headphones and shit. The meth-heads are getting impatient, and they've decided I'm a cop. One of them wants to blow my head off. Phil hears me use one of our code-words we set up, the one that says I'm in danger. Thing is, our security ain't available. Some internal screw-up. No uniforms in sight. It's just Phil in the van, unarmed. You know how he don't like to carry. So he jumps out and runs toward me. Next thing I know, he's standing outside the lot, yelling. He's asking the dealers for help, you believe that?"

"I don't get it," Erin said.

Katz shook his head in admiration. "Phil don't look like a cop," he said. "You've seen him. He looks totally harmless. Bald, glasses, kinda fat. He goes off about how his wallet's been stolen, he's been mugged, and can we help him. The meth-heads don't know what to make of it, but they're looking at him, not at me. I see my opening and I go for it. I grab the gun off the guy."

Erin nodded. "And you got the bust?"

"Hell no," Katz said. "I let that sucker rip and put two rounds within a foot of Phil."

"Jesus," Erin said. "Are you kidding?"

"Nope. Phil runs like hell. Then I give the gun back to the dealer. After that, they *know* I'm not a cop, they'd swear it in front of their own mommas. We keep going with the op and I get their distributors, their supply guys, everything. Two weeks later, we make a dozen arrests and take the whole gang down."

"You shot at Phil?" Erin said in disbelief.

"No way," Katz said. "I shot next to Phil. Maybe you haven't seen my range results, but I'm a damn good shot. Phil knew I wasn't gonna hit him, but those other guys thought I was trying to blast him. Phil rescued me, and he did it without blowing my cover. I owe him. And Ames might've been an asshole, but he was on my squad and those bastards killed him. So tell me who pulled this shit."

Erin studied his face. He seemed earnest, but good liars always did. She decided to tell a little bit of the truth and see how it played.

"As far as we can tell from the evidence, Stachowski's the one who shot Ames," she said quietly.

Katz blinked. "No," he said. "Phil, he don't even carry most of the time. I told you that."

"It was Ames's own gun," she said.

"Why'd he do it?"

"Why do you think?" Erin challenged.

Katz's heavy brow wrinkled. "Phil wouldn't shoot nobody without a good reason," he said. "Del must've pulled something."

"Like what?" she asked, watching him closely.

"I was supposed to meet Phil later," Katz said. "We had a meeting at ten, only it didn't happen, because he got shot. But I knew it was something important. He told me we was gonna sort some shit out, something about an undercover who needed our help."

"He told you that?" Erin asked.

"Yeah, we all knew," Katz said. "I mean, he didn't exactly spell it out, but we could guess it easy enough. So I figure he was meeting Del, but something went wrong. I guess Del was playing both sides."

"Did you ever see anything that told you he might be dirty?" Erin asked.

Katz shifted uncomfortably. "Nothing I'd take to IAB," he muttered.

"But you did see something?"

"You know how it is," he said. "You gotta count on these guys to watch your back, so you don't snitch."

"Yeah, I know all about the blue wall," Erin said grimly. "But that wall of silence might've gotten Phil shot. If Ames knew Phil was working somebody on the inside with organized crime, that guy's name would be worth money to the right people."

"We wouldn't none of us sell out one of our own," Katz protested.

"Are you sure of that?" Erin asked. "You know these guys better than I do."

Katz lost the battle to maintain eye contact. His gaze slid to the floor. "I used to be sure," he said. "It wasn't never nothing like that. It was just money, drug money. It'd just go into Evidence anyway. A little on the side wasn't hurting nobody."

"That's how it starts," Erin said. "Did you take money, Katz?"

"Yeah," Katz said so quietly she hardly heard him. "Once."

"How much?"

"Couple thousand, when we busted a stash house. We all took a cut. Never felt right about it."

"What'd you do with the money?"

"Banked it. It was gonna be for my kid, for college. But I can't do that, you know? Because then it'd be on him. I'd always know, even if he didn't. So it's just sitting there, in a savings account. I had to take it. If I hadn't, the others would've thought I wasn't a team player. Then maybe they don't watch my back so good. But Jesus, that shit eats at you. If it wasn't wrong, how come I feel like this about it?"

"I think you know the answer to that," she said.

"Yeah," he said heavily. "I guess maybe I do. Oh Christ, O'Reilly, is that what this is about? That goddamn drug money? Is that why Phil and Del got shot?"

"I don't think so," Erin said. "But that's how it started. Somebody on your team got a taste and wanted more."

He swallowed. Then he looked up again, and to Erin's surprise she saw tears in his eyes. "Okay," he said. "I guess I know how this goes now. Where's your IAB guy?"

"His office is upstairs," she said. "But I don't think he's in yet. The sun's not even up. Why do you want him?"

"I gotta turn in my shield and my piece," he said. "Hell, I deserve it. Damn it, I knew better. Del had his hands dirty, just like me. But why'd it have to be Phil? He didn't never touch dirty money."

Erin's thoughts were racing. She stepped forward and laid a hand on Katz's arm. "You want to make this right?" she said very quietly.

"That's what I'm trying to do," he said.

"Then help me. To do that, you need to keep your gun and your shield. And you need to keep your mouth shut, at least for a little while."

"Why? What do you want?"

"You've been undercover before," she said. "I need you to be my ears. Find out who was working with Ames. It's at least one of the other guys, maybe all of them. Then I need you to tell me. Can you do that?"

"You want me to spy on my own team?" he said. "On other cops?"

"I want you to find out who isn't really a cop," she said.

He swallowed. "That's a big ask."

"It's a big sin you're trying to balance out," she replied.

"Okay," he said unhappily. "How do I get in touch with you?"

She took out one of her cards and handed it to him. "Call me," she said. "Or text."

"Okay," he said again, more firmly. "I never meant it to go this far."

"It's a slippery slope," Erin said. "Little sins lead to big ones. That's what they taught me in Sunday school. But you can do this. For Phil."

"And for Cam," Katz said. "That wasn't no coincidence, was it?"

"What do you think?" she shot back.

"Not a chance," he said. "And if somebody's going after our families, I say fuck that. No way. Not on my watch. They're going down."

"Damn right," she said.

He squared his shoulders and opened the break room door, going back to rejoin his squad. Erin watched him as long as she dared, wondering if she'd made the right call. She thought he was okay, but if he wasn't, she might have tipped her hand. She wondered how Webb would have handled it. Or Carlyle. Or Phil.

Before she could head back to her own desk, Erin's path was blocked again, by Lieutenant Webb this time.

"What is it, sir?" she asked wearily.

He pointed wordlessly to the couch.

"What?" she asked.

"I can't order you to sleep," he said. "And I can't make you do it. But I'm ordering you to lie down and close your eyes, and to stay that way for at least ten minutes."

"That's not much of a nap," she said.

His mouth creased in something approximating a smile. "If you're still awake in five, I'll be very surprised."

"I can't sleep now," she said. "We've got things to do."

"You're not the only cop in this office," he said. "We'll carry the ball until you're back with us."

"Katzenberg seems all right," she said. "I don't think he's in on whatever this is. He'll tell us if anything seems weird."

"You trust him?"

"No. But I'm willing to listen to him."

"Good," Webb said. "We'll sort it out later."

He flicked off the light. Erin considered protesting, but decided her best protest would be to march out ten minutes later, wide awake, proving him wrong.

"Ten minutes," she snorted. She could handle anything for ten minutes. She'd just think about the case, and soon enough she'd have another lead to follow.

Webb's estimate of five minutes was a little off. She was asleep in three.

*   *   *

When Erin woke up, she found someone had draped a spare blanket over her. Something heavy was pressing down on her legs, which were so warm they were almost overheated. She opened her eyes and craned her neck to see a dark, furry ball lying on top of her lower body. A pair of large pointy ears protruded from the ball, which was making soft, squeaky snoring sounds.

She tried to ease her legs out from under her slumbering K-9 and was rewarded with a vicious cramp in her right calf muscle. Stabbing pain shot up her leg with breathtaking intensity. She sucked in the scream that tried to burst out, gritting her teeth and forcing herself to stay still until it subsided to a dull ache.

Rolf, disturbed by her motion, lifted his head and blinked sleepily at her. He unhinged his jaw in an enormous yawn, uncurling his tongue to full extension.

"Thanks, kiddo," she muttered. Her mouth felt thick, her teeth coated with that fuzzy sensation that came from going to sleep without brushing. Her hair was tangled and matted, her eyes bleary, and a low, throbbing pain was keeping time with her pulse behind her eyeballs.

In spite of all that, she did feel a little better. She sat up and swiveled her legs off the couch, stretching them out and massaging some life back into her calves. Rolf got to his paws and stretched in unison with her, yawning again.

Erin took out her phone and checked the time, which was 10:13 in the morning. She'd only been out for a few short hours.

"Okay, partner," she told Rolf. "Let's get back to work."

Webb and Piekarski were in the main office, sitting at their computers. Nobody else was in sight.

"Did Rolf give you a smooch, Sleeping Beauty?" Piekarski asked.

Erin made a face. "He's charming enough," she said. "But he's got really bad breath. Plus, he snores."

"Copy that," Piekarski said, grinning. "I have the same problems with Vic."

"Where is he, anyway?"

"Still at the hospital. I just talked to him a few minutes ago. They need all the help they can get over there."

"I also want one of our people near Stachowski," Webb said. "In case he wakes up."

"Or in case someone tries to get to him," Erin added.

"That, too."

"On that subject, what happened to our volunteers?" Erin asked.

"Carter got a lead," Webb said. "One of Ames's contacts in the drug business. He says Ames might be the key to the whole thing. They left about half an hour ago."

"And you let them?" Erin exclaimed. "Sir, they're our top suspects!"

"I know," he said. "But they don't. I'm going to let them run a little and see where they lead us."

"They might go for Mrs. Stachowski again," she said.

"Only if they can fly," Webb replied. "Manhattan's still on lockdown."

"Jesus," Erin said, walking to the windows. "How much snow is out there?"

"Better than two feet," Piekarski said. "And it's still falling."

"I think Katz may be stand-up," Erin said. "He confessed to grabbing some loose cash at a bust a while ago."

"And you think this makes him a *good* cop?" Webb asked with polite disbelief.

"I think he was telling me the truth," she said. "It's small potatoes, but he tried to hand in his shield. I'm pretty sure he wants to do the right thing."

"Women's intuition?"

She scowled at him. "Detective's."

He nodded. "That's good enough for me. What'd you get out of him?"

"He's going to watch the others and let me know if anything seems off about them," she said.

"We've got a mole of our own," Webb said approvingly. "While the bad guys are hunting for theirs."

"This is some *Spy Versus Spy* shit," Piekarski said. "Who's hunting whom?"

"Everyone's hunting one another," Erin said. "That's what makes it interesting. Did you find anything in their financials?"

"Some unexplained income," Piekarski said.

"The way Katz talked about it, skimming from busts is pretty normal for them," Erin said. "It doesn't mean they're on the bad guys' direct payroll."

"It's a place to start," Webb said. "Damn it, I thought the NYPD got rid of all the crooked Narcs back in the Seventies."

"Logan's team has a rep," Piekarski said. "We're the ones that can't be bought. Everybody knows that about us. You know what that means?"

"It means there are others who can," Erin said.

"It's not enough to take to IAB," Webb said. "We need hard evidence."

"The shooter won't have kept the gun," Erin said.

"Unless it's his duty weapon," Piekarski said. "You can't ditch your sidearm without raising a red flag."

"What sort of idiot would use his duty weapon to shoot another cop?" Webb retorted.

"The sort who wasn't expecting to have to," Erin said. "This shooting wasn't planned. The plan was to get Phil to talk, not to kill him. Phil jammed them up when he grabbed Ames's gun. Things happened pretty fast; maybe our shooter acted on reflex and training."

Webb nodded. "Good thought. Piekarski, call the Ten. It's a long shot, but see if you can retrieve the spent brass from their range."

"*All* of it?" Piekarski was appalled. "That'll be hundreds of casings. Thousands, maybe. There's no way we can run forensics on all of it!"

"It's a hail Mary," he agreed. "Like taping together shredded documents. But that sometimes works. I'd like to have something in our back pocket, just in case."

"There'll be no way to match the brass to a specific officer," Erin said.

"No," Webb said. "But it's possible only one of these guys was on the firing range recently. It'll help build the case, regardless. And I'm getting a little tired of justifying my orders."

"I'll call them, sir," Piekarski said.

Chapter 17

Erin didn't know what to do, and it felt bad. She was trapped by the snow. She had the Narcotics cops' financial records in front of her, but couldn't make heads or tails of them. The only member of their squad who'd ever been any good at piecing together financial data was Kira Jones, and Kira had transferred out. She was Internal Affairs now, and wouldn't have time or interest for a Major Crimes case.

Unless, of course, that case involved crooked cops. Erin slapped her forehead. This was exactly the sort of thing Kira could help with. It was Kira's *job* to help with it.

"Sir?" she called.

"Find something?" Webb replied.

"Not yet. But I'd like to take this to someone."

"Who?"

"Kira Jones."

Webb thought it over. "We don't want to haul IAB into this just yet," he said.

"She'll be discreet," Erin said.

"Lieutenant Keane's bound to find out," Webb warned.

"He'll find out anyway, sooner or later," she said. "I really think Kira can help."

Webb shrugged. "If that's what your gut tells you, go for it," he said. "I'm not seeing any leads here. We could use a fresh pair of eyes."

Erin thought about calling Kira's desk before going in person, but Lieutenant Keane would have records of his subordinates' calls. If he went looking, he'd know. So Erin got Rolf's leash and took him upstairs. It was better to keep things informal and unofficial.

It would have been hard for Erin to explain exactly why she didn't trust Andrew Keane. "Bloodhound" Keane was Internal Affairs, which meant most ordinary cops didn't like him, but there was something coldblooded about the man. He was a little too manipulative, a little too smooth, a little too much of a politician. He reminded her of a police version of Evan O'Malley.

And there was one other thing. Earlier that year, a Mafia thug had died in one of the Eightball's holding cells. The Lucarelli Family had known he was there and they'd reached into Erin's police station and murdered him. Erin figured the only way the Lucarellis could have done it was by having a leak—an Internal Affairs leak. She didn't know it was Keane; but she hadn't ruled him out either.

Kira had been quietly looking into the leak, at Erin's request, without official sanction. Maybe it wasn't an issue anymore. The Lucarellis had been crippled by internal strife, including the murder of Vinnie "The Oil Man" Moreno, the don who'd very briefly run the organization. They were much less of a threat than they had been.

All the same, Erin didn't like going into the Internal Affairs office on the third floor. It was like sticking your hand in a lion's mouth. Maybe the lion was well trained, maybe he wasn't, but if he was hungry did you really want to risk it?

IAB was quiet. The light was on in Keane's office, shining under his door, but only one of the desks in the outer office was occupied. To Erin's relief, Kira Jones had showed up for work in spite of the blizzard.

"Hey," Erin said quietly.

Kira started. Her head whipped around. When she saw Erin, she smiled. She dressed like a desk cop these days, in clothes a businesswoman might wear, but her ears had a few too many earrings for a corporate girl, and she'd recently re-dyed her hair for the Christmas season. It was a dark forest green, blending into crimson toward the tips.

"Hey yourself," Kira said. "I'm surprised you made it in."

"Are you kidding?" Erin said. "I've been out all night, running around like an idiot. This is the safest place I've been in the past twelve hours."

"Not many cops say that about IAB," Kira said, grinning. Then her smile faded. "I guess you're working the Ames/Stachowski shooting."

"That's right," Erin said. "What's IAB's take on it?"

Kira's eyes darted toward Keane's office. "That's up to the Bloodhound," she said. "And he hasn't told me anything. What's up?"

"Want to get out of the office for a few minutes?" Erin said. "Rolf needs a run around the block."

"You think you can get around the block? We've got two feet of snow out there!"

"We won't go far," Erin said. "Come on, the fresh air will do you good."

Kira shook her head, but she understood. Fresh air had nothing to do with Erin's request; what she wanted was to talk far from inquisitive ears.

"Okay," Kira said, standing up and pulling on her jacket, a holdover from her old Gang Task Force days. It was black leather with silver accents, more of a biker's coat than that of a desk-bound officer.

They went downstairs, through an eerily deserted lobby, past a bored-looking Sergeant Malcolm at the front desk.

"You're going out in that?" he asked. "You're crazy."

"Guilty as charged," Erin said with a smile. "On both counts."

"I don't want to have to call Sean and tell him his daughter got frostbite on my watch," Malcolm said. "You're not dressed right for the conditions. Don't you have a warmer coat?"

"I don't like bulky jackets," Erin said. "They make it hard to get to my gun in a hurry."

"If your fingers freeze and snap off, it won't matter if you can reach your piece or not," he said. "You won't be able to pull the trigger. You be careful."

"We won't be long," Erin said, patting Rolf. "Don't worry, we've got a rescue dog right here if we need him."

The snow was still coming down hard, blowing into their faces as they stepped onto the sidewalk. The walk had been cleared, probably more than once, but already had several inches of fresh snow covering the concrete.

"This is crazy," Kira said. "I mean, we get snow here, but not like this. They're saying it's going to be one of the worst storms on record."

"Maybe Hell froze over," Erin said.

"Maybe," Kira agreed. "Listen, Erin. I don't know what you're hoping to hear, but I haven't found anything on that thing we talked about. And I've been looking. I'm sorry."

"I'm not here about that," Erin said, raising a hand. "This is about Phil Stachowski."

"And the other guy? Ames?"

"Ames isn't a victim," Erin said grimly. "I'm pretty sure he's one of the perps."

"Oh my God," Kira said. "You mean...?"

"It looks like Phil shot him," Erin said. "In self-defense. I want you to look at the financials and phone records of the rest of Ames's squad. There's four of them."

"I need a warrant for the phone records," Kira said.

"Webb's got one," Erin said.

"Then why isn't this going through channels?" Kira asked. "Shouldn't he give it to Keane?"

"I'm asking you because I trust you," Erin said. "Right now you're the only one I trust in IAB. And you've got a great head for numbers. We need something on these guys, anything. I know one of them shot Phil."

"You used his first name," Kira said. "Twice."

"So?"

"You know him? Personally?"

Erin shifted uncomfortably. "What's that got to do with anything?"

"Erin, we can't let personal feelings intrude," Kira said. "We've got protocols and procedures for a reason."

"The protocols don't cover my situation," Erin said. "Trust me."

"Everyone thinks they should be an exception," Kira said.

"Can you do this for me?" Erin asked, putting a hand on Kira's arm. "Please? It's important."

Kira sighed. "If Webb can show me a warrant, I'll see what I can do," she said. "And I can keep it quiet, for a day or two. But after that, I've got to file a report with Keane. He's already got his eye on this case, and if he learns one of our victims shot the other, he'll be all over it. That'll make it an IAB case. And if he knows I hid something from him, he'll start watching me. More than he already does, I mean."

"I know," Erin said. "Thanks."

Rolf tugged impatiently on the leash. They were outside, they were supposed to be walking. Why were the humans just standing around talking? They could do that indoors. He managed to get Erin to go a few steps, toward the corner of the building. The K-9 cocked a leg and dyed a patch of snow yellow.

"I'd better let Rolf move around a little," Erin said. "He'll get cabin fever."

"I'll go see your boss," Kira said. "Then I'll get cracking."

"Thanks again," Erin said.

"You're going to get me in real trouble one of these days," Kira said.

"We're Major Crimes," Erin said. "We don't get in trouble; we *are* the trouble."

As the precinct door swung shut behind Kira, Erin's phone buzzed. She fumbled it out, pulling off a glove so she could activate the screen. It was a text from an unknown number. She brought it up close to her face and blew, clearing the snowflakes that were already settling on it.

"Need to talk," the text read. "Get to Bryant Winter Village ASAP."

Erin swore softly. Winter Village was over forty blocks north of the Eightball, which in these conditions was going to be like forty miles. Why did she need to go there? What had Katz found out?

Rolf paused again, looking back at her in loving exasperation. Erin was a wonderful human being, the best one in the whole world as far as he was concerned, but now she was staring at that little black plastic thing instead of giving him the walk they both needed. It was a good thing he was around to remind her what was important.

"Sorry, kiddo," she said, turning back toward the building. "The walk's going to have to wait. We've got police work."

Rolf couldn't believe it. But he was a good boy, so he followed her.

*   *   *

"You're going *where?*" Webb asked. Even over the phone, his disbelief was obvious.

"Winter Village," Erin said. "Bryant Park."

"To do what? A little ice skating?"

"I got a text from Katz. He's got something for me." Erin steered the borrowed Ford Interceptor around the corner. Despite its four-wheel drive, the car slewed sideways. The wheels churned helplessly for a moment, throwing up showers of snow, before they found a little purchase and the car lurched forward again. She was already missing her Charger, but it was in New Jersey. She'd gotten the blue-and-white-painted Interceptor from the Departmental motor pool as the only available vehicle with a K-9 compartment.

"Do you need backup?" Webb asked.

"Maybe. But I don't want to spook the bad guys."

"You know, there's three of them and one of you."

"Katz is on our side. That makes two good guys, plus Rolf."

"You think. You should've brought Piekarski and me with you."

"The car won't fit all of us," Erin pointed out. "Besides, Zofia isn't supposed to be doing fieldwork. She's pregnant, for God's sake!"

"Just me, then," Webb said. "You know, your commanding officer? The one who's supposed to give you orders?"

Erin sighed. "You want me to turn around and come pick you up, sir?"

"I want you to be safe. People are dying on the roads today. See that you're not one of them."

"I'm not going fast enough to get killed," she said. She was crawling along at twelve miles an hour, forcing her way through the deep snow.

"I don't like it," Webb said. "This feels off."

"I don't like it either," Erin replied. "But we need a break in the case. I'll be careful."

"And just how are you planning on doing that?"

She didn't have an answer, so she said nothing.

"Right," Webb said. "I'll contact the local boys and see what they've got available. If you get in trouble, don't be a damn hero. Call the cavalry. There's a lot of boys in blue, O'Reilly, and they're here to help us."

"Copy that, sir."

"And let me know what's going on."

"Will do."

Erin hung up and concentrated on her driving. The whole city had been reduced to white and gray, snow and concrete. Visibility was terrible and road conditions were worse. She saw a couple of other vehicles trying to make their way through the streets, but the stalled cars outnumbered the mobile ones. Manhattan had settled into a siege mentality, its inhabitants waiting out the storm.

"How'd these bastards get to Winter Village in the first place?" she asked Rolf. She didn't understand how they'd even had time to make the trip before texting her. Webb was right; something was weird about this whole business. But the way to find out the answer was to get there.

Rolf didn't know. He watched the falling snow and panted excitedly. He'd missed out on his walk, but he was wearing his K-9 vest, which meant he was working. Work was great. The only things better than work were food, his rubber Kong toy, and Erin. And since he worked with Erin, and often got the Kong toy for doing his job well, that made work the best.

His excitement was gradually dampened by the length of the drive, but not completely smothered. The Shepherd could be patient when the situation required it. He sat back on his haunches but didn't lie down. His tail kept twitching with suppressed excitement.

Erin had never seen Fifth Avenue so deserted. In other circumstances she'd be thinking about winter wonderlands and enjoying the spectacle of Manhattan's buildings draped in snow. But now she was cursing the weather and praying she wouldn't get stuck. The Interceptor was handling the drifts like a champ, but it was an SUV, not a damn tank. Snow was getting packed in the wheel wells. She could see faint tracks in the road where a few other crazed motorists had braved the streets, so she tried to follow them to make the going a little easier.

Bryant Park lay behind the New York Public Library. The city's PR folks called it an "urban oasis," which just meant a block of trees instead of skyscrapers. A broad, tree-studded walkway, lined with a concrete railing, ran around a large central clearing. In the summer this was a flat piece of grass, a pleasant meadow. When the weather turned cold, the city flooded it and turned it into a big outdoor ice rink.

Once the blizzard ended and the streets were cleared, the city would plow off the ice and New Yorkers would get out their skates. There'd be holiday lights, music, food stalls, the works. But now, as Erin circled the library on West 42nd and guided her Interceptor into a police space, she saw an uninhabited arctic wasteland.

Somewhere above the clouds the sun was shining, but that didn't make much difference at ground level. The thick gray clouds cast a murky twilight, illuminated from below by the streetlights. Erin unloaded Rolf and looked around. She saw no movement through the falling snow.

"This park's got to be four or five acres," she said. "Where the hell are these guys?"

Rolf didn't know, but he was ready to search.

Erin thought about texting Katz and asking for his location, but decided against it. If he was playing his cards close to the chest, it wouldn't be a good idea to send him a message. It could blow his cover. Better to arrive unannounced.

"We'll start at the fountain," she told Rolf. "If we don't see anyone, we'll try your nose."

They made their way up three low, broad flights of stairs, walking between little glass-walled shops offering food and souvenirs. The shops were decorated for the holidays but their interiors were dark and empty. The proprietors had stayed home.

The big concrete bowl of the Lowell Memorial Fountain loomed in front of them, frozen and still. Erin didn't know who Josephine Shaw Lowell had been, or why she deserved a fountain in her honor. Nor, at the moment, did she particularly care. Her nerves were jangling. This felt too much like one of those late-night horror movies where the heroine ended up walking through a deserted city. Maybe the shops weren't empty after all. Maybe they were inhabited by the shambling remains of their former customers and staff, hungry for Christmas brains.

"It's never zombies," she said, earning a head tilt from Rolf, who had no idea what she was talking about.

The two of them approached the fountain. It was as deserted as the rest of the Winter Village. Erin cursed. What had she been thinking, driving all this way on the strength of such a thin message? Even with Rolf's nose, there was no easy way to cover all this ground. She'd have to try a reply to the text, or else give it up.

"Detective!"

The word, coming from behind, nearly made Erin jump out of her shoes. She spun around to face three figures, swathed in heavy coats. Where had they come from? They must have been behind one of the shops, or else arrived right on her tail. She recognized the big, bulky silhouette of Katz. The other two must be Mingo and Carter.

Erin didn't like it. She'd gotten a clandestine, cryptic message, but how sure was she that it had really come from Katz? And if it hadn't, what was going on? It felt like a set-up, but she didn't know how or why.

"Detectives," she replied, keeping her voice level. "What's going on?"

"I was hoping you'd be able to tell us," Carter said, stepping forward. Red and green Christmas lights from the nearest shop glowed on his round, boyish face.

"It's a crazy coincidence, you showing up here," Mingo said.

"It's crazy all right," Erin agreed. She glanced at Katz, who moved his massive shoulders in a slight shrug.

"But it's no coincidence," Carter said. "We need to talk."

"Maybe we could go someplace more comfortable," Erin suggested. "Like Antarctica?"

Carter smiled. "Here's fine," he said. "It's private. Nobody's going to drop in and listen."

"Why does that matter?" Erin asked. "You sent me that text."

"Of course I did," Carter said. "We've got a deal to offer you. It's better we talk out here, away from those IAB bloodsuckers."

"I'm listening," Erin said, wishing she had her recorder running but having no way to reach it without tipping him off.

Carter came closer. Now they were only about ten feet apart. His hands were stuffed in his coat pockets, his head covered by a watch cap which was already dusted with snow. Mingo was off to one side, hands also in his pockets, watching.

Katz stood next to Carter, arms crossed, looking back and forth between them.

"I've been doing some checking up on you," Carter said. "And I think we can help each other."

"I hope so," Erin said.

"Phil Stachowski really stepped in it," Carter said. "And he was stupid."

"He's a lot of things," Erin said quietly. "I don't think stupid is one of them."

"It is now," Carter said. "Forget about him. He's out of the game. The guy's a vegetable."

"Jesus, Len," Katz said. "You don't gotta say shit like that."

"It's true," Carter said. "Either he dies, or he spends the rest of his life drooling in some mental ward. Whatever. We've got to think about ourselves, and what we're going to do now."

"And what's that?" Erin asked.

"Phil was infiltrating the O'Malleys," Carter said. "And that ought to matter to you as much as anybody."

"Why?" she challenged.

"Because you're on Evan O'Malley's payroll," Carter said. "For big money."

Chapter 18

Erin stared at Lenny Carter. "I'd love to hear how you came to that conclusion," she said.

"Wait a sec," Katz said. "Whaddaya mean she's working for O'Malley?"

"Keep up, Katz," Carter said impatiently. "You've got a brain; try using it. Of course she's working for O'Malley. And she's screwing Morton Carlyle on the side. That's all over the street."

"No," Katz said, shaking his head. "No way. She's one of the good guys."

Carter snorted in exasperation. "There's no such thing as good guys, dumbass! There's just people. Jesus! You're too dumb to be breathing! I suppose you think crime doesn't pay, even though we grab stacks of bills off the guys we take down every day! You think your shit doesn't stink? You're the same as me and every other jerk on the streets. We bust our balls out there, and for what? A lousy eighty grand a year. You can't even live in Manhattan on that! O'Reilly's smart. She saw which way things were going and she made her play. How much do you get for a contract, O'Reilly? What's the going rate?"

"You're well-informed, Carter," Erin said, ignoring the question. "Where are you getting your info?"

"Same place you are, I expect," Carter said.

"Len?" Katz said. "What's she talking about?"

"Quiet," Carter said. "The grownups are talking. You'll get yours, don't worry. We're all in this together."

Katz looked back and forth from Carter to Erin and back again. Bewilderment was stamped on his face; bewilderment and a growing sense of betrayal. He was a man who clearly had no idea who or what to trust.

"So here's the deal," Carter continued, turning his attention back to Erin. "Phil's got a guy inside. He was going to bring the whole thing down. And if that happens, you go down with it. You understand? If the O'Malleys go, everything comes out. All the hits you've done, for them and for those Italian bastards. Yeah, I know about the hotel bombing, too. Remember that poor Italian chick? What'd you get for taking her out?"

"Jesus Christ," Katz said. "Are you serious? Len? She's a goddamn gold shield!"

"She's a contract killer for the Mob," Carter said.

"But I thought..." Katz said helplessly.

"There's a lot of dollars on the table, O'Reilly," Carter said. "And if that's not enough, think of yourself. You want to collect your pension? Or do you want to do twenty to life upstate? Old Man O'Malley needs a name. You've been working the case. You must've found it. So who is it?"

"You really think I'm going to just tell you?" Erin replied. Her mind was racing as she spoke. She was torn between the need to keep up her undercover charade and her duty as a cop. She was facing two crooked detectives and one wild card. She had no idea which way Katz would go if things went sideways. She was wearing her vest, but that wouldn't be enough against three trained gunmen. Carter and Mingo had their hands in their pockets. Were they holding guns? She'd bet on it. Could she clear her own piece before taking fire? Unlikely. And even if she could, what then? Start shooting other cops?

Carter smiled. "So you do know," he said. "That's good. I really thought Phil was going to tell us. That stupid, crazy son of a bitch. Who would've thought he had the guts to go down fighting? Del sure didn't. He let Phil get way too close."

"Hold on," Katz said. "*You* shot Phil?!"

"I didn't have a choice!" Carter snapped. "He had Del's gun! He blew Del's brains out right in front of me! He was going to shoot me next. It was self-defense, you friggin' moron!"

Erin saw the expression of sheer horror on Katz's face. He really hadn't known. The big detective took a step away from Carter.

"You wanted to interrogate Phil," she said to Carter. "What was the plan? Beat the name out of him? Hook him up to jumper cables?"

"Something like that," Carter said. "The details don't really matter anymore, do they? He won't remember his own name even if he comes out of the coma. But I'd like to make sure of him. Your partner at the hospital, the big Russian. Is he in on it, too? Or can you buy him?"

"Vic's not buyable," Erin said numbly. "He wouldn't be interested."

"That's a shame," Carter said. "But I guess it doesn't make much difference."

"How much money?" she asked. "For the name?"

"Okay," he said. "Now we're talking. Let's negotiate. How's five large sound?"

"Like chump change," she shot back.

"Len, we're talking about a cop here," Katz said. "If they find out about him, aren't they gonna kill him?"

"That's not our problem," Carter said. "It's his. Would ten be better?"

"How much did you offer those losers to break into the Stachowski house?" Erin replied. It was a guess, but she saw immediately it had been the right one.

"The nice thing about working with junkies is they come cheap," Carter said. "Would you believe five hundred apiece? And they didn't ask for anything up front, so they were basically free."

"But they saw your face," she said.

"Only the dead one," Carter said, grinning. "I would've taken care of him on my end, but that wasn't necessary. I ought to send a thank-you card to Phil's old lady. She took that problem right off my plate. Who would've thought that chick could throw down like that?"

"How much are you getting from Evan?" Erin asked quietly.

"Evan?" Carter repeated. "I'm not getting jack from Evan! He doesn't call the shots, not like he thinks. Things have been coming loose for a long time now. He's on his way out. Once he's gone, we'll see who's there to pick up the pieces. I bet you've been planning to ride your boy Carlyle all the way to the top, but he's not the only horse in the race. I've got my money on a better one. Carlyle's smart, sure, but he hasn't got the stomach for this."

"So that's your plan?" Erin asked. "To get the name Evan wants, use it to worm your way in close, and then get rid of him?"

Carter shrugged carelessly. "A lot of times, these problems take care of themselves," he said. "The street takes out its own trash."

"How much?" Erin pressed. "For the name?"

"I'll give you fifteen," he said. "Final offer. Or else maybe we find another way to convince you. Mingo, what do you think of her car battery idea?"

"I like it," Mingo said. "I never tried it, but I know how. I got jumper cables in my car."

Carter's right hand came out of his pocket. He was holding a pistol, a Glock 18 just like Erin's. *Department-issue*, she thought distractedly. And it was pointed at her.

"That's the gun you used, isn't it," she said. "To shoot Phil. You'd better watch out. CSU has the casings, and my squad's getting a match from the Ten's firing range."

Carter blinked. He clearly hadn't considered that. "I didn't want to shoot him," he said. "But I did. Just like I'll shoot you if I have to."

"Len, don't," Katz said. He took a step closer to Carter. "You don't have to—"

Katz stopped short as Mingo drew his own gun and pointed it at him.

"Stay right there," Mingo said softly.

"Or what?" Katz said angrily. "You gonna shoot me too?"

"I'd rather not," Mingo said, giving a slight shrug, as if to ask what else he was supposed to do.

Carter sighed. "Just give me the name," he said. "Then we can all go home and forget about this. You'll be fifteen grand richer, and we won't have to hook up the alligator clips."

"You want a name?" Erin said, holding up her left hand and pointing her index finger at his round, false-innocent face. "Okay, I'll give you one. Rolf, *fass*."

"Rolf Fass?" Carter said in confusion. He started to say something else, but didn't have time to get it out.

Rolf hadn't understood a bit of what was being discussed. He'd just been standing next to Erin, watching her and waiting for orders. Snow had piled up on his fur, but he had a thick natural coat under his K-9 police vest and it didn't bother him. Once he heard his name and his "bite" command, however, he went instantly into action. He crouched, coiled his powerful legs, and exploded up and forward in a shower of snow, launching himself at the target Erin was pointing at.

Carter's words turned into a startled squawk. His hand wavered, the gun barrel sliding away from Erin's face. He pulled the trigger, more in reflex than intention. The Glock went off with an earsplitting crack.

Erin was already moving, shoving her hand under her coat in search of the grip of her own pistol. She'd gotten it clear of its holster and tried to squeeze the trigger. She saw the muzzle flash from Carter's gun. The gunshot was like a thunderclap. Something hit her head like a blow from a sledgehammer. Everything went brilliant white, then pitch black.

* * *

The first thing Erin felt was something warm and wet against her face. It moved, rubbing against her cheek and left eyelid. She heard a low, anxious whine. Then the wet thing came back and slapped against her again. There was a weird, strong smell, reminding her of spicy food.

She tried to move, but couldn't feel her hands or feet. Her fingers had gone completely numb. A bolt of pure terror jolted her awake. She came up suddenly, in a flurry of desperate motion. Snowflakes flew all directions. She kept moving, coming up onto her feet. Then her knees buckled and she went down again, planting a hand to brace herself. The hand disappeared into a two-foot snowdrift, swallowed to the shoulder. Her face hit the snow, little points of ice stinging her.

Erin lurched upright again and rubbed her face. Her hand came away stained red. She was bleeding, she realized dully.

In front of her, Rolf flattened his ears and whined again. He wagged his tail in low, back-and-forth sweeps. The dog was worried. He stepped forward and nosed cautiously at her, licking his lips. Then he tossed his head and snorted, pawing at his face.

As awareness returned, Erin looked wildly around for danger. All she saw was two lumpy shapes, half-covered in snow. Neither of them moved.

Two, she thought. *Not three.* What the hell had happened? How long had she been out?

Her head was throbbing and her vision was blurry, but maybe that was the snow. What had hit her? She tried to probe the injury, but her fingers were sluggish and unresponsive.

Her first-responder medical training prodded her memory. When you got hurt, shock pulled blood away from the extremities, prioritizing the internal organs. That meant, if you were out in the cold, your fingers and toes were at risk.

God, but she was cold. She was shivering, in spite of her jacket. The world didn't seem to have any color in it. But that was because of the snow, she reminded herself. The fresh blood in the snow certainly looked bright and red when she looked at it.

"Gun," she said, getting the word out with some difficulty through trembling lips. She'd tried to draw it; had she succeeded? She couldn't remember.

The holster at her hip was empty. She dropped back to her knees, searching the ground where she'd fallen. It wasn't easy, since she had to work by feel and she couldn't feel her damn fingertips. But after a few moments her right hand hit something hard and she came up with the Glock. She racked the slide, making sure it wasn't frozen. A bright brass-jacketed bullet popped out the ejection port and spun into a drift, vanishing from sight.

Erin forced her fingers to close around the grip of the pistol. She stumbled to the pair of fallen figures. The first was face-down in the snow. She planted a foot under the body and kicked it over. It rolled onto its side, revealing Detective Mingo.

She considered and immediately discarded the thought of checking his vitals. Even if she'd been able to take a pulse with her numbed fingers, the man at her feet had taken a bullet right over the bridge of the nose. His eyes were wide and glassy. He was still clutching his own gun in one icy hand.

Erin left him and turned to the other body. This one was propped against the window of one of the little shops in a sitting posture. His head was slumped down on his chest, but she could tell who he was from the size alone.

"Katz?" she said without much hope. A good half-inch of snow had settled on him. He was dead; he had to be.

His head rolled back and he looked up at her. He blinked.

If Erin had been more sensitive by nature, she probably would have screamed. Instead, she blurted out a curse and lurched backward, almost falling over.

Katz tried to sit up a little straighter and couldn't. He had blood all over him, dark and frozen, stiffening his clothes. He smiled shakily.

"O'Reilly," he murmured. "Sorry."

"Don't apologize," Erin said, wishing she could stop shivering. "Where are you hit? How bad?"

"Dunno," Katz mumbled. "Leg... maybe both. Shoulder, too. Maybe three in the chest."

"Holy shit," Erin said. She was astonished he was still breathing, let alone talking.

"Vest," he explained, gesturing with his right hand. That hand was holding his Glock.

"Hang in there," she said. "I'll call a bus."

She reached with her free hand into her hip pocket and hauled out her phone. The pocket was full of snow. The phone came out dripping, the screen black.

"Shit," she said, stripping off her glove and swiping the screen. Nothing happened. "Shit, shit, shit."

"Mine's... broken," Katz said thickly. "Fell on it. Mingo... shot me. Son of a bitch. Always told him I was... better shot than him. Emptied half his damn clip. I only got one off, but it was... pretty good shot."

"Yeah, it was," Erin said, trying the phone again. The screen remained stubbornly blank. "Where's Carter?"

"Dog grabbed him," Katz said. "He went down. Juiced the dog. Pepper spray, I think. Made dog let go... for a second. Carter ran. That way."

Katz waved vaguely behind Erin, in the direction of the Public Library.

"Is he hurt?" she asked.

"Think maybe you clipped him," Katz said. "Dog... got his arm. Dropped his gun. Getting... pretty... cold. Sorry..."

His head slumped forward again, his eyes rolling shut.

"Jesus," Erin said, trying to think what to do. Carter was on the run, but he was injured and possibly disarmed. Katz needed immediate medical help. Come to that, so did she. But they didn't have a working phone. Where was the nearest place she could go to make a call?

"Library," she said, alarmed at how slurred her voice sounded. She had to get indoors, and soon.

She didn't want to leave Katz, but what choice did she have? There wasn't a thing she could do for him out here. Rolf was looking up at her anxiously. The dog snorted again. His eyes were bloodshot from the pepper spray.

"*Fuss*," she told him. Then she turned and started slogging across the ice rink, heading for the New York Public Library.

Rolf, obedient to his "heel" command, took up his position beside and slightly behind her. He sneezed. His eyes were watering and he kept licking his chops, trying to get rid of the fiery aftertaste of the mouthful of pepper spray. That bad guy he'd bitten had definitely tasted worse than most bad guys. But that didn't mean he wouldn't bite him again, given the chance. The K-9 had wanted to chase him, but the human, *his* human, had been hurt. He'd decided, on his own initiative, to go to her instead. He didn't regret the decision; regret wasn't really part of Rolf's emotional makeup. He looked forward, not back.

Footprints, partially filled by snow, marked the way toward the library. Drops of Carter's blood had soaked into the snow, leaving an irregular trail of frozen crimson.

Erin and Rolf followed it.

Chapter 19

The ice rink was piled deep with snow, which made for hard going, but at least it wasn't slippery. Erin plowed doggedly onward, reeling a little with every step. Her sense of balance was off. The wound on the side of her head didn't seem to be bleeding anymore. She told herself that was a good thing. It was hard to believe she'd been shot in the head and was on her feet.

Rolf had saved her life. His lunge had spoiled Carter's aim so the bullet intended to go between her eyes had glanced off the side of her skull instead, digging a channel through her scalp. The force of the impact had still been enough to knock her out for a few minutes, but she dared to hope the bone hadn't been fractured and her brain hadn't been scrambled too badly.

She wondered how long she'd be able to stay up. For some reason, she thought of Ian Thompson. The former Marine had once gone five days in the Afghan mountains without sleep, carrying a wounded buddy. He'd had a concussion, too, but he'd gotten through by sheer determination. If he could do it, so could she.

"Dig deep," she murmured, quoting one of Ian's catchphrases. "Find more. Keep going."

The cold was almost a blessing. She didn't feel much pain, or anything else. If anything, she felt oddly warm now. In some distant, academic part of her brain, she understood that was a bad thing, but didn't remember why.

How big was the ice rink, anyway? She felt like she'd been slogging across it for an hour at least, but that couldn't be. The whole of Bryant Park was only a block long. But the snow screwed up her sense of distance and proportion. How much of a lead did Carter have? How badly hurt was he?

None of it mattered. Erin's priorities had narrowed to a single sharp point. She was a cop, chasing down a criminal, and she had to get to him before he got away and did any more harm. Nothing else was important. She'd sort out the rest of it later. If there was a later.

Her foot caught on something hard hidden beneath the snow. She pitched forward and face-planted. Her cheeks were so numb from the wind that she hardly felt the impact. She spat snow and scrambled clumsily back to her feet.

She was standing at the foot of a low flight of steps that led to a terrace at the rear of the library. Was there a back door? She didn't know. Carter's footprints led to the left, around the north corner of the building, so that was where she and Rolf went.

Now, with the massive wall of the library to her right, she felt less lost. Her world had something large and solid in it, which was oddly comforting. She stuck close to the wall, which seemed to provide a little protection from the weather, and kept going, putting one foot in front of the other.

Erin was so focused on walking that she nearly went right by the door. It was a small side entrance, a lot less impressive than the front door on Fifth Avenue. The door had been locked, but it was smashed open, standing a few inches ajar. She dully studied the splintered lock. How had Carter broken it?

"Shot it out," she said. So he still had a gun, probably a backup piece like the one she usually carried strapped to her ankle. Her own extra gun, damn it all, was in New Jersey. She hoped her borrowed Glock would be enough to see her through.

Her objectives were simple: get to a phone, call backup and an ambulance, run Carter down. That was good; she wasn't sure she could think clearly enough to handle complicated concepts. Holding her borrowed Glock in both hands, Rolf's leash wrapped around her left wrist, she shouldered her way inside.

The entryway was very dark after the blinding white of the blizzard. Only a handful of dim lights were lit. The library was closed, of course, like everything else in New York. To her right was a walk-in closet. She took a second to clear the space, verifying it was empty. She saw only bare hangers and coat racks.

Ahead were a couple of doors, one leading to restrooms, the other to some sort of conference room. The hallway branched left and right. Erin swung one way, then the other, sweeping the muzzle of her pistol across dark, empty space. On her right was the Children's Center, dark and deserted. But to her left was a bank of telephones at the foot of a staircase.

Erin went for the nearest phone. As she reached for it, she saw a pool of melting slush in the rough shape of a footprint.

She spun, bringing up her gun. She was just in time to see a muzzle flash from the landing, the bright burst of fire illuminating Lenny Carter's face. Carter fired three times in rapid succession. Erin reflexively squeezed off two shots in return, though her hands were so stiff she had no idea if she was aiming properly or not. A bullet whined past her ear and smashed into the phone behind her. Then Carter was gone, his footsteps echoing on the stairs as he climbed up and out of sight.

Erin risked a quick glance at the phones. By sheer, malevolent luck, Carter's volley of bullets had hit both of them.

Maybe they'd work, maybe they wouldn't. She didn't dare take the time to check.

"*Komm!*" she told Rolf, forcing her numb, tired feet up the stairs. Little needle-jabs of pain were starting in her fingers and toes as blood began to return to the frosted tissues. In a little while, she knew, they'd really start hurting.

She made it up the first flight of steps to the main entrance level. Carter might have headed for the front door, or he might have kept climbing. "*Such!*" she gasped to Rolf.

Rolf sniffed at the stairs. Drops of fresh blood had spattered the floor, giving him a perfect trail to follow. The K-9 charged upstairs to the second floor, tail wagging, dragging at Erin's arm.

By the time she finished the second flight of stairs, Erin's breath was coming raggedly and her hands and feet were burning. She felt something wet on her cheeks. It was either melting snow or tears. She didn't know which and didn't care. All she knew was that she was going to get Carter.

She somehow made it all the way to the top. Rolf wasn't even breathing hard. He was excited. The pepper spray didn't seem to have done him much harm. The snow had helped dilute the chemicals. The dog was having the time of his life. He was chasing a bad guy with his partner, doing what he'd been bred and trained to do. The scent of the frightened, injured bad guy went down the hall from the stairs. Rolf followed it.

They turned right at the rotunda, going into a reference room. On the left was a desk where a helpful sign informed Erin she could get a library card. Rolf was leading her on, straight through that room toward a set of doors at the far end.

Erin plunged through and found herself in one of the largest rooms she'd ever entered. She'd been here before, she realized dully, years ago. It was the Rose Reading Room, a gigantic cavern of a space, the length of a football field. No interior columns or reinforcements supported the ceiling. The vast area was filled with row upon row of reading tables and chairs, enough for five or six hundred people. A double row of chandeliers, all of them dark, hung from the ceiling.

Rolf pulled left, which saved Erin's life. She looked that way in time to see Carter, crouched behind one of the tables, aiming a gun at her.

She dove for the floor. He fired twice, the shots whipping over her head. She rolled clumsily, came up on one knee, and returned fire, sending three quick rounds his way.

There was a moment of silence, broken only by the harsh breathing of two humans and one dog.

"O'Reilly!" Carter called. "That you?"

"It's me," she replied grimly, scanning the room. She didn't see him. He must have ducked down below one of the tables.

"Did I get you?" he asked. He sounded almost cheerful.

"Which time?" she replied. She considered sending Rolf after him, but he knew about the dog. He might be waiting and aiming. She wasn't going to risk it, not just yet.

He actually laughed. "Either one," he said. "Does it matter?"

"Nope," she said. "You're a shitty shot, Carter."

"I guess so," he admitted. "Never was much good with my off hand. Your K-9 dinged my right arm pretty good. I think maybe it's broken. And I suppose we didn't do each other any favors, either. I thought you were dead."

"Not yet," she said. "Did I hit you?"

"Yeah," he said. "When you drew on me outside. Just under the vest, on my hip. Hurts like a son of a bitch. You're fast, you know that? I think I underestimated you."

"You wouldn't be the first," she said. "Why don't you throw your gun over here and give it up? It's over, Carter."

"You want the gun? How do you know I haven't got two?"

"Because you lost one back at the fountain," she said. "Katz told me. And I don't think you were carrying three."

"Bullshit," Carter said. "Katz is dead."

It was Erin's turn to laugh, even though her hands were hurting like they'd never hurt before. They were on fire, getting seared from the inside out, every nerve ending alive and screaming. She ignored the pain and kept laughing through the tears.

"You know, Carter," she said, "for a guy who wants to be a murderer, you're really bad at it. You didn't kill Phil, you didn't kill Katz, and you didn't kill me. Your buddies Mingo and Ames are dead, and you're hurt and hiding out in a damn library. You're done."

"I didn't shoot Katz," Carter said. "That was Mingo. I was too busy with your dog. Sorry about the pepper spray."

"Forget about it," she said. "Rolf's been shot, Tased, and smacked into walls. It takes a lot more than that to stop him. Give me your gun, now. Or I'll send him in for round two, and this time he'll break your other arm."

There was a pause. Then Carter laughed again.

"Why not?" he said. "It's not like I've got more bullets for the damn thing. Here you go."

A small handgun skittered across the floor, stopping a few feet from Erin.

"Okay," she said. "Now stand up and keep your hands where I can see them."

"We can still make a deal," he said. "Why don't we pin this whole thing on Mingo and Del? They go down, we walk away clean. And rich, if we get the guy the O'Malleys want."

"Stand up and we can talk about it," she said.

"You'll shoot me," he said.

"If I'm going to shoot you, there's nothing stopping me," Erin pointed out. "I can just walk over there and put two in your brain."

"That's a really good point."

Carter slowly stood up. He was three tables over from Erin. He was an absolute mess. His hair was disheveled, blood was dripping down his right leg, and his jacket sleeve was badly torn where Rolf had bitten him. His hands were visible and empty, but he was smiling.

"What?" she demanded. "What've you got to grin about?"

"You're not going to shoot me," he said.

"Don't tempt me," she growled.

"No, you're really not," he said. His smile widened. "Junkyard O'Reilly, professional killer, isn't going to pull the trigger. You can't. Not if I'm unarmed and helpless. And I am. No more weapons. I can't even fight back hand-to-hand, not with this arm."

"Shut up," she said. "I'm placing you under arrest."

"No, you're not."

"Watch me." She started toward him, keeping the Glock aimed at his face. He might be wearing body armor, so if he tried anything, she'd go for a headshot.

"No, you're not," he said again. "Because I know something about you now."

"Oh yeah? What's that?"

"You're not a murderer."

Erin felt a sudden chill that had nothing to do with the weather. "Bullshit," she said. "I've killed more people than you."

"When they were shooting back," he said. "But what about that Italian babe? The one outside the hotel?"

"I said, shut up. You've got the right to remain—"

Carter's eyes widened. "She's not dead!" he exclaimed. "You fixed the whole thing! And that means you've been Phil's guy this whole time. Holy shit!"

He started laughing. Erin felt the world spinning around her. She thought she was about to throw up.

"No, this is great," Carter went on. "Absolutely unbelievable. You pulled the wool over all their eyes. Evan O'Malley, Kyle Finnegan, Morton Carlyle, even Vinnie the friggin' Oil Man! But now you're stuck. Because if you take me in, I get my phone call. And guess who I'm going to call?"

"Are you blackmailing me, you son of a bitch?" Erin snarled. Her finger was inside the trigger guard. The range was about twelve feet. It would be a very easy shot, but even if she somehow missed, she had plenty more rounds in the magazine.

"Hell yes I'm blackmailing you," he said. "Here's the deal. I walk, or I spill your dirty little secret to all the wrong people."

"There's a third option," she said.

"Yeah." Carter was still smiling. "And it's what I'd do. It's what I thought you'd do. But it turns out you're not me. Katz, that thick-headed idiot, was right. There really *are* good guys, and you're one of them. You can shoot me, and then maybe you can go to Confession and tell your priest all about it. You think you'll ever be able to look your dad in the eye again?"

The Glock 18 had a trigger pull weight of five and a half pounds. Erin's finger tightened. She was exerting at least four pounds of pressure and her fine-motor control was still iffy. The trigger shifted slightly in her grip.

Carter was looking right at her, that mocking smile plastered on his youthful, psychopathic face. He was wrong. She could kill him. If she didn't, he'd already told her, he'd kill her, and Carlyle with her. He wouldn't even have to use his own hands to do it. All he needed was his voice and his goddamn phone call.

He was right, too. She couldn't haul him down to the Eightball and book him. But Erin O'Reilly was damned if she was going to let him slip away after what he'd done. Besides, if he walked, he'd still betray her. She knew that as surely as she knew anything.

Her tongue felt thick in her mouth. For a moment, she didn't think she'd be able to speak. But then the words came.

"Leonard Carter, you're under arrest for the attempted murders of NYPD detectives Philip Stachowski and Erin O'Reilly. You have the right to remain silent."

"This is such bullshit," Carter said. "I'm out of here."

"If you give up this right, anything you say can and will be used against you in a court of law." Her voice grew stronger as she recited the words, as familiar as the Hail Mary or the Our Father.

"See you on the flip side, O'Reilly," he said. He started walking toward the exit.

"You have the right to an attorney," Erin continued, turning and keeping him covered. "If you cannot afford an attorney, one will be assigned to you by the court. Do you understand these rights?"

"Piss off," he said and turned his back. He was in the doorway, not even bothering to look at her. He was absolutely sure she wouldn't shoot him in the back.

And she wouldn't. But she didn't have to. Erin glanced down at her dog. "Rolf, *fass!*"

Chapter 20

The first thing Erin did with Carter's phone was to call an ambulance for Katz. She knew she needed medical attention, too, but that would have to wait. Before that, she needed to deal with Carter himself. And she couldn't do it through official channels. Carter had made that abundantly clear.

Fortunately, she had access to some very unofficial channels. She couldn't remember the number of Carlyle's current burner phone; he changed phones so often. It was programmed into her own phone, but that didn't do her a lot of good at the moment. She looked up the number for the Barley Corner and called that instead.

"Barley Corner," a familiar voice said. "Sorry, but we're closed on account of the weather."

"Hey, Danny," Erin said. "I don't need a drink."

"Erin? Is that you?"

"Yeah. My phone got trashed and I need to talk to your boss. Can you grab him?"

"Sure thing. He's upstairs. Do you want to hold, or can he call you back?"

"Have him call this number."

She hung up and waited. Carter, lying on the floor near her feet, glared at her. He couldn't do anything but glare, since she'd handcuffed him and slapped a piece of duct tape over his mouth. She'd found the tape in a supply cabinet. You could never go too far wrong with duct tape. It wasn't precisely in line with the Patrol Guide, but she figured in a case like this it wouldn't hurt to bend the rules a little and help him exercise his right to remain silent.

She used the time tending Carter's bullet wound. It didn't look too serious. Her shot had gouged a chunk of meat out of his hip, but the bone hadn't been hit. He ought to make a full recovery, unfortunately. His right arm was badly swollen, but she didn't have the skills or the equipment to do anything about that. Rolf had gone for the right arm both times, just like he'd been trained to do.

The phone rang just as she was finishing bandaging the wound.

"Talk to me," she said.

"What is it you're needing?" Carlyle asked, without preliminaries.

"I need someplace I can stash a guy for a little while," she said. "It has to be discreet."

"Where are you now?"

"Public Library."

"This lad you're tucking away," Carlyle said. "What's his condition?"

"A little banged up, but he's not bleeding out."

"Are you able to travel?"

"Can you get a car to the 5th Avenue Public Library? I'm parked at the other end of the block. I don't know if I can get him that far on my own."

"Let me make a call or two. I'll have some lads there as soon as I can. It shouldn't be more than thirty minutes."

"We'll be in the Rose Reading Room, third floor. The library's closed, but the side door on 42nd is open. And these have to be reliable people, you understand? Only guys you'd trust with your life."

"Understood. Ta, darling."

A plan was coming together in Erin's head. It was desperate, but it just might work. She'd already set the first pieces in motion. Hiding Carter somewhere safe, where he couldn't communicate, was step one. But this wasn't some Third World police state; she couldn't just leave him locked in a basement. She needed someone official to take him. Captain Holliday would never agree to this. Neither would Lieutenant Webb. That only left one option. She didn't like it, but you had to play the cards you were dealt. She made another call.

"Precinct Eight Internal Affairs," the woman on the other end of the line said.

"Hey," Erin said. "It's me."

"Great," Kira sighed. "Why am I not surprised?"

"Don't worry," Erin said. "This hasn't got anything to do with you. Is the Bloodhound in?"

"He's in his office."

"Good. Can you give him a message?"

"I can transfer you."

"Don't. Just tell him I need him to meet me somewhere offsite."

"Where?"

"I don't know yet."

"What kind of a message is that?"

"The important kind. Things are happening fast, and I need to know he can meet me where I'll be. It's about an internal problem. I've got a cop in bracelets, injured."

"You've got *what?!* Never mind, I heard you the first time. Jesus Christ, Erin. What do you think you're doing?"

"What I have to," Erin said. "This is why I need IAB. I need Keane, and I need it to be quick and quiet. This doesn't go through normal process."

"I'll tell him. But then I'm letting go of this. I don't want any part of whatever the hell you're up to."

"Fair enough. I'll get you the location as soon as I have it. And thanks."

"Don't thank me yet. Keane might hang your head on his wall."

"If he does, I'll try to enjoy the view."

"Erin? Are you okay? You sound a little funny."

Erin barked a laugh. "It's a long story," she said. "Tell you later."

And she hung up. Then there was nothing to do but wait.

* * *

Twenty minutes later, her hands had mostly stopped hurting, but a glorious headache had blossomed where Carter's bullet had creased her skull. She heard the sirens as the ambulance arrived at the Winter Village, accompanied by several Patrol cars. The windows on the back wall of the Reading Room overlooked the ice rink and fountain, but the snow was still too thick to see what was going on. All she saw when she looked that way was a blurry glow of blue and red emergency lights.

After only a couple minutes the ambulance was on its way, lights and sirens still going. That was good news; they wouldn't have been in such a hurry if Katz was dead. It was also bad news; they wouldn't have been in such a hurry if they didn't need to get him to a hospital right away. Erin watched those lights disappear into the storm, drummed her fingers on the windowsill, and silently prayed.

Rolf, who'd been sitting and staring at Carter, abruptly turned toward the door and cocked his head. Erin put a hand on her gun and tensed.

"Erin, love, are you in there?" an Irish voice called cheerfully.

She relaxed and let go of the pistol, breathing a sigh of relief. "Yeah, Corky," she said. "C'mon in."

James Corcoran stepped through the door, smiling jauntily. "It's no day to be wandering about, love," he said. "You're lucky I'm mad enough to come to your rescue. Good Lord, you're a fright! I've never seen so much blood on a lass! And what's the matter with this poor blighter?"

"He tried to kill me," Erin said.

Corky shook his head. "What a blithering eejit," he said. "You'd think the scunners would know better by now. What's to be done with him?"

"Didn't Carlyle tell you? We need to stash him somewhere safe while I figure what to do with him."

"That's easy enough," Corky said. "We'll weight him down and pitch him off one of the bridges. No need to waste a bullet on the blighter. The crabs and wee fishes will take care of the rest of the business. His mum may miss him, but I'd wager no one else will."

"Corky!"

He grinned. "I forgot for a moment you were a copper," he said. "Nay, love, I'm yanking your chain. I've just the place. A laundry, just down the way, closed for repairs. Pipes burst in the cold, poor lads. Can he walk?"

"Yeah, but I don't think he'll cooperate."

"Oh, he'll do as he's told, or I'll slit him open and leave him for the dogs," Corky said, in a tone of voice that made it impossible to tell whether he was joking or not. He bent and hauled Carter to his feet. The dirty cop winced and cried out into his gag. Corky shook his head in disgust.

"What's this gobshite bleating about now? I scarce touched him."

"I think one of his arms is broken," Erin said without much sympathy. "Rolf bit him pretty hard. Twice."

Corky marched Carter downstairs to the side entrance, Erin and Rolf flanking him. Outside, a white van with no rear windows was illegally parked, engine idling. Corky tossed Carter unceremoniously in the back, then went around to the driver's seat. Erin put Rolf in back to keep an eye on Carter and took the shotgun seat. Corky started driving.

"I've been wondering what you've been up to," he said conversationally. "I was glad to hear from Cars. I thought maybe someone had done for him. All the lads are in a bit of an uproar. Who's the scunner in back, anyway?"

"Lenny Carter," Erin said. "He's a crooked cop."

"He's a copper?" Corky said in surprise. "Bloody hell, love! What is it you've dragged me into here?"

"I'll explain later," she said wearily.

"And your head?"

"I got shot."

"You know, for most of us, a bullet in the head's the end of us," he said. "I'd never go so far as to say you look like warmed-over death, love, but you're skating close to the edge of eternity. Shouldn't we get you to a hospital?"

"That's my next stop," she said. "But we need to take care of him first."

"Grand. Just a few short blocks."

Corky was as good as his word. Only a little while later, he eased the van up to the laundry storefront. He hopped out and unlocked the door. Then, after checking to make sure nobody was watching, they hoisted Carter out and transferred him into the laundry.

Erin got on Carter's phone again and called Kira.

"You're crazy," Kira said. "But I've talked to Keane. He's ready to come to you. Where are you?"

Erin gave the address. "I'll wait here," she said. "Just Keane, nobody else. Got it?"

"Copy that," Kira said. "Sit tight."

"Shall I hang about?" Corky asked, once Erin had hung up.

"Better not," she said. "You don't want to get involved."

"I'll be on my way, then," he said. "Tipping is customary, but I know coppers are notorious skinflints, so I'll not be expecting anything. And you needn't worry about the vehicle. I'll dispose of it in the usual manner."

"I don't even want to know," she said. "Thanks, Corky."

"What's the lad on about?" Corky asked, glancing at Carter, who was making muffled noises as loud as the duct tape over his mouth would allow.

"Nothing you need to worry about," she said.

"But I'm a mite curious," he said. Before Erin could do anything, he stooped and ripped a corner of the tape off Carter's mouth.

"She's a traitor!" Carter burst out. "To Evan! And you! She's never been on the take for real! It's all an act! Help me! You'll get forty—no, fifty grand! Cash! All you have to do is—"

Corky slapped the tape back over his mouth. Carter's eyes bulged and he tried to keep talking, but nothing intelligible came out.

"I thought perhaps he'd something useful to say," Corky said, shrugging. "I'm off, love. Try not to do anything I'd do."

"Never," she promised. Even tired and injured as she was, Corky was able to make her smile.

* * *

The laundry was damp and musty, probably from the burst pipe. Erin could practically smell mold taking hold in the walls. She tried not to think about it, concentrating instead on what she'd say to Keane. She didn't trust him. Whether he was corrupt or not, he was ruthlessly ambitious and probably a sociopath. He loved leverage more than anything, and she was about to give him a great big lever that would let him lean on her pretty hard.

But what else could she do? Letting Carter walk would sign her death warrant, and probably that of Corky and Carlyle too. She couldn't murder him. That was one line she'd never cross. Corky or Carlyle could make him disappear, would do it if she asked, but she wasn't going to put either of them in that position. That would be the same as doing it herself, only more cowardly. The only option open to her was Lieutenant Keane.

It took an endless hour for Keane to arrive. The snow had finally slacked off and nearly stopped. The plows were out, shoving their way through the drifts. They were clearing only one lane at a time. It'd be hours before the city could return to any sort of normal activity. But Keane had an official vehicle and could move if he had to.

He showed up in a black SUV with tinted windows, exactly the sort of car she'd imagined him driving. He parked in the same exact spot Corky had used. Erin saw he'd driven himself, instead of having one of his underlings chauffeur him. When she opened the door he was standing alone, immaculate in a black wool topcoat and dark blue scarf, black leather gloves on his hands, not a hair out of place on his well-groomed head.

"Detective," he said, favoring her with a slightly mocking smile.

"Lieutenant," she replied.

"This is highly irregular," he said.

"You're telling me," she said. "Come in."

He carefully kicked the snow off the soles of his shoes and followed her into the back room where she'd stashed Carter. Rolf, on guard, gave Keane a cool look and trotted to Erin's side.

"Who's this?" Keane asked, taking in the scene at a glance.

"Detective Carter," she said. "Precinct Ten Narcotics."

"I'm sure you have an excellent reason for keeping a wounded member of the Department handcuffed in a defunct laundromat," Keane said. "I'm waiting to hear all about it."

"This is the guy who shot Lieutenant Stachowski," she said.

Keane crossed his arms. "Explain."

"Lieutenant Stachowski has been running an undercover operation aimed at infiltrating the O'Malley gang for the past several months," Erin said.

Keane raised a sardonic eyebrow. "Do tell," he said.

"Recently, he's expanded the operation, in preparation for mass arrests," she said. "He's been stepping up surveillance on O'Malley higher-ups. In order to do that, he's needed the services of several additional officers. Stachowski is a cautious guy, and he knows the O'Malleys have ears inside the NYPD, so he insisted on using only officers he previously employed in undercover assignments. That included Carter's Narcotics squad. All of them had done undercover gigs in the past."

"I take it Detective Carter's motives were not as pure as originally believed?"

"His squad was five guys," Erin said. "Lieutenant Bowes was the commander. Then there were four detectives: Erwin Katzenberg, Domingo Sanchez, Delbert Ames, and Leonard Carter. They'd all done good work for the Department, but they'd also gotten a taste of something more. They'd gotten in the habit of skimming off the cash they grabbed during drug busts."

"Hardly unheard-of," Keane commented. "It's almost impossible to enforce, with all that untraceable money lying around. We do what we can."

"It's a slippery slope," Erin said. "Carter got greedy. So did Mingo Sanchez and Del Ames. Katz was the only one who felt guilty."

"What about Sergeant Bowes?"

"I don't know," she admitted. "I haven't met him. I don't know how deep into this whole thing he is. That'll be a job for you and your people."

"I see. Please continue."

"Carter was looking for ways to make more cash on the side," she said. "He hit on two ideas. The first was to use small-time pushers to do his dirty work. He'd bust guys, then offer to drop the charges in exchange for them doing little jobs for him."

"Such as?"

"Breaking into an NYPD Lieutenant's house, stealing his paperwork, and maybe assaulting his wife."

Keane smiled thinly. "That's an oddly specific example."

"Ozzie Cowan and Iggy Dutton were working for Carter," Erin said. "They broke into the Stachowski house in Hoboken, but Mrs. Stachowski killed Dutton and I arrested Cowan."

"Can you prove their connection to Carter?"

"Not specifically, but I can prove they were arrested by his squad. If Katz survives, he can help identify them."

"You said Carter had two ideas. What was the other?"

"He went to work directly for one of the O'Malleys," she said. "I assume it was their top drug dealer, but they've had some high turnover in that position."

"You might say that," Keane said. "Liam McIntyre was murdered by Colombian Cartel enforcers, if memory serves. His replacement, Veronica Blackburn, was also murdered, by persons unknown. And *her* replacement, in turn, scarcely had time to be promoted before he was shot by a rogue DEA agent and incarcerated. Who, exactly, *does* Detective Carter answer to?"

Erin had been thinking about that question. "It's not Evan O'Malley himself," she said. "And it's not Morton Carlyle or James Corcoran. Neither of them has anything to do with the drug trade, and I'd know if they were connected with him. So that just leaves Gordon Pritchard or Kyle Finnegan. Pritchard's an enforcer, not an earner. My best guess is Finnegan."

"You've had some experience with Mr. Finnegan recently, haven't you?" Keane asked.

"You could say that," Erin said. *I should've let him fall out that twelfth-story window*, she thought but didn't add. That would've solved a lot of problems.

"In either case, whether he reports to Pritchard or Finnegan, I suppose the story is largely the same," Keane said.

"Yeah," Erin said. "He told them about Stachowski's mole in the Family and they tasked him with finding out who it was. So he and Ames tried to get Stachowski to talk when they met at Central Park. But Phil wouldn't give up one of his people. He was unarmed, so they underestimated him. He grabbed Ames's gun and shot Ames. Then Carter shot him."

"I see. And did he discover the name of the mole?"

"Yeah," she said, looking Keane in the eye. "But he only just figured it out, and he hasn't had the chance to tell anyone else yet."

"I see," Keane said again. "So you thought it best to keep him under wraps and call me, in the hopes I would have some clever idea to preserve operational security."

"Something like that, yeah."

Keane studied Carter and Erin for a long moment, his dark eyes unreadable.

"You understand, if you want him processed outside official channels, it poisons the case against him," he said at last. "The city won't be able to prosecute him in open court."

Erin, tight-lipped, nodded. She'd already considered that.

"So you also understand, whatever happens to him, it will be strictly off the normal record."

"Yeah, I figured."

"And you are not, under any circumstances, to pursue his case further on your own time. Your access to him ends as of this moment."

"Copy that, sir."

"Very well," Keane said. "I hereby take custody of Detective Carter. This concludes your responsibility to the situation. You can be on your way."

Erin blinked. "That's it?" she blurted.

"I don't think you either need or wish to spend more time in his company," Keane said. "I would advise, actually I would insist, that you make your way to a medical facility. You appear to be significantly injured."

Erin touched the dried blood on her scalp and managed not to wince. "This? Forget about it. It's nothing."

"Need I remind you, you have previously suffered a traumatic brain injury," he said. "When you apprehended the late Michael Connor, as I recall. I would hate for that injury to be compounded by further cerebral trauma, which might jeopardize your promising career with the NYPD. The hospital, if you please."

"I don't have a car here," she said, a little petulantly.

"I'll be happy to call you a cab," he said. "A few of them should be running by now. The Department will cover the expense, naturally. Good day, Detective."

Chapter 21

After so many deserted parks, streets, and buildings, the Bellevue Hospital emergency room seemed crowded to Erin. A dozen patients were strewn around the waiting area, together with family members and a couple of nurses. A big guy with a buzz cut was moving among them, handing out blankets and taking information. When she and Rolf walked in, he mechanically handed her a folded blanket.

"Take a number from the lady at the desk," he said. "We're shorthanded, but we'll get someone to see you as quick as we can. Wait a sec, is that Rolf? Erin? That you?"

"Hey, Vic," she said, mustering up a smile. "How's the EMT cross-training going?"

"Holy shit! What happened to you? You got blood all over your face! I hardly knew it was you!"

"Oh, this?" She motioned to the side of her skull. "I got shot."

"Ha ha," Vic said. "Very funny. What really happened?"

"I got shot. Nine-millimeter. No big deal, it just skimmed me. I'm fine."

"Nurse!" Vic shouted, looping an arm around her waist. "We got a GSW to the head! I need a doc, stat!"

"Seriously, Vic," Erin said. "Stop being such a drama queen."

"Jesus drunken tap-dancing Christ, you got *shot* in the *head!* How is me taking that seriously being a drama queen? How'd it happen? Who did it?"

"Lenny Carter."

"I'm gonna kill that son of a bitch!"

"No, Vic, you're not," she said wearily. "I'll explain."

But she didn't get the chance just yet. Vic's exclamation had the desired effect, and an ER nurse descended on Erin. After a brief triage, consisting of the nurse probing the wound and shining a light in Erin's eyes, she found herself shunted into a room where she was told a doctor would be with her shortly. The hospital staff tried to pry Rolf away from her, but Rolf and Erin were having none of it and the dog stayed. So did Vic.

"Sheesh, Erin," Vic said once she was reluctantly lying down on the examining table. "You've been having all kinds of fun without me, haven't you."

"It was no fun," she said. "Did you hear about the gunfight at Winter Village? In back of the 5th Avenue Public Library?"

"Yeah. They brought in a detective all shot to shit a little while ago. Big guy, almost as big as me. Is that where you got tagged?"

"Yeah. Is Katz okay?"

"I dunno. I think your brother's working on him right now. Busy night for the O'Reillys. Does Webb know you're here?"

"He does now," Webb said from the doorway.

Erin and Vic started and looked toward the door. The Lieutenant stood there, looking as tired and worn as Erin felt.

"What're you doing here, sir?" Erin asked.

"I came to see about Detective Katzenberg," Webb said. "Little did I know one of my own detectives was admitted here, too. Did you ever think to let me know what was going on?"

"My phone got wrecked," she said. "Snow got into it."

"Too bad you were stuck somewhere remote, far from civilization, without access to other telephones," Webb said. "And you couldn't find a way to communicate with your commanding officer."

"Your sarcasm's rubbing off on him," Erin told Vic.

"I'm glad you're not dead," Webb said. "But I'm not happy. The last I heard, you were going to get some information from Detective Katzenberg. Then I learn, not from you but from the police radio band, that Katzenberg's been shot, along with another detective, and you're nowhere to be found. It took me almost half an hour to find out the other detective was male and couldn't be you. There's a BOLO out on the net with your name on it right now, did you know that?"

"You can cancel that, sir," Erin said sheepishly.

"I told them to call it off as soon as I learned you were here," Webb said grimly. "How badly are you hurt?"

"It isn't serious," she said. "The bullet glanced off. I was only out for a few minutes, I think."

"You were shot in the head and knocked unconscious," Webb translated. "How, exactly, does that equate to not being a serious injury?"

"I'm not dead," she said.

Webb looked at Vic, who shrugged.

"I'm on your side, sir," Vic said. "I think she's nuts. And I'm pissed at her, too. If you want to kick her ass, you're gonna have to get in line."

"For different reasons, I suspect," Webb said. "I'm mad because she dropped off the radar and I thought she'd been kidnapped or murdered. You're mad because she didn't bring you along."

"I'm also pissed about the kidnapping and murder thing," Vic said. "For what that's worth."

"I'm going to stand right here," Webb said. "I'm going to wait patiently until a qualified physician clears you. And then we're going to have a long conversation. Are we clear?"

"Crystal, sir," Erin sighed.

It was only a few minutes until Doctor Nussbaum arrived to check on her. He'd been her doctor after Mickey Connor had tuned her up, so he was familiar with Erin and her past physical trauma. He shooed the other detectives out of the room and gave her a careful examination, including asking all sorts of questions designed to test her short- and long-term memory.

"Well?" she asked once he was done.

"You're an exceptionally lucky woman," Nussbaum said.

"I got shot in the head," she said. "I don't think that's very lucky."

"The bullet ricocheted," he said. "I'll want X-rays to be sure, but unless you have a hairline fracture of the skull, the bone is largely intact. Concussions are tricky things, especially when you've suffered more than one. They have a cumulative effect. You really should try to avoid getting hit in the head again."

"I'll keep that in mind, doc," she said. "But I didn't get in front of the gun on purpose."

"Serious head trauma is no laughing matter," Nussbaum said. "Any contact hard enough to render you unconscious is a big deal. It's too early to tell, but I think you got away with this one. You also seem to have escaped serious frostbite damage. I'd say you dodged a bullet, but we both know you didn't quite manage to dodge it."

"But I'm going to be okay?"

Nussbaum smiled then. "I think so," he said. "But I wouldn't make a habit of being shot. In addition to the X-rays, we'll run an MRI and make sure you don't have a subdural hematoma. We'll keep you overnight, so we can monitor you and make sure there are no unexpected side effects."

"I'd like to go home," she said.

"And I'd rather you didn't unexpectedly keel over dead," he replied. "So it looks like one of us isn't getting what we want. Enjoy your stay."

"I'm not leaving a good review on your website," she growled.

"That's all right," Nussbaum said. "We prefer not to have repeat customers in the emergency room. If you'll follow Nurse Simons, she'll take you to the MRI and then to your room."

Erin grumpily followed the nurse, trailed by Vic, Webb, and Rolf. They ended up in a room that was, as far as hospitals went, pretty comfortable. As a police detective, she apparently rated a private room, if only so it would be harder to murder her. The nurse kept the other cops out while Erin changed into a hospital gown. Then, with a final admonition to be careful of her head and her sense of balance, the nurse left.

Vic and Webb came in before the door even had time to close. Webb pulled a chair to her bedside, while Vic lounged against the wall.

"Are you ready to make your report, Detective?" Webb asked.

"I don't have much choice," Erin said. "I'm not even supposed to go to the bathroom without help. I tracked a guy through a snowstorm with this head injury, and had a gunfight, but I can't be trusted to take a piss without some nurse holding my hand!"

"It's a liability thing," Vic said. "They don't want you falling down and suing the hospital."

"Speaking of liability," Webb said. "How many cops have you shot today?"

"Only one," she said. "And I just winged him. In my defense, he was about to shoot me."

"This would be Detective Carter?" Webb asked.

"Yeah."

"And where's Carter now?"

"I don't know."

"He's in the wind?" Webb asked sharply.

"No."

"I don't understand."

"His case has been taken over by IAB," Erin said slowly. "It's not a Major Crimes concern anymore."

"Is Carter in custody?" Webb asked.

"Yes, sir."

"IAB?"

"Yes, sir."

"When you start rattling off 'yes, sir,' I always get suspicious," Webb said. "Is there something you're not telling me?"

"Yes, sir."

He sighed. "Is it anything I need to know? Or should know?"

"No, sir."

"Who shot Stachowski?"

"Carter."

"Who shot Ames?"

"Stachowski."

"And who shot Katzenberg and Sanchez?"

"They shot each other."

"Why?"

"Katz was a good cop at heart. Mingo wasn't. Mingo shot Katz when Katz took my side, but Katz was tough enough that he didn't go down right away, so he blasted Mingo in the face."

"So what we've got is not one but two officer-involved shootings in which all the perps, and all the victims, are NYPD detectives?" Webb said.

"That's pretty much it, sir," Erin said.

"What a public-relations fiasco," Webb said.

"Glad we're not on the PR side," Vic said. "Me? I kinda like being notorious."

"You're always a PR fiasco," Webb said sourly, glancing at Vic. "The rest of us try to avoid it. O'Reilly, there's going to be a lot of scrutiny on this report, all the way to the PC's office. So I want you to think carefully, and then I want you to start talking."

Erin nodded. "Copy that."

"Captain Holliday will be coming to talk to you later," he added. "Since, by your own admission, you shot another detective."

"Non-fatally," she pointed out.

"Nonetheless," he said. "You might want a Union lawyer present when you talk to him."

"I think it's a good idea to keep the lawyers as far away from this as possible," she replied. "You'll understand why in a few minutes."

*   *   *

"That's it?" Webb said, half an hour later.

"That's it," Erin said. She'd hedged at first about what had happened with Keane. But in the end she figured, the hell with it. Webb and Vic deserved to know, and if she couldn't trust them, she truly couldn't trust anybody in the NYPD. Maybe she was just sick of all the secrets. It was time to get out of this undercover business.

"What a crock," Vic said. "IAB gets all the credit? After what Erin did?"

"You don't get it," Erin said.

"No," he said. "I don't."

"O'Reilly doesn't want the credit for this," Webb said quietly. "In fact, she doesn't want any part of it. And it's not going in the report."

Erin shot her commanding officer a grateful look, which bounced off him.

"I'm not happy about it," Webb went on. "Lieutenant Keane is breaking the law."

"Good," Vic said. "Then let's arrest *him*. I hate Internal friggin' Affairs, and that smug son of a bitch is the worst of the bunch."

"Even if we can prove it..." Webb began.

"Which we won't be able to," Erin interjected.

"That proof would also implicate O'Reilly," Webb finished. "Do you want to arrest her, too?"

"Not really," Vic muttered. "But why's this necessary?"

"If we put Carter in the system, he talks to the O'Malleys," Erin said. "Then they kill Carlyle and me."

"Why Carlyle?" Vic asked. "Wouldn't they think you'd played him for a sucker, too?"

"They'd have to assume he'd been compromised," Webb said. "And at that level of the Mob, anyone who's been compromised is a liability. From their perspective, either he's part of O'Reilly's infiltration, or he's the idiot who made it possible. Traitor or screw-up, however you look at it, he's done."

"And maybe Corky into the bargain," Erin added.

"Silver lining," Vic said. He'd never liked Corky.

"Keane doesn't have to keep Carter under wraps for long," Webb said thoughtfully. "Just until we're finished with the

O'Malleys. Once they're all behind bars, it won't matter what he says."

"At which point he walks," Erin said gloomily. "Keane warned me this would taint the case."

"Like hell he walks," Vic said. "This guy's shot a couple of cops. I won't be the only one who wants a piece of him. There won't be enough left of him to put in a takeout container."

"If he's smart, he'll start running the second his feet hit the street," Webb said. "Nobody in New York will trust him again. The NYPD will be looking for any possible excuse to bust him. I'll have Piekarski run through his financials again. We may be able to nail him for bribery and corruption even if we have to throw out the attempted murder."

"*Attempted* murder?!" Vic burst out. "Two cops are dead!"

"Carter didn't kill them," Webb replied. "Stachowski shot one, Katzenberg shot the other. And both of them were self-defense."

"Katz can testify against Carter," Erin said. "If he lives."

"We'll make something stick," Webb promised.

"I hate this job sometimes," Vic muttered. "How come we gotta have all these damn rules?"

"So people can tell us apart from the bad guys," Webb said. He stood up. "Thanks for the report, O'Reilly. Don't worry about filing anything. I'll type it up back at the Eightball."

"What version of the truth are we telling, sir?" she asked.

"The necessary one," Webb said.

"You should've blown the bastard's head off at the library," Vic said.

"You mean when he was unarmed and injured?" Erin replied.

"If he was holding a gun, how were you supposed to know it was empty?" Vic retorted.

"This conversation is over," Webb said coldly. "And I'm going to pretend I didn't hear that. O'Reilly, you're on medical leave until a doctor clears you for duty. A doctor, let me add, whose last name isn't the same as yours. I'll see you when you get back to work. Neshenko, I think you have a wounded detective to be guarding. And I don't mean the one in this room."

"Yes, sir," Vic said. "I'll get right on it."

"I'm sorry, Vic," Erin said once Webb was gone.

"For not shooting the guy?" Vic replied. "Nah, you did the right thing. I just wish it wasn't. I can't believe he's gonna get away with this!"

"He won't," she said. "You heard the Lieutenant. We'll get him on something."

"Financial crimes," he snorted. "What'll that be? Twelve months? Eighteen? He tried to kill you, Erin! You're only alive because you've got the thickest skull of any cop I know!"

"That's not true," she said. "Haven't you ever looked in a mirror?"

"Fair point," he said. "But I still should've been there. Between Rolf and me, we would've nailed him even if he knocked you down."

"It's okay, Vic. Anyway, it's not like Carter's running around free. Keane's got him locked away somewhere. How'd you like to be in his shoes right now?"

"No thanks," Vic said. "Why do you think Keane helped you?"

"That's what I'm more worried about," she said. "He was behind me getting transferred to Major Crimes in the first place. I'm a pet project of his."

"If he tries to get you to sleep with him, I'll make him choke on his own balls," Vic said.

"It's not like that!" she exclaimed. "I almost wish it was. Then I'd understand it better. I feel like everything Keane does is for his own reasons. I don't like owing him."

"If he screws you over, the ball-choking offer stands."

"Vic? Do you think of me like the sister you never had?"

He shrugged. "Don't get all soppy on me. Just get better and get off your ass so we can get back to work. Speaking of which, I better get going and make sure Stachowski's okay. We've got a couple reliable guys watching him, but Webb's right, I'll feel better if I've got eyes on him. Take care of yourself a little better than you've been doing."

"Back at you," she said. "Don't worry about me. The only thing that'll happen here is I'll be bored to death."

Then she lay back on the hospital bed and finally tried to relax. Rolf nosed at her hand.

"*Hupf!*" she said, resigned to the inevitable.

Rolf scrambled up onto the bed. There wasn't really room, but he curled between her knees and rested his chin on her belly. He heaved a deep sigh and gave her a mournful look.

"You wanted to be in here with me, kiddo," she reminded him. "You could've gone with Vic. He could've gotten you home, to your nice comfy bed."

Rolf didn't budge.

Chapter 22

The doctor wanted Erin to rest, so naturally a nurse came every couple of hours to wake her up. Apparently, with concussion victims, sleeping too long was a sign of something bad. Erin didn't know what and didn't care. The first time she was disturbed, she took it philosophically. The second time, she was surly. By the time the third hand gently touched her shoulder, she was borderline homicidal.

"Get away or I'll snap your arm off and cram it up your ass," she snarled without opening her eyes.

The hand quickly released and withdrew. There was a short pause.

"I'll come back later, shall I?" a soft Irish voice said.

Erin's eyes flew open. "I didn't mean you!" she said.

Carlyle smiled. "I fear I'm the only one present, darling, saving yourself and your dog. I'm sorry I couldn't come sooner. The roads are only barely passable, and I'd no desire to add to the burdens of the emergency workers by getting into a smash-up on the way."

Erin sat up in bed and rubbed her eyes. "What time is it?" she asked.

"Going on eight in the evening," he said. He held up an embarrassingly large bouquet of expensive-looking flowers. "Where shall I set these?"

"Windowsill, I guess," Erin said. "You didn't have to bring me those. I'm not really a flower girl."

He smiled. "I know, darling. But it's customary. Besides, this hospital's crawling with coppers. I fancied I'd be the target of fewer suspicious glances if my hands were filled with something innocuous."

"I'm surprised they let you in," she said. "Even with the bouquet. Didn't anybody ID you?"

"Oh, they know who I am," he said. "It seems they think if I'm wanting to do you in, I'll be able to do it from the comfort of our own flat just as easily. How are you feeling, darling?"

"My head hurts."

"I'd have smuggled in a bottle of Glen D, but your doctors would kill me on the spot."

She grimaced. "Yeah, probably a bad idea. I sure could use a drink, though."

"Corky tells me he discharged his responsibilities."

"He was a big help, thanks."

"Ian's ready to take me to the airport should we need to leave town for a while."

Carlyle said it lightly, but Erin could see he was dead serious.

"That won't be necessary," she said quietly, looking around to make sure they were really alone. The room was empty, as he'd said, and the door was shut. "My cover cracked, but it held. Only one guy knows."

"The lad you and Corky escorted?"

"Yeah."

"And he won't talk?"

"He won't be able to. Lieutenant Keane's got him, and Keane was already in on the secret. He'll be held incommunicado."

"How long?"

"As long as it takes."

"And how long will that be?" he asked. "With the good Lieutenant incapacitated, we've a spot of trouble ahead of us."

"We need to go ahead without Phil," she said. "We don't have any choice. We can't keep this up much longer. I figure a few extra days to sort out the chain of command, but then we're shutting Evan and his goons down."

"Will you be up for it? You've taken rather a beating of late, darling."

"I'm fine."

He nodded, but she could tell he wasn't convinced. "You've a security problem in your organization," he said.

"I've noticed," she said.

"Quite a number of bent coppers."

"Not as many now as there were a couple days ago."

"True enough," he said. "But your lot need to clean house."

"One thing at a time," she said. "We'll sort out the O'Malleys first."

"Are you needing anything?"

"I'll be checking out in the morning, assuming nothing weird happens overnight. Like you said, I'm not allowed to drink booze, and they'll probably have me on a liquid diet, so I can't have anything worth eating. If you can take Rolf for a turn around the block before you go, and find him something to eat, then bring him back up, that'll be plenty."

He took her hand. "I was worried about you, darling," he said, raising the hand to his lips and kissing the back of it.

"That's sweet," she said. "But I told you, I'm fine."

"Would you like me to sit up with you?"

Yes, she thought. "You'd better get back to the Corner," she said. "You need to do damage control. Carter was working for Finnegan or Pritchard, I'm guessing Finnegan. You need to put out a convincing story about what happened."

"Have you something in mind?"

"We'll say he got winged in the gunfight between Katz and Mingo," she said. "He grazed me and ran off into the snow. Nobody's seen him since. As far as we know, he's gone to ground somewhere, or else he's fled the city altogether, since the NYPD knows he's dirty. Better say Katz shot him, not me. It'll play better."

"If that's how you want it," Carlyle said. "What about Lieutenant Stachowski?"

"Tell Evan I'm trying a subtler approach," she said. "I'm working my way into his confidence, but it'll take a little time to open him up. And we have to wait and see how well he recovers."

"Grand," he said. "All we need is to stall Evan a short while."

"Exactly." She squeezed his hand. "Don't worry about me. I'm perfectly safe. You're the one who's going to be hanging out with a bunch of murderous thugs."

"That's a typical evening for me," he said. Then he bent down and kissed her forehead, careful to avoid the bandage wrapped around her skull. "I love you, darling."

*　　*　　*

The night was miserable, chopped up into two-hour segments by the annoyingly diligent nurse. But at sunrise, Doctor Nussbaum arrived with good news.

"Scans are clean," he announced, smiling. "How are you feeling?"

"Like I want to get the hell out of here," Erin said.

"You can be discharged," he said. "I understand you checked out AMA in the past."

"American Medical Association?" Erin was confused.

"Against Medical Advice," he corrected her. "This time that won't be necessary. But before you go, you've got a visitor."

"Junior!" she exclaimed, looking past Nussbaum. Sean O'Reilly Junior was peering around the doorframe. He gave her a weary grin and came in.

"Hey sis," he said. "I would've been in to see you sooner, but I've been really busy."

"So I've heard," she said. "Saving lives all night long. How's Katzenberg?"

"That's one tough guy," Sean said. "He was torn up pretty bad, but no vital organ damage, thanks to his vest. He's going to pull through just fine. He might even make a full recovery, but that'll take months. In addition to the gunshot trauma, he was out in the cold for quite a while. He's got frostbite damage to his fingertips. He should've been wearing gloves."

"He was in a gunfight," she said. "It's harder to pull the trigger with something on your hands."

"I'll never understand you and Dad," Sean said. "I respect you, but I don't understand you. I've never fired a gun in my life and I never want to."

"Can I see Katz?"

"No reason you wouldn't be able to. They've moved him out of Recovery into his own room by now, but if you ask around, you can find him. What about you? How are you doing?"

"You should see the other guy," she said.

"Mom's going to be pretty irritated," he said. "You're her only daughter. You can't be running around getting shot all the time."

"I wasn't planning on telling her about this one," Erin said. "And you can't. Remember doctor-patient confidentiality."

"I'm not your doctor," Sean said. "But your secret's safe with me, on one condition. Don't ever get shot in the head again."

"I'll do my absolute best," she promised. "I didn't do it on *purpose*. Do you have any idea how much it hurts?"

"More than some things and less than others," he said. "I'm just glad you're okay. Now I'm going home. One thing our jobs have in common is the overnight hours. I've been here since... God, I don't even know. You may not have slept well, but you got a lot more sleep than I did last night."

"Go home and get some," she said. "You've earned it."

"So have you," he said.

*   *   *

After Sean left, Erin changed out of the hospital gown. Her only option was the clothes she'd been wearing. She belatedly realized she should've asked Carlyle to fetch her some fresh things. She could smell day-old sweat and blood on the stuff, but it was still better than walking around in a cheap, ugly nightgown, her ass hanging in the air.

Rolf watched her dress with mounting excitement. Clothes meant a walk or, better yet, a run. By the time she fastened her belt and clipped her shield to it, he was prancing at the door.

"In a minute, kiddo," she said. "We need to make a couple of visits first."

Katz's room was on the same hallway as hers, only a couple doors down. A Patrol officer was lounging on a chair between the rooms, ostensibly to provide protection. He had a copy of the *Times*, open to the Sports section; a thermos of coffee; and an entire box of Krispy Kremes, of which two were already missing.

Fortified with a donut she persuaded the uniform to hand over, Erin went into Katz's room. The big cop was lying in bed, swathed in several yards of fresh white bandages. His eyes were open, but he was hardly moving. He was staring out the window at the sky. It was still overcast, but the clouds were lightening. The sun might actually come out soon.

"Hey, Detective," Erin said.

He turned his head, moving with exaggerated care. Clearly, doing just about anything caused him pain.

"Morning," he said quietly.

"How're you doing?" she asked.

"Hard to say," he said. "Can't feel much in my fingers. Doc says I'm lucky not to lose digits. As far as the rest of it, I'm cruising on morphine. Gotta say, this is some good shit. All these years working Narcotics, I finally get what all the fuss is about."

Erin smiled. "You'll be back on the street before you know it," she said.

He didn't return the smile. "Not a chance," he said. "I'm done."

"You don't mean that."

"Yeah, I do. I may be high as a friggin' kite, but I know exactly what I'm saying. I got my letter of resignation all set. Gonna get it to my Captain as soon as I can."

She stared at him. "Why?"

"I'm coming clean with it," Katz said. "All of it. The dirty money, the way I covered for those bastards, everything. I'm giving all the cash back."

"To the drug dealers?"

"No! To the City, where it should've gone in the first place. I can't do this anymore. You saw what happened because of it. People died."

"Bad cops died," she said.

"And a couple good ones got hurt," he said. "Phil's lady nearly got killed, too. Maybe if I'd said something, if I'd done something different, I could've stopped all this before it went this far."

"Katz, this wasn't your fault," she said.

"Some of it was," he insisted. "You were right. I had to do the right thing, but I left it too late."

"No, you didn't," she said. "You saved my life."

"And I killed a friend," he said. "Mingo made some bad choices, but he was my partner! We went through all sorts of shit together and I put a bullet between his friggin' eyes!"

"While he was shooting you," she reminded him.

He shrugged and immediately regretted it. "That ain't the point."

"What is the point then, Katz?"

"I can't do it no more," he said. "And not 'cause of the holes in me. I gotta get out, gotta start over fresh. I just talked to my Union lawyer. She says I ain't gonna serve time, and I don't gotta worry about losing the pension since I wasn't on the Force long enough nohow. So I figure I'll get well, then I'll sort out what happens next."

"Katz? Do you know how to do anything else?"

"Sure!" he said, smiling for the first time in the conversation. "I know how to push drugs. Maybe I'll play for the other side."

He chuckled as he said it, and they both knew he didn't mean it.

"Did you get him?" Katz asked. "Lenny, I mean."

"Officially, no," Erin said.

"And unofficially?"

She nodded. So did Katz.

"If you need a reference, have them give me a call," she said.

"Copy that," he said. "You know, I didn't believe Lenny. About you being dirty. Not for a second."

Erin, caught off guard, found her eyes filling with unexpected tears. "Thanks," she managed to say. "For saying that. And for saving my life."

"No," he said. "Thank you. You saved me."

"Did I?"

"Of course you did," he said.

Erin didn't have an answer to that. Instead of saying anything, she managed a nod and started for the door.

"And since you're up and around, and I'm not," he said. "Can I ask you a favor?"

"Of course."

"If you see Phil Stachowski, or his wife, can you tell them... you know?" Katz looked away, embarrassed.

"Will do," she promised. "I'm going to look in on him right now."

But she didn't think he'd be in any position to hear Katz's message.

Chapter 23

Vic was outside Phil's room. He'd gotten a bottle of Mountain Dew and a couple of Twinkies from a vending machine. He was munching one of the yellow snack cakes.

"Gonna see our buddy before you shove off?" he asked, after swallowing.

"Yeah," Erin said. "How is he?"

Vic looked at the floor. "In a coma," he said. "He's breathing on his own, but they're gonna fit him for a feeding tube pretty soon. The wife's in there with him now."

"Camilla? She's here?"

"Yeah. Just showed up, after the plows came round."

"The kids aren't here, are they?"

"Just the missus."

"Maybe I should come back later," Erin said.

"Go on in," Vic said. "I don't think they'll mind."

Erin knocked twice, to let Camilla know she was coming. "*Bleib*," she murmured to Rolf, who cocked his head at her but stayed put. Then she eased the door open and slipped inside.

Camilla Stachowski was sitting next to Phil's bed. The bedside table and windowsill were covered with cards, flowers, and photographs. A family photo of Phil, Camilla, and their daughters was front and center. It was the Christmas photo Erin had seen on Phil's desk. Camilla was pale-faced but her eyes were dry. She was holding Phil's hand.

"Excuse me," Erin said, almost whispering.

The room had a solemnity about it, like a funeral. Phil lay very still. A saline bag hung on a hook above the bed, the plastic tube running into his arm. Electrodes were hooked up to various machines. If it weren't for the heart monitor's slow, rhythmic beeping, he might have been dead. The doctors and nurses had cleaned him up; his head was bandaged and he wasn't bleeding. But his skin was sheet white and his chest barely moved with each breath.

Camilla looked up at her. "Good morning, Detective O'Reilly," she said, using the same soft tone.

"I don't mean to intrude," Erin said awkwardly. "I was on my way through and I wanted to stop in."

"You're injured," Camilla said, seeing the bandage on Erin's head.

"It's not too bad," Erin said. "I thought you should know, we got the guy who shot Phil."

"I'm glad," Camilla said, without much feeling. "He won't be able to hurt anyone else."

"Yeah," Erin said. "I just wish we could do more."

"I've been talking to him," Camilla said, her eyes going back to her husband. "The doctors don't know if he can hear me or not, so I tell myself he can. That way I can at least be here and... and feel like we're not alone."

Her voice quavered just a little, but she tightened her jaw and recovered. "I tell him about his daughters, and how much they miss their dad. I talk about the vacation we were planning for February. I tell him he's always done our taxes, so I'll need him to be home before April; otherwise I'll have to hire somebody. And I try not to think about..."

Camilla's voice trailed off. Erin laid a hand on the woman's shoulder.

"Do the docs have a prognosis?" she asked.

Camilla shook her head. "This sort of injury is so rare," she said. "The neurosurgeon is very, very good. I've been reading up on him. He's worked miracles, and that's good, because that's what we need. I hold Phil's hand, and sometimes I think he's holding mine back, but it's just my imagination. Are you religious, Detective?"

"Yeah, I am," Erin said.

"Do you pray?"

"When I can."

"Will you pray for Phil? For us?"

Erin swallowed the lump in her throat. "Absolutely," she said. Then, "Can I sit with you? For a little while?"

"I'd like that," Camilla said.

Erin found a second chair in the corner and pulled it over, taking a seat beside Camilla. They sat in silence for a few minutes. Then Camilla started talking again, but not to Erin.

"Phil," she said. "Do you remember our honeymoon? When we went up to Canada, around Niagara Falls? The leaky pipe in the hotel? How it started raining indoors after midnight? I was so upset, because I wanted everything to be perfect, but you laughed. You said, 'This is a marriage. You think this is the last time a pipe's going to break? Things are going to go wrong. Life's not about avoiding trouble, it's about dealing with it. And it's so much better to face it together than alone.'"

Camilla's voice hitched again and became hoarse. "Phil, I'm so glad you've been by my side all this time. I never wanted to be alone. God, Phil, I need you. And Nora and Grace, they need their dad. Please, God, if you can hear me, don't take my Philip. Not yet."

"Amen," Erin whispered. There was nothing else to say.

She sat there as long as she felt like she could. Nothing changed.

Camilla took a tissue from the box by the bed and dabbed at her eyes. "Thank you, Detective," she said. "I know you have places you need to be. I'll be all right here."

"I'll check in on him," Erin said. "When I can."

Camilla nodded. "There's a lot of your comrades downstairs," she said. "Everyone's worried about him. You're the sixth or seventh officer to come. They keep leaving cards and flowers."

"Phil's a good man," Erin said.

"The best," Camilla said.

"And he's brave," Erin said. "He got hurt protecting one of us. You know what the Bible says about that?"

"'Greater love hath no man,'" Camilla quoted.

Erin stood up. "You can call me," she said. "Any time, if there's anything you need. Anything at all."

"Thank you," Camilla said.

"I'll see you later," Erin said and started for the door.

"Oh my God," Camilla said.

Erin's head jerked around, but Camilla wasn't looking at her. The woman was looking at her husband.

Phil's hand was curled tight around his wife's. He was gripping her fingers.

"Phil?" Camilla whispered. She looked more frightened than before. Erin understood that. Hope could be a terrifying thing.

The wounded man's jaw slowly opened and closed. His lips worked fitfully, but no sound came out.

Erin ran to the door and flung it open, scaring the hell out of Vic. Rolf, who'd lain down beside the Russian, sprang to his paws, ears perked, ready for action.

"Get the doctor!" she snapped at Vic. "Right now!"

"Copy that," Vic said, already sprinting toward the nurse's station at the end of the hall. Erin let the door swing shut, leaving Rolf poised and confused.

Erin hurried back to the bedside. Camilla was standing now, bending over the bed, holding Phil's hand in both of her own. And Phil's eyes were open.

"Can you hear me?" Camilla asked.

Phil nodded. His lips quivered. He licked them and, in a voice so soft Erin could scarcely hear it, he spoke.

"Cam."

Tears were spilling out of Camilla's eyes, pouring down her cheeks. She didn't even notice. "Yes, it's me," she said. "It's me. I'm here."

"Am... am... alive?"

"Yes, Phil, you're alive." Camilla was laughing now, through her tears. "You're in the hospital. Bellevue. You've been hurt, but you're going to be okay."

"Remember..." Phil said, seeming to have trouble finding the words. "Carter... Ames."

"It's okay, Phil," Camilla said. "You don't need to talk right now."

"Have to... find... O'Reilly."

Camilla started. "Detective O'Reilly?" she repeated. "She's here, Phil. Right now."

Erin stepped shyly forward, not really wanting to intrude on this private moment. "Hey," she said. "I'm here. Everything's fine, Phil. Your wife's right. Don't try to say too much yet. Just rest."

Phil's eyes fixed on her. He gathered his strength and drew in a long, shuddering breath.

"I didn't tell them a thing," he said, quietly and distinctly. Then he sagged back, exhausted by the simple effort, and let his eyes slip shut again.

"I know," Erin said. "And Phil? Katz says he's sorry."

Phil gave no sign if he'd heard her words.

"You just rest now, Phil," Camilla said. "We'll take care of you."

The door flew open and a doctor and two nurses rushed in, pushing a crash cart. Vic trailed behind them, worry all over his face.

"What happened?" the doctor demanded, his eyes leaping from one machine display to the next.

"He woke up," Camilla said with tearful, exquisite delight.

The medical team flew into action. Erin retreated to the fringe of the little group. After a moment, Camilla joined her, getting out of the doctor's way.

"Jesus, Erin," Vic said. "I thought the poor guy was choking on his tongue or something. You could've said it was good news, couldn't you? Damn near gave me a heart attack."

Erin couldn't answer right away, because Camilla had pulled her into a spine-cracking hug.

"Oh, God," Camilla said over and over. "Oh, God." All the strength she'd been holding onto the past couple of days had dissolved into emotion. The tough, self-reliant woman who'd blasted a home invader with a shotgun was nowhere in sight.

"It's okay," Erin managed to say, patting Camilla's back.

"So, he's getting better?" Vic said.

Camilla released Erin, wrapped her arms around Vic, and hugged him, too. At that moment she would have embraced anybody she could reach.

"Uh..." Vic said, completely at a loss.

After a moment, Camilla let go of him. She turned back toward Erin. "What did he mean?" she asked. "What he said about not telling them anything? It seemed important."

"He was protecting one of his people," Erin said. "The bad guys were trying to get a name out of him. He's telling me our officer is safe, that he didn't give up the name."

"Of course he didn't," Camilla said proudly. "He'd never betray a friend. I told you that."

"I don't think you need us hanging around this room right now," Erin said. "We'll get going. I'll tell the guys downstairs. They'll be over the moon. I'm so, so glad."

"Thank you," Camilla said. She was still crying. "I know it's going to be hard, that it's a long road, but I've still got him. I thought I'd lost him."

Erin thought back to an ambulance ride she'd once taken, to holding Carlyle's hand while she watched the life draining out of him, to the sheer desperation and despair of losing a loved one.

"I hear you," she said. "But you didn't. And he's going to need all that love you've got."

"He'll have it," Camilla said, more firmly. "Every bit of it."

Chapter 24

The bathtub was a little pool of Heaven. Erin was up to her neck in warm, liquid bliss. She was a shower girl under normal circumstances, but the cold had gotten into her bones. Now, finally, she was starting to feel warm all the way through. It might not be a bad idea to stay there forever, until she melted away.

She'd fed Rolf, then given him a bath to rinse the lingering pepper spray out of his fur. That stuff was amazingly persistent. Even after the shampoo, he still smelled like a bad taco truck. After that, a bath of her own had been the next logical step. She wouldn't have expected Carlyle to have bubbly bath soap in his apartment, but she'd found it in one of the cabinets. Now her head was floating on a sea of fragrant foam. Her chin dipped into the bubbles and her eyes slipped shut.

Her street instincts were operating at a particularly low level, but they still nudged her awake with the realization someone was watching her. She blinked sleepily and looked to the doorway, already knowing what she'd see: Rolf, staring at her with his big brown eyes.

Instead, Carlyle was standing there, one arm on the doorframe. He smiled.

"Feeling a bit more human again, darling?" he said.

Erin stretched out her feet, wiggling her toes in the warm water. "Yeah," she said. "How did things go with Evan?"

Carlyle sat down on the toilet seat next to the tub. "All's well," he said. "The lad's not happy, but he understands these things take time. He's not forgotten you, but you've a bit of breathing room, and that's all we need. What news of Lieutenant Stachowski?"

"He's awake," she said, her good mood draining out of her. "He knows who he is, and who his wife is. He remembers who shot him, and why. That's all great news, I guess. But he's in really rough shape. He'll be in the hospital for weeks, probably months. He's got critical brain trauma and they haven't even started figuring out what that means long-term. He'll have serious problems for the rest of his life."

"It's a terrible thing," Carlyle said.

"Damn right it is," she said. "His career's over. There's no way he'll be back to work; not now, not ever. What a goddamn mess. The Department's lost five cops over this, two good ones and three bad ones, and for what? To protect me!"

"Erin, this wasn't your fault," Carlyle said, unknowingly echoing her words to Katz. "If those lads hadn't been traitors, none of this would've happened. You needn't pay for their sins."

"Why not?" she asked bitterly. "Phil's paying for them. He may never walk again. Maybe he's missing big chunks of his memories. Maybe he won't be able to taste food, or make love to his wife. God damn it, he didn't deserve this!"

"You're right," Carlyle said. "He didn't. That's why you wear that gold shield, darling. To avenge the innocent."

"I failed," she said. "Carter's going to get away with it."

"You're so certain of that?" Carlyle replied. "He's been abandoned to Lieutenant Keane's tender mercies, aye?"

"Yeah, what about it?"

"Does the good Lieutenant strike you as a particularly merciful fellow?"

Erin shook his head. "Now that you mention it, no."

"What do you fancy he's doing with Detective Carter at this very moment?"

"I have no idea. Probably figuring out how he can use him to leverage his own career."

"Perhaps," Carlyle said thoughtfully. "I was just thinking how convenient it might be for everyone concerned if Detective Carter quietly disappeared. Or perhaps if he suffered a sudden crisis of conscience and took his own life."

The bath water no longer felt so warm and comforting. Erin sat upright, shedding water and bubbles from her shoulders. "Are you serious?"

"I was considering that Mafia lad who hanged himself in your holding cell," Carlyle said. "That was convenient as well."

"You think Keane is going to make Carter disappear?"

"I'm merely thinking like what I've been these past two decades."

"Jesus," Erin said. "I'd better—"

"Aye?" Carlyle asked politely, after waiting a few moments for Erin to finish the sentence. "You'd best do what?"

She slumped back. "I have no idea," she said again. "Shit, I nearly shot him myself. I wanted to."

"Speaking of lads you've wanted to shoot in the past, I ran into Corky downstairs," Carlyle said.

"What'd he want?"

"To try a new cocktail."

"What was it?"

"Something blue," Carlyle said with distaste. He tended to be a straight whiskey man, except on special occasions. "Some monstrous concoction of Curaçao and tequila, unless I'm mistaken, served over ice. He seems to have developed quite a taste for tequila since his tropical sojourn."

"I'd rather have something warm on a day like this," Erin said. "They said on the radio it's the third-worst storm in New York's history. More than twenty-eight inches of snow."

"But we've weathered it," Carlyle said. "Just as we'll weather the next one. Who's in charge of your operation now?"

"I don't know," Erin said. "Captain Holliday's going to figure it out. Maybe he'll take over in person. This'll delay us, but only a little."

"It'll all be over by Christmas?" Carlyle suggested with a twinkle in his eye.

"I'm starting to think it'll never be over," Erin said. "Some of this stuff is going to last a lifetime."

"Was he angry with you?" Carlyle asked. "Lieutenant Stachowski, I mean."

"No," she said. "He was glad I was there."

"And he would've died to protect you."

"I never asked him to!"

"You didn't have to," Carlyle shot back. "Just as you'd have done for him. Honor his sacrifice, darling. Finish the job he wants you to do."

"Carter figured it out at the last minute," she said. "Phil didn't talk, but if Carter had the chance to make even one phone call or text, that would've been it. Do you know how close we came?"

Carlyle smiled. He knelt by the tub and put a hand on her bare shoulder, ignoring the soap suds that darkened the cuff of his jacket. "Do you know another word for nearly dying, darling?"

"What?"

"Living." He leaned in and kissed her lightly on the lips. "It's cold outside, but it's warm in here, and we're not dead yet."

"That's right," Erin said. "We're alive."

The building shook slightly, the bathroom window rattling in its pane, as a snowplow rumbled past, piling up the last of the snow on the sidewalk. Outside, New York was coming awake and alive again. One storm was over. Another was coming.

Here's a sneak peek from Book 24: Brain Damage

Coming 6/24/2024

A present was waiting on Erin's desk in the Precinct 8 Major Crimes office. Vic Neshenko, Zofia Piekarski, and Lieutenant Webb were all at their computers, either working or pretending to work. Nobody so much as said a word to her and Rolf as they entered. But Vic and Piekarski were watching her out of the corners of their eyes, which made Erin immediately suspicious.

The package on her desk was a box about the right size to hold a basketball. It was gift-wrapped in the bright pink and purple paper a six-year-old girl would want on a birthday present. A pink bow decorated the top.

There was no getting away from it, so Erin tore open the paper. She stared at the gift for a moment.

"Har, har," she said dryly, hefting a brand-new bicycle helmet. It was pastel pink, with a threaded hole in the upper forehead. This hole, the package informed her, was for a rainbow-striped unicorn horn, included in the package. The helmet had big cartoon eyes with long eyelashes.

Vic was snorting with suppressed laughter. Piekarski was giggling. Even Webb had a smile on his face.

"Welcome back, O'Reilly," Webb said. "Detective Neshenko and Officer Piekarski thought you ought to have a little something to commemorate your recent adventures, and to greet you when you came back on duty. I assume your visit to the neurologist went as planned?"

"Clean bill of health, sir," Erin said. "So I guess I won't be needing this." She set the helmet on the corner of her desk, where it stared at Vic with its enormous eyes.

"You sure?" Vic asked. "You can use the horn when you head-butt the bad guys. Hell, you won't even need to pull your gun. Just the look of that thing will scare the hell out of them."

"How is this scary?" she asked.

"You'd have to be crazy to wear something like that on the street," Vic replied. "And criminals are scared of crazy people."

"*I'm* scared of crazy people," she said. "Anything happen this morning?"

"The Homicide boys down in Queens want to know if we're willing to take a look at something," Webb said.

"Who's dead?" Erin asked.

"Pizza delivery guy," Vic said. "Somebody beat his head in. Patrol unit found him in his truck, still behind the wheel."

Erin deflated. "That sounds like a pretty normal homicide," she said. "Mugging gone wrong. What makes this a Major Crimes case?"

"Something else you'd rather be doing, O'Reilly?" Webb asked.

"No, sir. It just seems a little weird they'd bring it to us. Are they shorthanded?"

"No, they're just idiots," Vic said.

"Oh, God," Erin said. "You don't mean..."

"Yeah," Vic said with relish. "It's Lyons and Spinelli, your old pals from the 116. You sure you don't want to wear that helmet?"

Erin rolled her eyes. "That's just what I need. Those two bozos seeing me dressed up like a little girl? No thanks. I can't believe they'd call me."

"You're not the only member of this squad," Webb said. "You're not even the commanding officer, in case you've forgotten. Anyway, it was Lieutenant Murphy, your old CO, who called us. He thinks something's a little weird about this one."

"Weird how?"

"A man gets beaten to death in his company vehicle, but the windows aren't broken and his seatbelt's still fastened," Webb said. "Plus, he's got a record."

"I was just checking his priors," Piekarski said. "Floyd Shelton, age thirty-two, took two falls for burglary. He served two nickels upstate, only got paroled four months ago."

"A felon killed under suspicious circumstances?" Erin said. "That's more like it."

"I'm glad it meets with your approval," Webb said. "We've been waiting on you. CSU is processing the scene as we speak. I've had the others running background. I'll ride with you and let the lovebirds carpool."

"Tweet tweet, sir," Piekarski said.

"Cold pizza for lunch," Vic said. "This is gonna be a good day, I can feel it."

"Don't eat the evidence, Vic," Erin said.

* * *

"We ought to talk about your future," Webb said.

Erin braced herself. She kept looking out the windshield, avoiding her commanding officer's eye.

"You've been a detective less than two years," Webb went on. "But you've had what you might call an eventful career."

"You could call it that," Erin agreed.

"You've also been in more critical incidents than I can count," he said. "Gunfights, serious injuries, hostage situations, you name it."

"What's your point, sir?"

"You've been running on all cylinders," Webb said. "Don't you think it may be time to take a breather?"

She shot him an incredulous look. "I can't do that!" she snapped. "Not now!"

"I know, you've got something important in the works," he said. "But that'll be wrapped up within the next few days. It might actually be over by New Year's. Once you've taken care of that, you might seriously consider doing something else."

"Like what?" she asked. "I'm a cop, sir. This is all I know how to do."

"You'll be a cop with a great deal of pull," Webb said. "This is a career-making move. If you play your cards right, you can write your own ticket."

Erin didn't say anything. She turned her attention back to the road.

"What?" Webb demanded. "I was watching you right there. It was like someone flicked a switch behind your eyes. I'm trying to give you some good advice. What did I say that was so awful?"

"Nothing," she sighed. "It just sounded like the sort of thing Lieutenant Keane would say."

"You say that like it's a bad thing."

"Do *you* like him?"

"Whether I like him isn't the point. He's smart, he's ambitious, he's the youngest—"

"The youngest Lieutenant in the NYPD," Erin interrupted. "Yeah, I know. He's also a ruthless, sneaky son of a bitch who'd pimp out his own mom to get ahead. I don't want to be him."

"Obviously," Webb said. "And you don't have to be. But you want to think what you'll be doing a year from now, or five years. I'll be retired in a few more years, if I haven't kicked off from a heart attack. You're young. Relatively young, I mean."

"Thanks," she said wryly.

"You've got eight more years with the Department if you want to put in your twenty," he said. "You can't go that whole way like you've been doing. There'll be nothing left of you to collect your pension. It adds up, O'Reilly. All of it. The injuries, the stress, the trauma. You keep writing checks on your future, sooner or later they're going to bounce."

"Are you *worried* about me, sir?" she asked.

"It's my job," he said.

"And now you sound like my dad."

"Your dad wore a shield for a quarter century," he reminded her. "If he's got advice about being a cop, you might consider listening to it."

"So which is it? You think I should be advancing my career, or taking medical retirement?"

"I think you can't be a street detective forever. Do you want my job?"

Erin laughed. She couldn't help it. A vision of herself popped into her mind, fifteen years older and fifty pounds heavier, smoking like a chimney and counting the days to retirement.

"I'm serious," Webb said. "You could make Lieutenant one of these days. Maybe sooner than you think. That's assuming you don't get yourself crippled or killed."

"Thanks for the career counseling," she said, trying not to sound too sarcastic.

"Just keep it in mind," he said. "Opportunities are slippery things. If you don't grab on hard, they slide right past you."

"Do I detect a note of regret, sir?"

"A note?" Webb said. "My life's a whole symphony of it."

*   *   *

The pizza truck was in a parking garage just off Union Turnpike. The garage served DaSilva Memorial Field at St. John's University. Erin wasn't thrilled about that. The last time she'd been involved in a case at a college, she'd stepped on a few administrative toes and the head of campus security had demanded her resignation. But several NYPD vehicles were already on scene, together with a car bearing a security label, so maybe the red tape had already been cut away.

Among the official vehicles were the Crime Scene Unit forensics van, the coroner's van, a pair of NYPD blue-and-whites, and an unmarked sedan. Erin knew the last one was a police vehicle from the spotlight over the left rearview mirror, but also because it was familiar. The last time she'd seen it, her old enemy Detective Spinelli had been driving it.

Someone had already strung yellow tape around the victim's pickup. Two cold-looking Patrol officers stood guard, while the evidence techs and the coroner did their thing. A pair of plainclothes guys watched, hands in their pockets. Erin recognized them, even from the rear. The big, broad-shouldered one was Detective Lyons. The little one that looked and moved like a weasel was Detective Spinelli. She hoped he'd at least gotten rid of his sleazy little mustache.

Vic and Piekarski arrived right behind Erin, Webb, and Rolf. They approached the scene together, already looking around for possible clues as to what had happened.

"These Homicide dicks are assholes," Vic said to Piekarski in a stage whisper. "But don't worry. If they get out of line, I'll give them a boot-leather enema."

"Are you offering to protect me because I'm female, or because I'm pregnant?" Piekarski hissed. "Because neither one is a compliment."

"I'm protecting you because I love you," Vic said indignantly. "And besides—"

"Can it, Neshenko," Webb interrupted. "You can fight with your girlfriend when you're off the clock. On duty, your ass is mine. And so is hers."

"When he says that, he doesn't mean your actual ass," Vic said. "He'd never go for that. Not that it isn't a great ass. I mean, a really great—"

"Shut up," Piekarski said.

Spinelli heard them coming. He turned around, giving Erin a view of a sharp-featured face that still sported its ridiculous excuse for facial hair. He gave her a sour look.

"Your troubles are over," Vic announced. "Major Crimes is in the building."

"Good thing we're in a nice, spacious garage," Spinelli replied. "It's almost big enough for your ego."

"You think we want to be here?" Vic shot back. "You guys called us, remember?"

"I apologize for my subordinate," Webb said blandly. "Believe it or not, he's on his best behavior. So, I trust, are you. We're here to help and we're all on the same team. What've we got?"

"Single victim," Lyons said, giving Erin a contemptuous glare. "Black, mid-thirties. Doc says cause of death is blunt force to the skull, probably a hammer. We're thinking robbery, smash-and-grab."

"Pizza delivery guys still get paid in cash a lot of the time," Spinelli said. "Plus tips."

"Yeah," Vic said. "A couple hundred bucks sounds like a fantastic motive for murder."

"I saw a guy get killed for seven-fifty in pocket change once," Spinelli retorted. "These guys aren't geniuses and they come cheap."

"Plenty of idiots in all kinds of professions," Vic agreed. "Cheap losers, too."

"We were told the victim was found in the driver's seat, still wearing his belt," Webb said.

"That's right," Spinelli said. "Car was parked right where it is now. A school custodian found it about ninety minutes ago. Doors closed, engine off. Nobody around. He thought it was weird, so he came up and knocked on the window. He figured the driver was asleep, but then he saw the blood in the guy's hair and called campus security. They called us."

"Were the car doors locked?" Erin asked.

"Yeah," Spinelli said.

"Both of them?" she pressed.

Spinelli shifted uncomfortably.

"You did check the passenger door too, didn't you?" Vic asked.

"CSU is still processing the scene," Spinelli muttered.

"I think we'd better take a look for ourselves," Webb said.

The delivery car was a battered Toyota pickup from the late Nineties, wheel wells rusted out, a logo for Ninja Pizza ("Slice and Dice!") painted on the doors. A cartoon of a black-masked ninja held a slice of pizza in one hand and was flinging a pair of dice with the other. Sarah Levine, the Medical Examiner, was in the process of examining the body behind the wheel.

"Morning, Doctor," Webb said.

Levine checked her watch, which read about ten-thirty. "Correct," she said. "But time of death was during the night. Judging from body temperature, the victim's heart stopped between one-thirty and two."

"How did we get an ID on him?" Erin asked.

"We called Ninja Pizza," Spinelli said. "They had a driver who didn't clock out at the end of his shift, and one of their trucks was missing. They gave us the name, so we e-mailed his boss his mugshot. He gave us a positive ID. CSU just printed him, and the prints are a match. It's Floyd Shelton, all right. Or it was."

"Good quick work," Webb said. "Have you been to Ninja Pizza yet?"

Spinelli shook his head. "We haven't had time. We've been canvassing the scene. Unfortunately, with the field closed and the snow piled up so high, nobody else seems to have been around."

"Nobody saw nothin,'" Vic said with a sardonic smile.

Erin was looking at the dead man, watching Levine making her observations. "You said he got hit with a hammer?" she prompted.

"The trauma to the cranium is consistent with a blow from a hammer," Levine said. "He was struck three times, resulting in a depressed-skull fracture and massive intracranial hemorrhage. Unconsciousness would have been instantaneous, with death following within five to ten minutes. If you observe the impact points, you can see the impact was made by an octagonal metallic object. This is consistent with some styles of hammer."

"Octagonal? Like a stop sign?"

"Correct. There is surprising variance in striking surfaces of hammers across different brands. Some are circular, some octagonal, some square. This narrows the possible number of murder weapons considerably."

"Hey guys," Erin said, directing her words to the nearest CSU tech. "Did you find a hammer anywhere? With or without blood on it?"

"Not yet," the technician replied. "But we're still looking."

"Looks like he got hit on the right side of his head," Erin said, trying to examine the injury with the same clinical detachment Levine always brought to bear.

"Correct," Levine said again. "All three blows struck his right temple."

Erin looked across the front seat of the car. The passenger door, like the driver's door, stood open. Another CSU guy was dusting the handle for fingerprints, which seemed optimistic to Erin. It had been a chilly night and the killer had likely worn gloves.

"Was that door unlocked when you got here?" she asked.

"Yeah," the CSU guy said. "But the driver's door wasn't. The Patrol boys told us they used a Slim Jim to get it open so they could check his vitals."

"The killer was in the truck," Erin said.

"Obviously," Levine said. "It would not have been possible to strike him with a short-handled hammer from any other location, especially since he was secured by his seatbelt."

"The killer was sitting next to him," Erin said. "And our guy wasn't expecting to get hit. He was looking the wrong way. Otherwise he would've been hit at least once in the face. If he'd been looking at the passenger, the headrest would've gotten in the way of these wounds."

"The ballistic arc of the hammer would have been interrupted," Levine said. "It would have resulted in a glancing blow at best. Your hypothesis is sound."

"No pizza," Vic announced. He'd been examining the cargo box behind the pickup's cab.

"Are you saying the bad guys stole the pizza along with our victim's pocket change?" Webb asked.

"Maybe," Vic said. "Or maybe he'd already made his delivery."

"Pizza delivery guys don't carry passengers," Erin said. "I've never seen them operate in pairs. So who was the passenger?"

"Someone he was meeting here?" Vic suggested.

"Maybe it was a hooker," Lyons said. "And he was getting a blowjob, so he didn't see it coming."

"His pants are zipped up, genius," Vic said, rolling his eyes.

"We still might be looking for a girl," Lyons insisted.

"It's possible," Webb said. "But male or female, I think they're more likely to be an accomplice than a romantic partner."

"Who said anything about romance?" Lyons asked. "I was talking about blowjobs."

"Stay classy, Lyons," Erin said under her breath.

"From what I see, we've got a convicted felon who's been murdered," Webb said. "The most obvious explanation is that he was involved in some sort of crime, and one of his associates killed him. That suggests either a conflict of personality, or an argument over the loot."

"Let's find out who got robbed last night," Piekarski said.

"Good idea," Webb said. "See how many burglaries or robberies were reported last night. CSU has this scene in hand. Lyons and Spinelli, would you mind staying here and making sure the evidence is properly collected?"

"Glad to," Spinelli said through clenched teeth. He didn't like taking orders from an outsider, even when they were phrased as polite requests.

"The rest of us are taking a trip to Ninja Pizza," Webb said.

"I wonder if they have sushi as one of their toppings," Vic said. "I'm hungry."

Ready for more?

Join the Clickworks Press email list
for the latest on new releases, upcoming books and
series, behind-the-scenes details, events, and more.

Be the first to know about new releases in the Erin
O'Reilly Mysteries by signing up at
clickworkspress.com/join/erin

About the Author

Steven Henry learned how to read almost before he learned how to walk. Ever since he began reading stories, he wanted to put his own on the page. He lives a very quiet and ordinary life in Minnesota with his wife and dog.

Also by Steven Henry

Fathers
A Modern Christmas Story

When you strip away everything else, what's left is the truth

Life taught Joe Davidson not to believe in miracles. A blue-collar wood-worker, Joe is trying to build a future. His father drank himself to death and his mother succumbed to cancer, leaving a broken, struggling family. He and his brother and sisters are faced with failed marriages, growing pains, and lingering trauma.

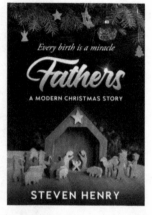

Then a chance meeting at his local diner brings Mary Elizabeth Reynolds into his life. Suddenly, Joe finds himself reaching for something more, a dream of happiness. The wood-worker and the poor girl from a trailer park connect and fall in love, and for a little while, everything is right with their world.

But suddenly Joe is confronted with a situation he never imagined. What do you do if your fiancée is expecting a child you know isn't yours? Torn between betrayal and love, trying to do the right thing when nothing seems right anymore, Joe has to strip life down to its truth and learn that, in spite of the pain, love can be the greatest miracle of all.

Learn more at clickworkspress.com/fathers.

Ember of Dreams
The Clarion Chronicles, Book One

When magic awakens a long-forgotten folk, a noble lady, a young apprentice, and a solitary blacksmith band together to prevent war and seek understanding between humans and elves.

Lady Kristyn Tremayne – An otherwise unremarkable young lady's open heart and inquisitive mind reveal a hidden world of magic.

Robert Blackford – A humble harp maker's apprentice dreams of being a hero.

Master Gabriel Zane – A master blacksmith's pursuit of perfection leads him to craft an enchanted sword, drawing him out of his isolation and far from his cozy home.

Lord Luthor Carnarvon – A lonely nobleman with a dark past has won the heart of Kristyn's mother, but at what cost?

Readers love *Ember of Dreams*

"The more I got to know the characters, the more I liked them. The female lead in particular is a treat to accompany on her journey from ordinary to extraordinary."

"The author's deep understanding of his protagonists' motivations and keen eye for psychological detail make Robert and his companions a likable and memorable cast."

Learn more at tinyurl.com/emberofdreams.

More great titles from Clickworks Press

Death's Dream Kingdom
Gabriel Blanchard

A young woman of Victorian London has been transformed into a vampire. Can she survive the world of the immortal dead— or perhaps, escape it?

"The wit and humor are as Victorian as the setting... a winsomely vulnerable and tremendously crafted work of art."

"A dramatic, engaging novel which explores themes of death, love, damnation, and redemption."

Learn more at clickworkspress.com/ddk.

Share the love!

Join our microlending team at
kiva.org/team/clickworkspress.

Keep in touch!

Join the Clickworks Press email list
and get freebies, production updates, special deals,
behind-the-scenes sneak peeks, and more.

Sign up today at clickworkspress.com/join.